PITY PRANK

WHITNEY DINEEN

This book is a work of fiction. Names, characters, locales, and situations are the work of the author's overactive imagination and the voices in her head. Any resemblance to people living or dead, events, etc., is purely coincidental. And I don't mean maybe.

Made in the United States. March 2026

Print ISBN: 979-8-9912328-8-3
E-book ASIN: B0FWHWC6RY

https://whitneydineen.com/newsletter/

33 Partners Publishing

ALSO BY WHITNEY DINEEN

Pity Series

Pity Date

Pity Party

Pity Pact

Pity Parade

Pity Present

Pity Play

Pity Please

Pity Prank

The Mimi Chronicles

The Reinvention of Mimi Finnegan

Mimi Plus Two

Kindred Spirits

Relatively Series

Relatively Normal

Relatively Sane

Relatively Happy

Creek Water Series

The Event

The Move

The Plan

The Dream

Seven Brides for Seven Mothers Series

Love is a Battlefield

Ain't She Sweet

It's My Party

You're So Vain

Head Over Feet

Queen of Hearts

At Last

She Sins at Midnight

Going Up?

Love for Sale

The Accidentally in Love Series (with Melanie Summers)

Text Me on Tuesday

The Text God

Text Wars

Text in Show

Mistle Text

Text and Confused

A Gamble on Love Mom-Com Series (with Melanie Summers)

No Ordinary Hate

A Hate Like This

Hate, Rinse, Repeat

Visionary Fiction

The Celestial Contract

Conspiracy Thriller

See No More

Non-Fiction Humor

Motherhood, Martyrdom & Costco Runs

Middle Reader

Wilhelmina and the Willamette Wig Factory

Who the Heck is Harvey Stingle?

Children's Books

The Friendship Bench

To my favorite neuro-sparkly girl. I love you with my whole heart! You make the world a better place.

CHAPTER ONE

FINLEY

I'm currently trying to decide if I should expand my business by renting the recently vacated storefront next to mine. Staring out the Happy Snaps window, I itemize the pros and cons. Pro: the additional square footage would allow me to leave up different backdrops and sets, thereby letting me offer more options to my photography clients. Pro: the bigger my space, the more successful I appear. Con: the cost. I'll have to work longer hours to offset the expense. Con: there will be more space to keep clean. Con: large spaces make me feel like I don't have control. Con: I don't have control. Ever. Anywhere in my life.

My heart rate accelerates to a rapid enough pace that I reach for the cold bottle of water sitting next to me. *Sip. Breathe. Sip. Breathe.* After repeating my favorite calm-down technique a total of seven times, I finally regain my equilibrium.

Back to my inner debate. A large part of my client base comes to me for sexy—but perfectly respectable—boudoir photos. I don't shoot porn; I capture true romance and fantasy.

A lot of photographers rely on AI filters to set the mood. I think those are crutches for people of limited creativity. I pride myself on my extensive imagination, and props take up more square footage than I currently have.

Yet I need to be careful because I have a history of making rash decisions that haven't always panned out. Like the time I convinced myself a black diamond ski run couldn't be that much harder than the bunny slopes I'd recently mastered. My ankle still hurts when the weather turns.

My attention is briefly diverted by a larger than normal speck of dust dancing along a sun beam. It shimmers exuberantly and sways to a cosmic rhythm only it can hear. I can't help but wonder why these particles never seem to go anywhere. Imagine being weightless *and* airborne and still not making a break for it. If I had the same opportunity, I'd be halfway to Mars.

When I was little I fancied these illuminated wisps were fairies from another dimension. I thought if I concentrated on them hard enough they would impart the secrets of the Universe to me. They would explain things like, why do people always seem intent upon running in a straight line?

I never saw the appeal of rushing for the sake of rushing. For me, running was about the journey. It was about freeing my soul from its heavy confines. An occasion to flail my arms and feel the wind on my armpits—something I imagined dragonflies experienced every time they took flight. Boy, did that make me jealous.

My first course of action before letting loose was to release my hair from its confines—generally a silky scrunchie. The increased motion would make my follicles bob up and down like they were engaged in a Medusa-esque dance of their own. Unfortunately, on the basketball court, there was a strict rule that all hair had to be pulled away from the face. As such, my high post days didn't allow total freedom.

While that was a definite downside, the upside was that nobody made fun of me when I ran with my arms up in the air. They just assumed I was waiting for a pass. I could jump and prance all I wanted without appearing *too* abnormal.

My mom once told me that when I was in preschool, Damian

Kirk asked Miss Fettering what I was doing. My teacher contemplated the question long and hard before responding she thought I was running. I don't think Mom told me this story to make me feel bad about my preferred style. She was probably just giving me a heads up that if I altered my execution a bit, I might be able to eradicate some of the abuse I took in my formative years.

The thing is, I never realized I was being made fun of. At least not until sometime around fifth grade. In my mind, I was friends with everyone. I liked them and they liked me. We were a joyful pack of contrasting personalities living in harmony. I blame Little Bear for my astonishing naïveté. I mean, heck, if a bear, a little girl, a duck, and an owl could all be best friends, why couldn't a room full of humans? *What an innocent little girl I was.*

Joelle Stinger was the first to overtly bully me out of my delusions. She would snatch my hat off my head and throw it in a mud-puddle; she would always push me in the hallway; and at lunch, she'd take my sandwich and grind it under the heel of her enormous purple Air Jordans.

I remember being confounded by the way she expressed friendship—because yes, even then, I couldn't fathom someone not wanting to be my friend. It wasn't until her mother called mine saying she'd heard her daughter was bullying me that the reality of the situation became clear. I was not universally liked. By the eighth grade, I started to question whether I was the stereotypical weird kid who always showed up in those angsty teenage movies. I was one headgear away from becoming a cliché.

I'm completely lost in my reverie and don't realize there's a person standing in front of me until she clears her throat. "Oh, hey, hi." I stumble over my words while staring at the rigidly prim woman across the counter. Her vaguely annoyed expression says it all—she thinks I'm a silly airhead. *Take a number, lady.*

"Hello." Her tone is not only brittle, it's condescending. "My colleague, Margaret, recommended your services. She said you were the best photographer in town." While I should enjoy the compliment, from her it sounds more like an accusation.

Margaret and Bob Rogers are my favorite clients. Half the business I currently have is from their referrals. Although, I thought they were both retired, so the "colleague" portion of this woman's comment is a little lost on me.

Without asking for clarification, I inquire, "Are you and your husband looking for something special?" Margaret and Bob have recently been reenacting covers from those bodice-ripping romance novels sold at the drug store. For the life of me, I can't see this woman wanting to do the same, but who am I to judge? Maybe her ice queen demeanor hides the heart of a wild woman. I hope that's the case, for her husband's sake, anyway.

"I'm not married." Her left eyebrow arches abruptly, nearly touching her hairline. She brushes the razor edge of her blonde bob aside, hooking it behind her ear. *Yikes, even her ears are pointy and sharp.*

"Oh, okay. I can certainly take some nice pictures of *you*. What did you have in mind?"

"I don't want pictures of me. I'm here to book a session for a man named Thomas Culpepper."

"And you want me to do for him what I do for Margaret and Bob?"

"Who's Bob?" she wants to know.

"Margaret's husband."

"I thought her husband was named Randal."

At this point, I probably should have considered the possibility we were talking about different Margarets, but I didn't. Social cues have never been my strong suit and as such I've gotten to a place where I ignore half the things that don't make sense to me. It's either that or accept feeling like I've perpetually lost the plot.

Forcing a smile, I announce with great authority, "Margaret's husband is *Bob*." Which in my defense, is true in the case of Margaret Rogers.

With a shrug, Miss Snippy tells me, "Then that's what I want you to do. If it won't be too much trouble." Her half eye-roll is a clear indicator she's being sarcastic—another indirect use of expression I have a challenging time understanding.

"No trouble at all." I pull out a notepad from under the counter and pull off the top sheet. Picking up my favorite felt tip pen—Papermate Fine-tip Flair—I ask, "Do you have any special instructions?"

Her green cat eyes narrow like my question is too ridiculous to be believed. I normally enjoy interacting with the public, but that isn't currently the case. "I'll just take the standard package." *Margaret and Bob never do the standard package.*

"That's only two wardrobe and background changes," I tell her.

"That will be more than enough." Talk about a lack of imagination. She pulls a Coach wallet out of her Coach handbag—an uptight brand if there ever was one.

Glancing at the payment screen, she says, "Four hundred dollars? You'd better be good."

"I am," I assure her before adding, "The cost includes hair and makeup, set changes, one nine by twelve print of each pose, and of course all of the digital files." Her eyebrow arches again. "We could be at it for hours," I add.

As she taps her credit card on the screen, I open the calendar on my laptop. She agrees to have the man I'm assuming is her boyfriend here one week from today at ten a.m. Then she walks away without so much as a goodbye. After two steps, she turns around. "If the shots are any good, I might be interested in hiring you to put together a calendar for us."

Tingles of excitement shoot across my scalp. "Like one of those firefighter calendars?" I wonder why I never thought of offering those before. I could probably make enough on them alone to pay for an expansion.

Snippy Von Sharpstein looks confused. "I don't know anything about firefighter calendars, but if they do them, then yes. I suppose like that."

I don't believe for one second she's never seen those smoking hot pictures of shirtless public servants, flexed muscles glistening in baby oil—an occasional puppy thrown in for good measure. Clearly, she wants me to think she's above such common enjoyment, which makes no sense at all. Especially as she just booked a sexy session for her man friend.

As my new customer walks out the door, I look down at a copy of her receipt. Constance Brucker. The name suits her. Uptight and rigid. I hope Thomas Culpepper gives me more to work with. If not, there's no way four hundred dollars will be enough.

CHAPTER TWO

THOMAS

"Yes, Mom," I mumble into the phone while shoving my toiletries into a bag. My mother has once again called to itemize all the reasons I should not have accepted a job in Wisconsin. She repeats her favorite lament for what must be the hundredth time. "There's so much cheese there."

"There's nothing wrong with cheese," I tell her.

"There is if you have high cholesterol or you're fat."

"Good thing my cholesterol and weight are perfectly normal."

"It's probably not even good cheese. Just pedestrian cheddar," she spits like there's something wrong with my favorite fromage.

"I promise to take you to a cheese factory when you come visit me. That way you can complain to them directly. Perhaps suggest they change their evil ways and focus on a nice triple cream Explorateur."

Ignoring my offer to let her vent her complaints directly to the source, she demands, "Visit you? Why in the world would I visit you *there*?"

"Because I'm moving there?"

"Thomas," my mom drawls exasperatedly like she is about to

state something so obvious a clairvoyant could see it across continents. "I predict you're going to miss New York City so much you'll be flying home every weekend. You'll be back for good in six months."

"I'm going to love Wisconsin." My tone is confident, which is not really the case. I grew up in Manhattan. I've lived here my whole life. If not for a recent upsetting event, I probably would have happily died here without ever entertaining the thought of another address.

"If you're that sure you're going to love it, why aren't you selling your apartment? Answer me that."

My apartment consists of the top two floors of a prewar brownstone on the Upper West Side—Central Park adjacent. At the very least its value will double in the next ten years. In the meantime, its rental will pay for the taxes and upkeep. Which I explain to my mother, yet again.

"You're keeping it because you're planning on coming home," she insists.

"Think what you want, Mom, I need to get going. Today is my last day at the hospital and I don't want to be late."

"You're still meeting us at Croquette at seven, right? Your father is coming straight from the airport." My dad is flying in from Rome where he's been speaking at an international cardiology conference. Instead of embracing retirement, he prefers to fly around the world and talk about his favorite topic, the human heart.

"I'll be there," I say before hanging up.

I love my mother. I really do. It's just that she can be a lot. She and my dad met at Duke University where they got their undergrad degrees. They're both from small southern towns, but the minute my mom stepped foot in Manhattan forty years ago—where my dad did his residency before accepting a job here—she shed any small-town vibe she might have once possessed. She set out to prove she was someone to be reckoned with, and she succeeded. I don't know of one person who has ever been able to put my mother in her place, and believe me, Manhattan society has tried.

After tossing my bag into a large suitcase, I zip it up and roll it toward the front door. This way, after supper with my family, I can have the car swing by my place and, within minutes, be back on the road on my way to Laguardia and my new life.

My last day at work flies by with record speed. Two heart attacks, one second-degree burn, one injured biker who played chicken with a taxicab and lost, two cases of pneumonia, two stab wounds, and a burst appendix. Being an emergency room doctor in the Big Apple is nothing if not exciting. Which is exactly why I'm leaving.

Three months ago, there was a subway accident that brought thirty-seven wounded into our ER. Thirty-seven men, woman, and, yes, children. It was my day off, but I was called in. My co-workers and I worked for ten long hours, treating lesser injuries and prepping the more extensive cases for surgery. It was grueling and awful, and honestly, more than I could process.

We get a lot of gory wounds in the city, but they usually come in one at a time. Thirty-seven at once was a life-changing event, especially as we lost a record twenty. After a week of getting practically no sleep, I started to see a therapist. Two sessions in, she asked if I'd ever thought about working in a less stressful environment.

"I'm an emergency room doctor," I told her. "ERs are traumatic by nature."

"True," she agreed. "But they're not all as intense as the ones in New York City."

While that might seem like an obvious statement, her words hit me like a football to the side of the head. I didn't have to work in the city. I could easily take a job upstate, or in Connecticut. There were plenty of smaller towns within commuting distance if

I decided I wanted to keep living in New York. That same week, I contacted a headhunting firm and told them I was considering relocating. My criteria included a smaller hospital, a town with a lower crime rate, and somewhere along the Eastern seaboard. I got everything except for the location part.

One month later, I received an offer from a hospital in Wisconsin. Elk Lake is a smallish vacation community in the southern part of the state. While not in my preferred area, I was immediately enchanted when I saw the pictures on the internet. Each image looked like an old-timey postcard.

The lake itself was full of small boats surrounded by sandy beaches hosting joyful families and assorted sun worshippers. Main Street was straight out of one of those old Judy Garland movies my grandmother used to love. The hospital looked like a doll house version of New York Presbyterian.

I told myself there was no way I could live in such a small town, yet I couldn't seem to get Elk Lake out of my mind. So much so, I agreed to take a meeting with the hospital board. I figured seeing it with my own eyes would either make it obvious I was crazy to consider such a move, or it would seal my fate. It did the latter.

After meeting with Constance Brucker, the hospital administrator, I signed a one-year contract. She wanted a three-year commitment, but I talked her down. While my heart was telling me this move was the right thing, my head still wasn't sure.

The hostess at Croquette greets me flirtatiously. "Dr. Culpepper, how nice to see you again." Her eyes make the slow peruse from the top of my head to my work loafers. "Your parents and sister are waiting for you." She purrs like a spoiled Siamese offering to share her bowl of cream.

Avoiding extended eye contact, I follow her toward my parents' favorite table situated under an impressive chandelier.

My dad looks tired but even so, his crow's feet are pointed upward in joy at being back at my mother's side.

My mom is wearing a classic black St. John pantsuit that makes her look formidable. She calls her wardrobe her armor, and it's a fitting description. My sister, Vivienne, is the only one not dressed for an upscale Manhattan eatery. She's wearing overalls that are covered in paint, and her auburn hair is pulled back in a messy ponytail. She's an artist who specializes in giant canvases, ensuring she's often covered from head to toe in her medium.

My family greets me like they haven't seen me in a year. Dad stands up and gives me a hug. "Son, how have you been?"

My sister throws her napkin at me and laments, "I can't believe you're leaving us!"

My mother merely turns her head to the side for a kiss on the cheek. Once I've performed my duty, she tells my sister, "He'll be back."

Sitting down in the empty chair across from my family matriarch, I tell her, "In a year, maybe. But then again, maybe not."

"I don't believe that for a minute." She focuses on her menu before deciding, "I'm getting the roasted chicken."

My dad smiles at her. "You know you want the Bolognese."

"I already had pasta once this week," she declares. "Too many carbs will make me look like a manicotti."

"What if *I* get the Bolognese?" he asks her. "Will you share it with me?"

"Do what you want, Jason." The small upturn at the corners of her mouth says it all. As long as she orders something healthy, she can eat as much of his food as she wants without feeling any guilt about it.

My parents have a love story for the ages. I dream of having the same kind of relationship someday, but thus far that hasn't been in the stars for me. While I've dated quite a bit, the life of an ER doctor isn't always conducive to a fulfilling social life.

Meeting women can also be a challenge. Dating within the medical field might sound ideal, but if you don't work the same shifts, you never see each other. And if you do have the same schedule, you wind up talking about work so much it feels like you never get away from it.

My sister announces, "I'm going to have the roasted vegetable and couscous salad. Then I'm getting the crème brûlée for dessert." Vivienne never likes to start a meal without knowing how it's going to end.

"We can get *one* for the table," my mom tells her pointedly while shifting her gaze to my sister's attire. Even though she's stopped complaining about Vivie's clothing, she still likes to make it known she doesn't support her bohemian ways.

"*You* get one for the table," Vivienne hisses. "I'm not sharing." My sister doesn't enjoy our mother's favorite pastime of counting calories like the success of our species depends upon it.

After telling the waiter what we want, I announce, "My realtor found a nice house for me to rent near the hospital. It has three bedrooms and two baths so there's plenty of room for all of you to come visit me."

"You can walk to work then." Vivie sounds relieved on my behalf.

"It'll be weird driving again," my dad elaborates.

As most New Yorkers don't let their children learn how to drive in the city—talk about trial by fire—I didn't get my license until I went away to college. "I haven't driven a car since I rented one last summer when I went to the Hamptons." That resulted in one fender bender and one slightly more serious run in with a light pole. *I swear I put the car in reverse.*

"You shouldn't buy a car," my mom announces. "You should lease so you can turn it in when you come home."

"I don't know what I'm going to do yet." I give her a pointed look to suggest her continued harping on my coming home is starting to wear thin. After all, she's not a native New Yorker. She knows life exists on the other side of all the bridges leading into Manhattan.

"I'm looking forward to coming to see you," Vivie says. "It'll be nice to visit a new state."

"You've never been to Wisconsin, have you?" I ask her.

"Why would she?" our mom demands.

My sister winks. "I hear the cheese is spectacular." We share a laugh as our mother rolls her eyes.

My family is the only real downside to my not being in New York. Even though we all have busy lives, we get together two or three times a month for a meal, which is a touchstone I've always counted on.

I feel a physical pang as I wonder who I'm going to be spending my free time with while living in the Badger State.

CHAPTER THREE

FINLEY

"I can't believe you're going to be a mother." My good friend, Allie, is sitting across the table from me, busily making lists of things she still needs to buy. She and I only met a few months ago, but we really hit it off. Her parents are my regulars, Margaret and Bob.

"I'm having a hard time believing it, too," she says. "It's certainly not happening the way I thought it would." Allie and her ex experienced several miscarriages before he decided to cheat on her and get his mistress pregnant. After their divorce, she moved home to recover. She worked at the bakery for several months before she started teaching at the local high school. That's where she met Margie Flynn.

Allie gave Margie a place to stay when the girl's parents kicked her out after she refused to have an abortion. They got to know each other very well, so when Margie decided to put her baby up for adoption, she asked if Allie wanted to do the adopting. Allie jumped at the chance.

"How does Noah feel about you becoming a mom?" Noah Riley is Margie's childhood crush and current boyfriend.

"He's excited for me." Her eyes twinkle when she smiles. "I think he's excited for him, too. Noah loves kids."

"Do you think the two of you are going to get married?" My friend's love story has Hallmark Channel written all over it. Noah moved back to Elk Lake to coach their alma mater's basketball team. He coaches the boys and Allie coaches the girls. I wish I could star in one of those "going home" love stories. But that would require my moving back to Central Illinois, which is something I will never do.

Allie lifts up her coffee cup but puts it back onto the table without taking a sip. "I've loved Noah since we were kids. And while I hope to marry him someday, I don't want him to ask just because I'm going to be a mom."

I assure her, "The only reason he'd ask you to marry him is because he loves you as much as you love him."

Allie's sigh is long and steady. When it peters out, she says, "I can't believe how well my life is turning out. After Brett, I thought I'd be alone forever."

"What a gargoyle," I hiss. "I hope his legs fall off at the knees. I hope he gets alien abducted and relocated off planet. I hope his new wife leaves him for another woman. I hope …"

Before I can further expand upon the revenge fantasies I have for Allie's ex, she reminds me, "His wife had quadruplets. Life will be anything but easy for Brett."

"Good," I tell her before changing the subject. "Now, if only Noah had a nice friend you could set me up with." I don't want to spend my life alone, but the truth is I've not had great results dating. Clearly, as I'm still single.

"I made him promise to keep a lookout," she tells me. Her eyes narrow until it feels like she's trying to peer inside my soul. "You're extremely pretty, you know. Quirky girl next door, with a touch of sass."

"Quirky?" I nearly choke on the word. I work very hard to be normal, and her observation suggests I'm failing.

"Yeah, you know …" She points a finger as I stir my tea three times before tapping the rim of the cup. "You've got that tea ritual, for instance."

My hand stops mid-strike before I can accomplish the final tap. I tell myself not to finish, to be stronger than my compulsion, but I fail. *Tap.* "Oh, this?" I try to laugh it off. "I guess I've always done it this way."

"Before every sip?" Yeah, clearly she thinks there's something wrong with me. And while I used to, as well, I'm now much more comfortable being me.

Instead of confirming what she already knows, I ask, "How else am I odd?"

Allie brushes her long auburn hair from her face. "I didn't mean any offense. I think you're delightful."

She sounds sincere, but I still want to know. "How else, Allie?" Not that I'm going to change my ways, but it's good to get feedback now and again.

She hems and haws for a minute before saying, "You've got that texture thing going on."

"What texture thing?" I silently order my fingers to stop petting my fuzzy pink sweater. They're resisting. It is my furriest one, after all.

"You're very touch-oriented," she tells me. "You like soft things."

"Most people like soft things." I know I sound defensive but I can't help it. "You like soft things, don't you?"

Allie's eyes take on an unreadable expression. "I do, but I don't normally go up and touch people on the street."

I shrug my shoulders. "*Once,* maybe twice. But only to compliment them." *And cop a feel of luxurious fabric while I'm there.*

"Fourteen times that I've noticed," Allie tells me. *Oh, my god, she's been counting.*

"Fourteen?" That sounds like an awful lot, even to me.

"It's cute," she says. "People don't seem to mind at all. In fact, I'm sure they're flattered."

Three times is cute, fourteen might be construed as a compulsion. "I didn't think I did it that often."

"Artistic people are known to appreciate texture."

Did she say artistic or autistic? Staring at my tea, I pick up my spoon, stir it three times and tap the rim twice. *Shoot, I've done it again!* For some reason unbeknownst to me, I decide to distract my friend from my habitual stirring and tapping by blurting out, "I'm on the spectrum." While I'm no longer embarrassed about my neurodivergence, I don't exactly broadcast it. Most people see it as a stigma.

Allie sits up straight and her mouth drops open in what I hope is surprise.

"I'm not mentally challenged," I assure her. At least not in the way she might assume.

"Of course you're not." She sounds like she believes me, which is good.

"But I'm not super smart like in *Young Sheldon,* either," I add. How I've wished that was the case. If I could multiply seven-digit numbers in my head or invent a new kind of physics, I'd probably be a lot more comfortable broadcasting my condition.

"Finley, I don't think any less of you now that I know you're autistic. Heck, life is a spectrum. We're all on it somewhere, right?"

"In theory," I tell her. "In reality, most of you fit nicely into the box society has decreed acceptable. Meanwhile, I'm often outside of that box, wondering how to get in." With a pointed frown, I add, "But it's covered in barbed wire and tracker jackers." Nod to *The Hunger Games,* my most favorite post-apocalyptic form of entertainment.

Allie releases a snort at my description. "Why in the world would you want to be like everyone else?" If I didn't know better, I'd be inclined to believe my friend admires me. Yet there's just too much social stereotyping for that to be true.

"It's not that I want to be like everyone else; I just don't want to be so different as to stand out."

"Why?" she wants to know.

I lift one finger and announce, "There's the stirring. I don't particularly want to do it, but I have to. Routine is very reassuring to me." Another digit goes up. "Then there's my love of certain textures—which is pure satisfaction. But along with that goes my revulsion of other surfaces." Before she can ask, I tell her, "Aluminum foil makes me very nervous. I also hate the feeling of sand anywhere on my body."

"What else?" she wants to know.

"I have a number fixation." Allie's gaze narrows in confusion. "I love the numbers three, five, seven, fifteen, and twenty," I tell her.

"How is that a problem?"

I inhale deeply before explaining, "I like to breathe in slowly to the count of seven, but I feel lightheaded if I exhale the same amount. I can usually only make it to five, then I have to inhale to the count of two and force myself to exhale five, so the numbers work out."

At this point I'm fully expecting Allie to stand up and tell me it's been nice knowing me before she runs for the exit, never to be seen again. Instead of doing that, she says, "That has to be a lot of work."

"It is," I assure her.

"Can you ever breathe without counting?"

My chin bobs up and down three times. "When I'm sleeping."

My friend looks moderately panicky at hearing this. "That sounds exhausting."

"I've been doing it for as long as I remember. It's just normal at this point."

"I've always thought autistic people avoided eye contact. I mean seriously, I would have never known you were on the spectrum." She hurries to ask, "How did you find out?"

"Like you," I tell her, "my parents thought I was just a little different. They never guessed I had anything diagnosable going on. But when I was fifteen, I failed math. I was never a straight A student, but I never got anything lower than a C, until then." I inhale deeply before adding, "My teacher told my parents I was very smart, but I refused to apply myself. I knew that wasn't the case, but I didn't want my mom and dad to know I was stupid."

"So, what happened?"

"My mom found a tutor who came over to the house twice a week. Four weeks in, she told my parents I was unteachable. She suggested they investigate putting me into a special education program. My mom was so mad, she fired the woman on the spot and drove me two hours away to Chicago to see a specialist."

"Who said you were autistic."

"Eventually," I tell her. "It turns out there's a lot that goes into the diagnoses. ADHD, compulsive disorders, and learning disabilities are all individual diagnoses, as well as being common in people on the spectrum." I conclude, "It takes time to figure out exactly what they're going to embroider on your sash."

"Embroider on your sash?" she repeats.

"Yeah, you know, like Miss America contestants."

Allie laughs. "You're adorable, Finley. Seriously, I'm glad you're not like everyone else. A world of beige makes for a boring life."

"You're not beige," I tell her.

"Not usually, but I can be," she says. "I don't think you could ever be boring."

My head tips to the side so that my blonde hair sits on my shoulder. After a count of three, I flip it to the other side. I don't want my left shoulder to feel left out. I respond, "That seems like a weighted compliment, but I'll take it."

"Is being autistic the reason you don't drive?" my friend wants to know.

I hate that question. As far as the world is concerned, a trained monkey in a diaper can learn to drive, so if you don't, you must be a real idiot. "Autistic people can get drivers' licenses," I tell her.

"Then why don't *you* have one?"

"I get overstimulated easily," I confess. "Lights, pedestrians, traffic, horns. There's a lot going on."

"I'm surprised you played college basketball. That had to be a lot of stimulation, too."

"I used to wear clear earplugs to help mute the noise," I tell her. "Either the refs didn't notice them, or they thought they were hearing aids. Either way, no one mentioned them until my junior year. After that it became an issue, and I wasn't allowed to wear them anymore. Which led to me quitting. That buzzer, man. It's like being stabbed in the eardrum."

Allie laughs abruptly. "It really is." As the girls' high school basketball coach, she'd know. "Then there's all the whistle blowing and yelling in the stands."

"As bad as all of that is," I tell her, "nothing is worse than ten pairs of court shoes screeching across the floor."

Her grimace is one of camaraderie. "Do you have any special interests that are tied to your diagnosis?"

"Like Sam from *Atypical*?" I ask, referencing yet another television show that has dipped its toe into the neurodivergent well. Not surprisingly, the only hit programs about being on the spectrum illustrate stereotypical behaviors. And while I've truly enjoyed both shows, neither portrays my particular brand of sparkle. I'm neither brilliant nor overtly awkward, although the latter takes some work. Most autistic people pass for normal, most of the time.

"Yeah, like Sam," she confirms.

"I'm not obsessed with Antarctic penguins, if that's what you mean. I do tend to hyper-focus, though. When I get into a project, hours can feel like minutes."

"Give me an example."

"When I was in college, I took a drawing class. The assignment was to make a sketch of an interesting nose. I started at six o'clock at night and the next thing I knew it was six in the morning, and my alarm was going off."

"You spent twelve hours drawing a nose?"

"I did."

"You must have gotten an A."

Shaking my head, I tell her, "I drew an aardvark nose. My professor claimed to have asked for a human nose. Personally, I don't think he did but as I was the only one to jump species, he won the argument. He gave me a C for at least doing the assignment meticulously."

"That seems unfair."

"I agree," I tell her before changing the subject. "Any chance we can talk about something else?"

Allie reaches across the little bakery table and takes my hands in hers. Looking me straight in the eye, she declares, "We can talk about anything you want. But please know, I don't think any less of you because you have a touch of the *'tism*. If anything, I'm a little bit jealous that you're such a unique person."

A thousand embarrassing memories try to break out of my subconscious at the same time. Pushing them back into the basement of my brain, I reply, "I appreciate that, Allie. I really do. I'm comfortable being me now, but it's not been an easy journey getting here."

"I bet," she says sympathetically.

"It's hard enough being a teenager without learning that everything you thought you knew about yourself might not be true."

"Did it cause a big identity crisis?"

Instead of answering directly, I decide to practice my use of metaphors, and ask, "Does a Sasquatch have big feet?"

While I'm truly over feeling embarrassment about my differences, I'm reminded why I don't like to discuss them. When people find out you're autistic, they ask a thousand questions that, whether they realize or not, have a tendency to make the afflicted person feel … well … afflicted.

CHAPTER FOUR

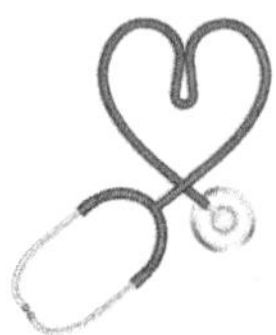

THOMAS

It turns out there aren't a lot of travelers arriving in Madison after eleven o'clock at night. I'm glad I scheduled a car to meet me at the airport instead of waiting until I landed.

After retrieving my luggage, I roll it out the sliding doors and look for the ride that's picking me up. According to the app, it's supposed to be a Tesla. Imagine my surprise when a man steps out of a giant, retro, black Cadillac—seriously, the car is bigger than some NYC apartments. "Thomas Culpepper?" he calls out.

"That's me," I respond while looking from the left to the right for witnesses in case he's really a mobster who time traveled here from the eighties to fulfill a hit someone hired on me. *Talk about a sure sign I'm a native New Yorker*. Most people would never consider such a possibility, but I worked with a doctor once who operated on a crime boss's wife. She didn't make it and her husband decided to enact revenge. Long story short, my co-worker survived, but left the city and took early retirement.

When I don't move toward the car, the driver asks, "You need me to come over there and push your suitcase for you?"

I step forward. "Sorry, it's been a long day."

After popping the trunk, he lifts my luggage and throws it in with the ease of a dock worker used to handling heavy cargo. "I don't usually work this late," he tells me. "But I had a fare that took me all the way to Chicago this afternoon. I figured I'd stop and pick you up on my way home."

"How long did that take?" I ask, while opening the front door to sit in the passenger seat next to him.

"Two hours to get there." He scoffs. "You'd think they'd just take a train or bus, but some people have more money than brains."

I pull the seatbelt strap across my shoulder and snap it into place. Somehow, the inside of the car seems bigger than the outside. "I was expecting a different ride," I tell my driver.

He snort/laughs. "I used to tell folks to look for Adelaide, but I didn't get as many trips that way. People are kind of snooty these days."

Even though I would have probably forgone the pleasure of this ancient vehicle, too, I decide to play the diplomat. I pat the fading burgundy leather seat next to me. "I bet this used to be the hottest ride around."

"It sure was. I didn't have Addie back in those days though. I picked her up at auction a couple of years ago. Can you believe she only had a hundred and fifty thousand miles on her?"

A hundred and fifty? "Wow, what's she at now?" I'm hoping he says a hundred and fifty-five.

"Two hundred thousand and twelve! Amazing, right?"

"It really is." I suddenly worry she won't have the life in her to get me to Elk Lake.

My driver turns the key on the ignition which roars to life like a tiger waking up from a sound sleep. "Name's Kevin Picknell," he says. "But you can call me Pickles. They've been calling me that since the second grade and the nickname stuck."

"Thomas," I tell him, even though he already knows my name from my reservation. "You said you decided to pick me up on your way home. Do you live around Elk Lake?" I don't really have a deep burning desire to know, but I like to make small talk with my drivers. It makes time fly by faster. And being that Kevin —I'm not sure I can call another person Pickles—and I will be on the road for at least an hour together, it would be awkward if we didn't chat.

"I was born in Elk Lake Hospital, and I've lived there for my whole fifty-seven years," he tells me. "I married my high school sweetheart, and we raised our kids in the house I grew up in."

"That's a pretty sound endorsement," I tell him. "I did the same thing you did, but I was born in New York City. Haven't been married yet and I don't have kids, but I've spent thirty-six years there."

Kevin turns the wheel sharply and merges onto the main road. "Why'd you leave?"

I give him an abbreviated version of my story. "It's stressful being an emergency room doctor in the city. I decided to see if I like small-town life any better."

"Better than New York?" I'm convinced he's going to offer to take me back to the airport when he adds, "You're never going to want to go back to the Big Apple. Elk Lake is heaven, man!"

"How's the pizza?" I ask. "I'm a bit of a snob."

"We got pizza. It's pretty good too, but our fried cheese curds are the real prize. Trust me."

"I've never had a fried cheese curd," I confess.

Kevin stares at me in shock before slamming on the brakes to keep from rear-ending the car in front of us. "That's like telling me you've never had a beer or a grilled cheese sandwich."

"I've had both of those," I assure him. "Cheese curds just aren't a big thing in New York."

Shaking his graying head, he tells me, "Your first meal out in Elk Lake needs to be at the diner on Main Street. Order the curds with all the sauces and then you gotta tell me which is your favorite."

"Tell you? You want me to call you or something?" I don't

normally stay in touch with my drivers. In fact, I've never done that.

"Nah." He waves his hand to the side. "Just come over to my house."

This is getting weirder and weirder. "To your house?"

"I live next door to where I'm taking you. Didn't I tell you that?"

"No, you didn't."

"Thought I did. You know, that's why I decided to pick you up on my way home."

This has been an odd interaction and I'm not sure my mother would approve. Even so, it's not unwelcome. In fact, I think I just made my first friend in Elk Lake. "Well, then," I tell Kevin, "I'll do that."

"I'll do you one better," he says. "I'll go to the diner with you and walk you through it. You know, if you want."

"That would be great," I tell him, not quite sure if it would be or not. But now that I know my driver and I are neighbors, it probably isn't a bad idea.

Kevin and I spend the next forty minutes talking about an array of topics that cover everything from his stance on the trans movement (judge not lest ye be judged, he's decided) to his deep-rooted hatred of the Chicago Bears—they'll never be as good as the Packers. Apparently, it doesn't matter that the Bears have won more Super Bowls. The Packers have beaten the Bears in every encounter they've had since 2011, so that's the end of that. The Packers have his heart.

As soon as we pass the Welcome to Elk Lake sign, Kevin says, "Welcome home, Tommy." It seems he's decided to use my childhood nickname, which honestly doesn't bother me. My sister and dad still call me Tommy.

Kevin proceeds to give me the scoop on every building we pass. "That's the Elk Lake Lodge," he says proudly as we pass a large hotel set back in the woods. "It's owned by some fancy pants billionaire from Chicago, but he's a good enough guy."

As we approach the intersection at Main Street, he points down the road to the right. "The diner's on the left. Movie theater is across the street." Turning to the right, he adds, "Grocery store is two blocks that way."

"How many grocery stores are there in town?" I ask him. I shop at the Red Apple in my neighborhood, but D'Agastino's, Zabar's and Fairway are close-by options. They all have their specialties.

"One," he tells me. "But we got two cheese stores, a bakery, and the diner. There's also a pizza place, a pub, a couple other restaurants …" He pauses for a beat before adding, "The bait and tackle shop on the lake serves the best tater tots in the state."

Note to self: Even with such a glowing recommendation, resist the urge to order food at the same place they sell fishing worms.

"It sounds like I'll be well taken care of," I tell him.

Kevin makes a sharp left before taking the first right. "We're here." He pulls into the driveway of the house I recognize from the realtor's photos. The white two-story Cape Cod-style house looks like the picture-perfect starter home for a young family. All it needs is a swing hanging from the oak tree in the front yard, and maybe some flowers in the window boxes that adorn the first-floor windows.

Kevin jumps out of the car and gets my suitcase from the trunk. I join him after a moment. "I've never lived in a real house before," I confess. "You know, with a yard and everything."

My neighbor's face contorts into a look of pure horror. "That's not good, Tommy. People need grass. It's a scientific fact."

I side-eye him to see if he's teasing me, but he looks serious. "I should probably find a gardener before spring then," I tell him.

"What for?"

What does he mean, what for? "To mow the lawn?"

"Tommy, Tommy, Tommy, you don't hire a gardener to mow the grass. If you don't want to do it yourself, you get a neighborhood kid. I'll make you a list," he offers.

With a nod of my head, I reach into my coat pocket for my

wallet. Before I get it out, Kevin tells me, "You paid on the app. You're all set."

"I was going to tip you in cash," I tell him. "Cash is king for tipping, am I right?"

"You know what's even better?" he asks. "Taking me out for my favorite cheese curds. You can pay."

"That sounds like a fair deal." I reach out and shake his hand before pushing my suitcase to the front door of my new place. Leaning down, I lift the doormat and search for the key that's supposed to be there. It's not.

"No key?" Kevin calls out.

I turn around and shrug my shoulder. "No key."

"Try the flower box under the picture window," he suggests.

I walk across the grass to check, but there's nothing but dirt inside. "Nothing."

Kevin holds up one finger and runs across the yard next door. Walking inside, I hear him call out, "Shelly! I need you!"

A short red-head walks outside in a fuzzy bathrobe. Her hands are on her hips as she admonishes, "Is that anyway to say hello to me after you've been gone all day?"

Her husband leans down and kisses her cheek. "Hi, honey. Sorry. I just brought our new neighbor home from the airport. He can't find the key Judy was supposed to have left for him."

She peeks around her front porch to look at me. Then she waves. "I'm Shelly!"

"Thomas Culpepper," I say.

"Call him Tommy," Kevin tells her.

"It's under the fake rock next to the porch swing," my neighbor yells. "Everyone and their brother knows to look under the mat if they want to break into a house," she yells.

And now they know about the fake rock on the porch, but I don't mention that. I simply find the very unrealistic-looking plastic rock and pick it up. Opening it, I pull out the key and hold it up in Shelly's direction. "Thank you."

"No problem, honey. I'll see you in the morning. I'm going to bring over some muffins for you."

Kevin runs back across to my driveway and gets into his car. As he pulls out, he rolls down the window. "We'll set up dinner soon, okay?" Then he waves and takes Adelaide home.

To be honest, I haven't spent much time wondering what my neighbors were going to be like in Wisconsin. But if pressed, I don't think I would have ever come up with a duo like Pickles and Shelly. So far, I'm not disappointed.

CHAPTER FIVE

FINLEY

I'm standing in what used to be the baby store next to my studio. While the extra space will be nice, I'm going to have some work ahead of me to make it useful for my needs.

My realtor is saying something, but my thoughts have already started wandering. All background noise is blending into a sort of low distant humming. That is, until I hear Anna say something about an infestation.

Turning sharply away from the wall I'm considering tearing down, I gasp, "What infestation?"

"Mouse. But don't worry, that's all been taken care of. The exterminator came last week."

"Good." I turn around again and try to imagine what it would be like to see directly into my store from here. "You're sure I can remove the wall?"

Pulling the contract out of her purse, Anna tells me, "As long as you sign a three-year lease. If you break it earlier, you'll have to put the wall back up at your own expense."

I nod my head up and down—wait for it—*five times*. "Okay. I'm ready."

Anna smiles excitedly. "You won't regret it, Finley. I'm thinking you can use this side of your business for boudoir shots and keep the rest as is for your primary business." Little does she know the boudoir shots have become so popular they're now my main source of income. Yet she's got a point. If I keep the rooms separate I won't make the families who come in nervous when they see sexier staging. Plus, then I'll only have to add a doorway.

Taking the pen handed to me, I walk over to the Tiny Tots counter and sign at the X. I give the contract back to my realtor. "Thanks for negotiating this for me, Anna. I feel a lot better about the new terms." They previously wanted a five-year lease.

"It's my pleasure." She hands me a set of keys. "You'll want to change the locks."

"I'll invite you to the grand opening once I'm up and running," I tell her. "In the meantime, I want to do a nice family picture for you as a thank you."

"I won't say no to that." Patting her slightly rounded stomach, she adds, "But let's wait until baby two arrives, okay?"

"It's a deal," I tell her.

Anna is besties with Faith, who owns the bakery down the street. They've been tight since childhood, and every time I see them together I feel a pang of envy. I can't imagine how cool it must be to have a friend who's known you for your whole life. Allie is pretty much my only friend in town, and we've only been hanging out for a few months. Having said that, I have high hopes one day she and I will be as close as Faith and Anna.

"I've got an appointment at ten," I tell Anna, "I'd better get moving."

Waving my contract in the air, she replies, "I'll drop this off with the landlord. And congratulations again, Finley. This is going to be a great move for you."

After walking out the front door, I lock up before speed walking next door to Happy Snaps. I've lived in Elk Lake for three years and have had my shop for nearly that long. I spend more conscious hours here than I do at my apartment. As such, I've made a real effort to make it as comfortable and homey as possible.

As soon as I enter, I notice a man sitting on one of the two overstuffed shabby-chic chairs by the window. He looks up and makes direct eye contact, which causes every thought in my brain to pour out like sand in a sieve. *Holy Hot Stuff, Batman*. This man is extraordinarily handsome, but his appeal is more than just physical. He emanates a kind of golden energy that's positively intoxicating.

"Hi there." As soon as he stands up, I can feel the room start to sway. I stagger to the counter so I don't fall over. He's well over six feet and from what I can tell he's built like he spends hours at the gym every day.

"H … h … hi, yourself. Thomas Culpepper?" I ask, both hoping he is and isn't at the same time. How in the world will I be able to take sexy pictures of this man and keep my wits about me? I can't even look at him fully clothed without stuttering.

"That's me." He flashes a brilliant smile which makes me wonder if he's ever starred in toothpaste commercials. His hair is the softest looking wavy chocolate brown I've ever seen. My hand lifts of its own accord like it's trying to reach out and touch it. Which of course I know I can't do. At least until it's time for me to style his hair for the shoot. I practically drool at the thought.

Thomas looks at my hand suspended in mid-air before copying the gesture and waving at me. "Hel-lo." He breaks the word into two syllables like I'm new to the English language and might not understand otherwise.

I drop my hand immediately and try to regain my composure. "Constance is very excited about these shots."

"Really?" He looks confused.

"Really," I assure him. "She's ordered the basic package to start, but if she likes what she sees …" In lieu of finishing my sentence, I give him an exaggerated wink.

"I didn't realize this was such a big deal to her," he says.

"Oh, it is. A *very* big deal."

Thomas's hazel eyes narrow in confusion before he bends down to pick up the bag he brought with him. "I brought some different shirts."

"Oh, we won't need shirts." There's no way I'm covering up this man in unnecessary clothing. *No way.* Unless of course it's a pirate shirt, wide open and billowing in the wind. Lucky for him, I have such an item in my costume collection.

Thomas's gorgeous brow furrows, drawing my attention to the golden flecks in his eyes. "I brought a doctor's coat too, if you prefer that."

"A doctor's coat?" I love the idea of turning him into a sexy doctor. It's decided then—we'll do a pirate look and a doctor one. Constance is going to *love* these.

Motioning to Thomas, I tell him, "Follow me into the backroom and you can get ready there."

As he approaches, I inhale his spicy aftershave. *Cloves, cinnamon, and orange, oh my!* "You smell great." The words are out of my mouth before I can stop them. That's another fun thing about me—I don't always think before speaking, which can sometimes make other people uncomfortable. Like the time I told a woman in the grocery store that her pants made her butt look amazing. While meant as a compliment, it was clear she wasn't used to such forthright comments from a stranger. I figured that out when she walked out of the store, leaving a full cart behind.

The last thing I want to do is make Thomas nervous. I hurry to tell him, "You smell like my favorite Christmas cookies."

"Huh. I've never heard that one before."

"It's a compliment of the highest order," I assure him. "My mom makes the best orange spice shortbread you've ever tried." Just when I think I've saved the moment from getting too awkward, I groan suggestively and declare, "Yummy!" Thomas's eyes pop open wider in an expression I once again worry is fear.

The backroom of my store is one big unfinished space with a variety of backdrops scattered about. I point toward the barber-style chair in front of a big lighted mirror in the corner and tell him, "Let's start there. I'll get your hair and makeup done first and then we'll settle on wardrobe."

"Hair and makeup?"

"Yeah, you know, so we can get the look we're after."

"I thought I was okay the way I am."

"You're fantastic," I assure him. "Really great! But I want to make sure we capture your character to the fullest."

"I'm a doctor," he tells me. I'm starting to think Thomas might be the one new to the English language.

"Doctor, pirate, sexy duke with a superiority complex … you can be anything you want and I'm here to make that happen."

Thomas sits down in the makeup chair looking highly uneasy. "I really am a doctor." Then he asks, "Do you get a lot of pirates and nobility in here?"

"Tons," I assure him.

Thomas sits down with the same amount of enthusiasm he might have knowing he was about to be electrocuted. "I'm pretty sure I don't need hair and makeup," he says again.

"I'm not putting lipstick on you, Thomas." Picking up a bronzing palate, I tell him, "Just a bit of contrast to sharpen your angles."

"Why exactly do I need sharper angles?" How is it possible that he's even sexy when he's acting stupid?

Turning to look him square in the eye, I ask, "Why do you think you're here?"

"I'm here to get my picture taken for …"

"Constance," I finish his sentence for him. "You're here for Constance. And you want to make her happy, don't you?"

"I … suppose?" He isn't selling it.

"You suppose? She's paid me four hundred dollars to take very specific pictures of you and that is exactly what I'm going to do. Do you understand?" He nods his head almost imperceptibly. "This is my job, Thomas. My *job*," I tell him. "It's what I do for a living. It's how I pay my bills."

"Yes, but …"

"Constance came in here *herself* to tell me what she wants, and as *she* is my client. I'm not going to let her down."

Thomas sits as still as a statue while I brush bronzer on his cheeks and jaw. By the time I'm done with him, he could have posed for a Michelangelo statue of a Greek god. I can't take all the credit for that though—he practically is one on his own.

Once I'm convinced his face couldn't look any better, I put the makeup brush down and face my model once again. This is the moment I've been waiting for. After turning the chair so his back faces the mirror, I lift my hands and run all ten of my fingers through his hair. Holy heck. It's even softer than it looks. It's better than all my furry sweaters combined. It's like running my hands through a litter of baby minks. It's softer than the Barefoot blanket I spent way too much money on. But only because it lost some of its softness after being washed. Until then, it was worth ten times as much.

Dear Santa, all I want for Christmas is to rub Thomas Culpepper's head every day of my life until I die.

Reluctantly, I remind myself that Thomas is Constance's boyfriend, not mine. Yet I don't understand how that can be because this man is so vital and alive. Constance has the warmth of a vampire bat in winter. But they got together somehow and now it's my job to give my client the best fantasy material I can.

She never has to know it's doing the same for me.

CHAPTER SIX

THOMAS

There have been a handful of times in my life where I was certain I'd completely lost the thread. Like the time I walked into a conversational Russian class instead of French 101. Or when my sister convinced me to take a ballroom dancing class with her, and the first number they taught us was the Macarena, in sign language. I still don't know what that was about.

There are moments so utterly ridiculous you feel like someone slipped you a mickey and you're hallucinating. None of those instances are stranger than what is currently happening to me.

"Just take off your shirt and I'll rub baby oil on you until you're glistening."

I stare at the photographer tasked with taking my picture for the hospital wall of staff photos like she's completely lost her mind. Yes, she's beautiful. Yes, I'm attracted to her, somewhat against my will. But there is no way I'm going to let her slather me up with oil for a picture that's supposed to assure people I'm a competent doctor.

"That won't be necessary," I tell her all the while trying to keep her from unbuttoning my shirt.

"Thomas," she says sternly like my sexy anatomy professor from sophomore year of college. "Let me do my job."

I take a step back while clutching my shirt modestly. "I don't understand what any of this has to do with why Constance hired you." I sound borderline scared, but darn it, I'm not comfortable with any of this.

"She has a plan," the photographer says cryptically before adding, "A very good plan, if you ask me."

"What plan?" I demand. *To embarrass me in front of the town?*

Finley sighs loudly before crossing her arms like she's losing patience with me. "It's not my place to tell you."

"If you don't tell me," I respond, "I'm going to leave before you take any pictures of me." I emphasize my threat by turning to face the exit.

"You can't leave! I promised Constance two different looks and I'm going to deliver." The photographer takes a step toward me, and adds, "I just rented out the store next to mine and I need every job I can get right now to pay for it. That means, I need you to do what you're here to do and I need you to do it well."

Now I feel bad. I don't want to stress her out, but at the same time I'm not some boy toy for her to manhandle. *Womanhandle.* You know what I mean. "What's Constance's plan, Finley?"

She looks up at the ceiling and sighs loudly like I'm her errant child pouting because she won't let me eat a bucket full of candy. "If I fill you in, you absolutely cannot tell Constance I gave you a heads up. She might want it to be a surprise."

I stare her straight in the eye, but she's having a hard time holding the contact. Which makes me even more anxious. "I promise I won't tell her."

Finley glances at her feet before hesitantly returning her gaze to mine. "Constance is thinking about putting together a calendar." She shrugs her eyebrows up and down suggestively. "Like the firefighters have."

After releasing the most unmanly gasp on the planet, I manage to demand, "Why?"

"Women love those things," she assures me. "It's great fantasy material, don't you think?"

"Maybe?" The big question here is not the marketability of such an item, but why would my new boss book me to do one without telling me. That's just wrong. And weird. And not at all something I could have imagined her doing.

"Those firefighter calendars bring in a lot of money," Finley tells me. "A lot."

Is that why Constance is doing it? Is she trying to raise money for the hospital? Even so, she should have informed me and then got my consent first.

Finley interrupts the litany of questions running through my head. "But only if the pictures are good."

Finally, a lifeline. "Is that what she said? Only if the pictures are good?"

She nods her head, not once, but five times. "That's what she said."

A slow smile crosses my mouth. I've just found my out. I'll do Finley's photoshoot, if for no other reason than to get it over with. I just won't do a very good job. I have to send the message to Constance that I'm not the man she thinks I am.

"Fine," I tell Finley. "I'll do it."

"Seriously?" she sounds as shocked as I have been ever since stepping foot into this place.

"Yup. Let's do it so I can go home." *And wipe all this makeup off my face.*

"Take off your shirt," Finley orders. "Then come over here." She grabs a bottle of baby oil sitting on the makeup table. I approach cautiously, even though I know what she's going to do. After opening the cap, she pours a fair amount in her hands. This woman has totally knocked me off my footing and has honestly made me feel more than a little insane.

One step. Two steps. Three steps. I'm in front of her. "It might be a little cold," she says while simultaneously slapping oily hands on my skin.

I shriek before practically jumping out of my skin. "It's not cold, it's freezing!"

"I keep it in the refrigerator," she says, like that's the obvious place to keep baby oil. "It's cold on purpose."

"What's the purpose?" I'm shivering like I've been thrown in a snowdrift. Naked.

Finley starts to make circles with her pointer fingers around my chest region. "It's to, you know … perk things up."

"Perk things up?" Her meaning is suddenly clear. "Ah, I see."

"Thank goodness. I didn't want to have to say the words."

"You didn't want to say that you were trying to make my nipples erect?" I challenge her with my eyes.

She blushes like a maiden aunt from the turn of the eighteenth century. "Correct."

"You're the one who takes these pictures," I accuse. "Not me."

"I take tasteful romantic photos. There's nothing dirty about them." She lifts her nose in the air like I've somehow offended her. "I enhance people's personal lives by letting them live out their fantasies, *tastefully*." She repeats the last word, like just by saying it, she's making it so.

"Are you going to rub this oil in, or not?" I ask with more than a hint of challenge in my tone.

She stares at my skin like performing that task is on the top of her list of things she wants to do before she dies. But instead of finishing what she started, she averts her gaze and demurely tells me, "You can go ahead and do it yourself. I don't want to make you uncomfortable."

If that was her intention, she failed. I have never been more disconcerted in my entire life. Having said that, I *am* ready to start having a little fun.

Once I'm sufficiently shimmering, Finley hands me a billowy white shirt to put on, which I do in record speed. Then she leads me toward a backdrop of a tumultuous seascape. Smacking at my hands to get me to release the death grip I have on my shirt, she orders, "Let your arms hang at your sides. Then turn and face the wind."

I gaze stage left to find an industrial-sized fan facing me. Finley hurries over and turns it on. She starts it on low and I'm immediately chilled again. "Any chance you can turn the heater on?"

She shakes her head. "We want you perky, remember?" *How could I forget?* She cranks the fan two more times before my hair starts to blow. Finley turns on the lights illuminating the set and declares, "It's go time!" Then she picks up her camera.

I do my best impersonation of Ben Stiller in *Zoolander*. I unleash his trademark "blue steel" smolder while puckering my lips like I'm blowing kisses. Then I furrow my brow and force my eyes to open so wide I can feel my IQ falling.

Finley lets her camera dangle from the strap around her neck. "What are you doing?"

"Modeling?" As I'm still in character, I sound as dumb as I look.

"Don't try so hard," she orders. "Just channel your inner pirate." She prompts, "You're a rugged man of the sea. You're an adventurous outlaw searching for buried treasure. You're ..."

I interrupt, "Going to hang at dawn for kidnapping the governor's daughter." Her look of confusion has me explaining, "*Pirates of the Caribbean.*"

"Ah, okay then. If that's your motivation, let me have it." She's nothing if not a consistent cheerleader. Which I suppose most of her clientele must respond to. Just not me.

"Ahoy, matey!" I shout while waving my arms mightily like I'm trying to hail a taxi in Times Square.

Finley once again stops taking pictures. "Ahoy, matey?"

"Isn't that something pirates say?" This is going to be more fun than I thought.

"Not sexy pirates," she assures me. "They say things like, 'Come over here, wench, and kiss the lips off of me.'"

"Seriously? Where do you get your information?"

"My client, Margaret, reads historical romance novels," she says like any idiot should have known.

"I've never read one," I assure her.

Her pointer finger shoots straight up. "Wait here," she says like she senses my greatest desire is to make a run for it.

Crossing the room, Finley picks up a book sitting on a small table and brings it over to me. I nearly laugh out loud when she hands it to me. *This* is the look she wants? The man on the cover is staring at the camera like he's got laser vision and he's trying to cut the photographer in half. His shirt is open and—wait for it—he's obviously on the chilled side. His hair is blowing as though he's standing in gale force winds and he's holding a sword at his side like he's going to single-handedly save the world from god knows what.

"This is exactly what we're going for," Finley assures me.

Now that my assignment has been clarified, I turn to the camera with devious intent and start having more fun than I can ever remember having.

CHAPTER SEVEN

FINLEY

Inserting my spoon into the teacup, I rotate it the requisite three times before performing the double tap. Then I pick up the mug and take a sip. I made orange clove in memory of Thomas Culpepper's delicious-smelling aftershave.

Staring intently at my computer screen, I cannot for the life of me believe this pirate is the same sexy man who came into my shop. There isn't one decent picture. Not one. Which never happens. Even if the model is reluctant, I can always get one good shot—usually when they drop their guard and don't realize I'm still snapping away. Not Thomas Culpepper though. He is by far the worst model I've ever worked with, and that includes the baby who projectile vomited onto my new camera lens.

Picking up my phone, I call Allie. Before she can say hello, I ask, "Can you come over?" Her apartment is only a block from mine.

"How about if I bring a pizza? I was just getting ready to order one."

"Extra cheese," I tell her.

I spend the next thirty minutes trying to find one respectable pose and one facial expression—not necessarily in the same photo. I'll Frankenstein them together if I have to. There's nothing. Not even the doctor shots, and Thomas *claims* to be a doctor. How hard could it be for him to look like one?

The knock on my door causes the teacup to nearly jump out of my hands. Clearly, more time has passed than I noticed. After mopping up the spilled liquid with my sweatshirt, I get up and walk across the room to let my friend in. I take the large pizza box from her while asking, "Want a beer?"

"Sure." She slides her coat off and drapes it over a stool at the counter. "You sounded upset. You okay?"

I reach into the refrigerator and grab two long-neck bottles before placing them on the counter. Popping them open, I hand one to Allie. "I had a session today with the most amazingly gorgeous man I have ever laid eyes on. Sizzling." I add the last for emphasis.

"Sounds like fun," she says enthusiastically.

I lead her into the living room and point to the spot I recently vacated on the sofa. "Take a look."

My friend sits down and puts her beer on a coaster. Then she focuses on the computer screen before looking up at me. She looks back and forth several times before asking, "This is the most beautiful man you've ever seen?"

"I know, right?!" I place the pizza box onto the coffee table before plopping down next to her. Then I wrap my arms around one of my furry, white, decorative pillows—I need *all* the comfort right now. "The thing is, in person, he's a total hottie. He just can't model to save his life."

Allie picks up the laptop and brings it closer to her face. "Is he cross-eyed?"

"In nearly every frame," I assure her. "But not in real life. In real life his eyes are a delicious hazel green. They also point in the same direction at the same time."

"Huh." She's obviously as perplexed as I am.

Reaching over, I click to the next page to show her the "doctor" photographs. She bursts out laughing. "These are horrible, Finley."

"Yup." Beating my head into the pillow, I tell her, "I don't know what to do. The woman who ordered them is going to ask for a refund for sure."

Allie's face contorts into what I'm assuming is supposed to be a look of sympathy, but comes off more like pity. "You might have to give it her."

"I might," I moan. "The problem is, I hate feeling like I've failed. I've never taken such bad photos. Ever."

"It's obvious your model was the problem." She reaches over and opens the pizza lid. Pulling out an extra cheesy slice, she brings it to her mouth and takes a bite.

"He *was* the problem, but I've always been able to put people at ease so I can get the shot I'm after." I tell her about how Thomas didn't seem to understand why he was there and how that added a lot of stress to the day.

"How could he not know what his girlfriend had in mind. I mean, he came with a lab coat and everything."

"He claims he really is a doctor," I tell her. "If that's true, you'd think he would know how to smolder like one."

"Yeah, well, real doctors don't exactly smolder, do they?"

"They would if they looked like him," I declare excitedly. Jabbing my pointer finger at the computer, I add, "But instead of looking sexy, this guy looks mentally diminished."

"He really does."

"It's not only about money," I tell Allie. "It's about my name, my reputation. I can't have this woman going around town telling people I suck at my job. Elk Lake isn't big enough to absorb that kind of ding to my reputation."

Allie grabs the throw off the back of the couch. "Is everything in here covered in fur?" she asks. *How has she not noticed this before?*

"Fake fur. I don't believe in killing animals for their skin."

Returning to the subject at hand, I tell her, "There's no way I can show these pictures to my client."

"What else can you do?"

"I could ask Thomas to come back for a reshoot."

"Do you think he'd do it?" she asks while kicking off her shoes and putting her feet up on the coffee table next to the pizza box. *Her socks look super soft.*

"No," I tell her. "I could barely even get him to stay for these."

"Then you're going to have to send them," she says. "Tell your client her boyfriend is simply not a model."

My shoulders slump low and I rest my head on the pillow. Even the fur isn't helping me feel better. "I suppose, but I hate accepting defeat. I pride myself in my ability to put my clients at ease, and this"—I sit up and make a wild gesture toward the computer screen before continuing—"makes me feel like a world-class failure."

"We can't win every race we run," she says.

What is she talking about? "I don't run. At least not if I'm not being chased by a gun-wielding lunatic."

Allie gives me that eye again. The one that says she thinks I'm an odd duck. "Email them and get it over with," she tells me.

I reach out and take my laptop out of her hands. Then I pull up my email and start to type.

Dear Ms. Brucker,

Here are the photographs you hired me to take of Thomas Culpepper. I'm sure you will be as surprised by them as I was. In my defense, Mr. Culpepper clearly did not understand the assignment, and he was unwilling to work with me on the shots you requested.

I don't believe Mr. Culpepper and I are a good fit. Please accept my deepest apologies and I wish you luck getting your photos elsewhere.

All the best,
Allie Rogers

I don't offer to refund her money, yet, because I really don't feel that I'm to blame. If she demands her money back, then so be it. I reluctantly hit send. Once my message enters the ether, I feel a definite weight lift off my shoulders. Luckily, Margaret and Bob have a session booked for tomorrow and I know without a doubt that every frame will be near perfection. If they weren't in their sixties, they could be romance cover models.

Yet, I can't help but feel disappointed I couldn't get Thomas on board. Even without any modeling instinct, the man is stunningly handsome. Imagine what he could do if he got with the program and unleashed his inner beast?

CHAPTER EIGHT

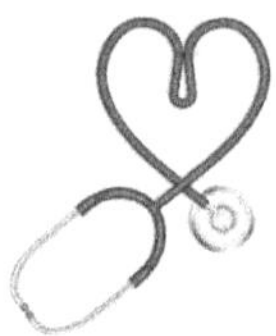

THOMAS

I've only been at Elk Lake General Hospital for a week. While it's emotionally more manageable than my last hospital, I'm struggling to feel useful. Tonsillitis, the flu, and gall stones are no fun, but they're all highly treatable.

Having said that, my co-workers are nice, and the small talk is largely the same. The only difference is here they talk about eating burgers at the diner and bowling instead of consuming oysters at Daniel and hitting the latest clubs.

I have a meeting with Constance Brucker this afternoon, and I'm not looking forward to it. She's been out of town all week, so I have yet to get her feedback on my photoshoot with Finley. I'm not sure how I'm going to be able to look her in the eye after that disturbing break of trust. Imagine expecting your new hire to take his shirt off and get greased up before taking pirate photos. It defies reason.

After eating a bowl of chili in the hospital cafeteria—which is actually very good—I make my way to the business offices on the other side of the building. I check in with Constance's secretary and sit in the small reception room to wait. After only a few minutes, my brittle-looking boss comes out of her office to welcome me.

"Thomas, how are you?" *Is it me or is she the one having a tough time making eye contact?*

"I'm okay, thank you." I follow her into her office and sit down at one of the chairs across from her desk.

Once she settles, she shuffles some papers before turning her attention to me. "I bet it's a lot slower paced here than in New York."

"You could say that." I shift uncomfortably in my chair, wondering when she's going to bring up the pictures.

I don't have to wait long. "So …" Constance inhales sharply before jumping in. "I understand things didn't exactly go as planned with the photographer I hired to take your photo."

The heat of resentment starts to creep up my neck and into my face. "You could say that. I wasn't expecting such a surprising concept for the shoot."

"What exactly did you expect, Thomas?" Her eyes pop open like I'm the wild card here.

"I don't know, maybe a nice professional headshot for you to hang on the wall?" I retort.

"If that's the case"—she continues to study me in that unsettling manner of hers—"I can't help but wonder why you insisted on dressing up like a pirate."

"I did what now?"

She clicks the mouse on her desktop and turns the monitor slightly in my direction. The pictures of my photoshoot fill the space. "Are these, or are they not, you?" She sounds thoroughly shocked. Actually, more unimpressed than shocked. Either way, she's not pleased.

I lean in toward the screen to get a better look. Dear god, they're even worse than I could have imagined. So bad, in fact, they make Zoolander look like a real pro. "This wasn't my idea," I tell her forcefully. "The photographer made me do it."

"That's not what she said." Constance clicks on her screen

again before reading, "Mr. Culpepper clearly did not understand the assignment, and he was unwilling to work with me on the shots you requested."

What? "She said you wanted me to dress like a sexy pirate and a sexy doctor. She said you wanted to use the images in a calendar like the ones firefighters have." I spit this out so fast I sound like a little kid tattling on a classmate.

"I wanted a normal picture of you to hang in the hospital entryway."

"Which is exactly what I went there to get for you," I tell her. "But Finley was positive you wanted these."

"What kind of calendars are those firefighters coming out with?" Constance asks before once again turning her attention to the computer. She clicks away before exclaiming, "Dear god. Why aren't they wearing their uniforms? Why are there so many puppies?"

"I think they use them to raise money," I tell her. "Finley was under the impression you wanted to do the same thing with the doctors here."

The look of revulsion on her face is comical. "Have you seen the other doctors here?" she says. "Could you imagine Dr. McCarthy starring in a picture like this? Or Dr. Randolph?"

Harry McCarthy's stomach would need its own month, and Edith Randolph must be nearing seventy. I simply shake my head.

Constance picks up her telephone and punches in a number. She puts the call on speaker so I can hear. The bright, chirpy voice on the end of the line answers, "Happy Snaps, this is Finley."

"Ms. Harper." My boss sounds downright disdainful. "This is Constance Brucker."

"Ms. Brucker. I assume you received the pictures." Finley sounds worried, which for some reason makes me feel bad for her.

"I did," Constance tells her. "And I'm highly confused by them."

Finley releases a low growl of frustration. "Me, too. I mean, your boyfriend is a smoke show, but he clearly does not know how to model."

Constance doesn't clarify that I'm not her boyfriend. Instead, she says, "Dr. Culpepper wasn't there to model. He was there to have a headshot taken for the hospital wall."

The silence is nearly deafening. In fact, I'm half-convinced Finley hung up the phone, but then she practically whispers, "Excuse me?"

"I specifically told you to do the same thing for him that you did for my colleague, Margaret Clinton."

"Margaret *Clinton*?" Finley chokes on the name.

"Yes, Dr. Margaret Clinton. She hired you to take professional photographs for her website."

"*Dr.* Margaret Clinton?" Finley repeats. "I thought you were talking about Margaret Rogers."

Constance shoots me a look like she's talking to a mentally challenged person. "Who is Margaret Rogers?"

"She's a client. She and her husband, Bob, come to me regularly to have boudoir pictures taken of them. Remember? I mentioned her and Bob, and you said you thought Margaret's husband was named Randal?"

"Margaret Clinton's husband *is* named Randal," Constance assures her.

"Oh, dear." Now I really do feel terrible for Finley. "I'm sorry, I probably should have clarified that," she says.

"Yes, you should have. I'm going to need you to go ahead and refund my payment so I can find a *professional* to take Dr. Culpepper's picture." Constance is a cold fish if there ever was one. Even I feel like I'm sitting in the principal's office waiting for punishment. I can't imagine how Finley feels.

Feeling the need to jump to the photographer's aid, I speak up. "I can always go back for a reshoot." After all, I'd hate for her to lose out on the money she needs for her expansion.

"You'd go back there?" My boss sounds appalled. "After all she put you through?"

It was awful, but it was also kind of funny if you think about it. "I would," I tell her. "If that's okay with Finley."

Dead air again.

"Is that all right with you, Miss Harper?" Constance demands impatiently.

"I … uh … suppose. I mean, sure … yes. I can do that."

"Would tomorrow work for you?" my boss asks me. When I nod my head, she asks Finley, "Does three o'clock tomorrow afternoon fit into your schedule, Miss Harper?"

"Sure," Finley squeaks. I can't imagine how embarrassed she is. She's got to be wondering how to face me after such a debacle. I'm kind of wondering the same thing. The woman did rub freezing cold baby oil on my chest.

"And Miss Harper," Constance feels the need to add, "we will not require your services for a calendar." Then she hangs up.

Poor Finley.

I make a motion to stand up, but Constance waves her hands for me to sit back down. "We have our hospital Spring Fling gala coming up in a few weeks. I hope you're planning to attend."

As this is the first time I've heard of it, I don't have any plans yet. "Message me the details and I'll put it on my calendar," I tell her.

Before I can leave, she says, "I wonder if you'd like to be my date."

"Your date?" As in, she wants to date me, or she just wants to help me navigate new terrain by introducing me around?

Instead of giving an indication what her intensions are, she simply says, "Unless you already have an attachment here in Elk Lake."

I really don't want to go on a date with Constance Brucker. Not only is she not my type—as in, she's way too rigid—but she's also my boss. It would be wrong on multiple levels, which is why I tell her, "I've actually started seeing someone."

She shrugs her bony shoulders. "It can't be serious yet."

Who says something like that? "Perhaps not, but I'm not the kind of man who dates multiple women at the same time."

"How provincial," she drawls snootily. "Well, let me know if things don't work out with her. Then we can go together." It's almost like she assumes our attending the Spring Fling as a duo is a done deal.

"Will do," I tell her before leaping to my feet and fleeing.

Now more than ever, I'm questioning whether this job is going to be the one for me. I want to keep an open mind, but I also don't want to feel pursued by my own boss. Especially Candace. If you'd asked me previously, I would have guessed she was either married to an equally stuck-up older man or she was single and collected Dalmatians to enhance her wardrobe.

Maybe I'll talk to Kevin about it tonight and see what he thinks. My new neighbor and I are going to the diner for those cheese curds he's promised will change my life. He's bringing Shelly, who has made it her job to bring me different baked goods every other day since my arrival. I've probably put on five pounds, but it's been quite enjoyable.

The Picknells are a definite plus for staying in Elk Lake. I barely even knew my neighbors in New York. The only problem is that everything is so slow paced from what I'm used to, and I'm starting to worry I'll die of boredom here. That, and you know, now my boss is making a play for me.

I briefly imagine what it would be like to tell my mother I'm coming back to the city. That thought makes me decide to double down on trying to make this work. It's not that I don't want to hear that she told me so, it's that she won't only say it once. It will become her mantra, and she'll use it every chance she gets. Forever. Until I die. Because even though she'll probably die first, she's the kind of woman who would haunt me to make sure I never forgot she was right.

CHAPTER NINE

FINLEY

I have not been able to get Thomas Culpepper out of my head since Constance Brucker called to read me the riot act. I could not feel like a bigger idiot than I currently do. The woman hired me to take headshots of Thomas. *Headshots.* No wonder he was freaked out when I tried to take his shirt off. Not to mention the baby oil. He probably thought I was a predator. *I can't believe I have to see him again tomorrow.*

Plopping down on the Regency-styled coverlet I have draped across the chaise lounge that Margaret and Bob are going to use this afternoon, I think back to the day Constance booked the photoshoot. There were likely cues galore she wasn't looking for sexy pirate shots. Starting with the obvious. She was referred by Margaret Clinton, not Margaret Rogers. I looked up the file I have on Margaret Clinton, and all I can say is the images were so unremarkable it's no wonder I forgot about them.

I should have trusted my instinct that Constance was a super cold fish and not someone who liked to steam things up in her relationship. That would have probably been something most people would have felt safe assuming. But I question my perception of others all the time. At least, I have since being diagnosed. There's no identity crisis quite like finding out everything you thought was real, wasn't.

Back when we learned of my "specialness," I begged my parents not to tell anyone. My adolescent notion of what it meant to be autistic made me want to keep that newly discovered part of myself hidden.

My parents, on the other hand, felt the best way to proceed was to be forthcoming. My father thought the school would be better able to help me with math, and my mom wanted to rub their faces in the fact that I wasn't stupid. I was *special*. I was sure they would start treating me like I was special needs, but my mom disagreed. As the parent, she won the battle, but not the war.

Even though I had gotten mostly A's and B's since the first grade, once the school found out I was autistic, they did treat me differently. Suddenly, they were talking about taking me out of the mainstream and putting me in honest-to-God special ed classes. Which are great if you need them, but all I needed was a little extra help in math. And perhaps a tip or two on how to understand sarcasm. I'm still working on that one, although I have learned to watch for the telltale eye-rolling, often accompanied by dramatic sighing.

The long and short of it is that my last year and a half of high school bit the big one. I started second-guessing everything and everyone. *What did they mean by that? Was there a hidden message? Do they really like me or are they making fun of me?*

It was so awful, I purposely neglected to mention my autism on my college applications. In retrospect, I wonder if they might have made an earplug concession for me in basketball had they known, but I still didn't want to be thought of as the *special* kid. Imagine the kind of press it would have attracted to be the first openly autistic college basketball player at the U of I. No, thank you.

"Finley, we're here!" I hear Margaret's voice before I see her.

Margaret and Bob are an old school preppy kind of couple. Seriously, they look like a country club duo if I've ever seen one. There is nothing about their outward appearance that suggests they like to have boudoir photos taken.

"I'm in the back," I shout before jumping up from the chaise. I don't want it to look like I'm loafing around.

The vision of my clients walking through the door makes me smile. They're parent-like in their conservative clothes and demeanors. "I'm happy to see you," I tell them. "Did you bring the book cover you want to recreate?"

Margaret waves it about her head with her black leather glove-clad hand. My grandmother used to have the exact same pair. "It's called *Sheathed*!" she says excitedly. "It's about the young daughter of a viscount who falls for her tutor, who's really a spy in disguise."

"Exciting," I tell her, appreciating her obvious enthusiasm. I don't read bodice rippers myself, but Margaret's passion for them has almost gotten me to try it. *Almost.*

"I brought along an eye-patch," Bob says. "I know the man on the cover isn't wearing one, but I think the idea of it adds a little more mystery, don't you?"

"Sure," I tell him. I have no real opinion on the topic. I figure, whatever makes them happy. I briefly wonder why I wasn't thinking that the day I took pictures of Thomas. He clearly wasn't happy.

"Why don't you two get ready," I say. "I'll run next door and pick up coffees. You want your usual?"

"Two decaf, low-fat Americanos with one raw sugar each," Bob confirms. Even their coffee order suggests they're a boring middle-aged couple.

I hurry out the front door of Happy Snaps and stride down the street to Rosemary's. The bakery has been part of Elk Lake's history for more than thirty years. Their gingersnaps alone make the trip worthwhile, but I have yet to try anything mediocre.

Faith Helms, the owner, and my realtor's best friend, greets me. "Good morning, Finley."

"Hey, Faith," I say, offering her a big smile. There are some people in this world that are so genuinely kind they make you feel like the sun is shining even at night. Faith is one of those people.

After I give her my order, she says, "I see you've got Allie's parents again, huh?" She must know everyone in town by their coffee orders. After I nod my head in confirmation, she adds, "I'd love to see some of the stuff they do."

"I'm sure they'd show you if you asked," I tell her. Margaret and Bob are unexpected exhibitionists. Not only do they like to have their picture taken, but they also let me use some of them to advertise with. That's how Allie and I met. I had a sandwich board of her parents in front of my shop, and she nearly ran her car off the road. She came in and demanded to know what was going on.

"I was thinking it might be fun for Teddy and me to do something like that for our anniversary," Faith says. "I'm just worried he'll be hesitant because he'd never want the press to find out." Her husband, Teddy, is an honest-to-goodness Hollywood movie star who's best known for his portrayal of Alpha Dog in the Wonder pictures.

"I can't imagine how the press would ever know," I tell her. "We could do it all hush-hush. I'd even sign a non-disclosure agreement if you'd like."

Her eyes sparkle with anticipation. "Let me talk to him and I'll get back to you."

Faith puts three large gingersnaps in a bag and hands it to me. With a wink, she says, "A little added spice for the spicy couple you're shooting."

"That's very nice, thank you." I remind myself that this town is filled with the loveliest people. Even if Constance does badmouth me, I'm guessing most won't believe her. At least I hope not.

For me, the worst part of being on the spectrum has been that I don't really trust how others perceive me. I've learned that just because they act like they like me doesn't necessarily make it so, which goes to the trouble I have reading tone.

I've gotten better at it in recent years, but in college, there was a girl who lived on my floor who I thought I was friendly with. She was a little odd, but I've always been very accepting of people's differences. One day, I mentioned her to my roommate and Lilly told me I needed to stand up for myself and quit letting Felicia make fun of me right to my face.

I replied that I didn't know what she was talking about. I told her that we were friends. That's when she set me straight. Apparently, Felicia used to tell people what an airhead I was. She even had a nickname for me—Flakey Finley. My inability to discern her true feelings made it clear she was right.

In adulthood I've learned how to mask who I really am. Or at least I thought I had. Ever since Allie told me that she thinks I'm quirky, I'm starting to second-guess everything all over again. It's not a feeling I welcome, either.

"Finley? You there?" Faith looks concerned, which makes me wonder how long I've been spacing out.

"Here. Good," I tell her while forcing a smile. "Just let me know what you and Teddy decide and we'll set something up." I wave awkwardly before turning around and walking out of the bakery.

One of the reasons I became a photographer was that I like spending time with people. I like studying them and capturing their moments of joy. Doing so while wearing a camera around your neck makes this acceptable. Whereas, staring at people like you're trying to commit their image to memory makes them nervous. Note to self: asking them to take their shirts off and greasing them up with baby oil also makes them uneasy, especially when they aren't expecting it.

CHAPTER TEN

THOMAS

It's March so it's still cold and crisp outside. It rained again today, as it's done every day since I arrived. As such, my walk from the hospital to the diner is a pretty soggy journey. Turning onto Main Street is a sensation unlike anything I ever experienced at home. New York streets are constantly busy. Pedestrians, taxi cabs, and cyclists are everywhere. There's a continuous hum of activity accentuated by sirens and honking horns. The streets of Elk Lake feel nearly abandoned in comparison.

Opening the door to the diner is like walking back in time. Its raw vintage-ness appears authentic and not staged. The red vinyl booths are straight out of a movie from the nineteen-fifties. There's even a juke box.

Looking around, I spot Kevin and Shelly in a back booth. I point at them before telling the hostess, "I'm meeting some friends."

When I arrive at the table, Shelly stands up and gives me a hug. "Look who's here!" I can't imagine she's really this excited to see me, but one thing I've learned about the people of Elk Lake is that they're very free in expressing their feelings. There's no passive-aggressive pretense that seems to thrive in big cities.

I return Shelly's hug before extending my hand to Kevin. "I'm glad we're doing this." After driving all the way from the airport with him, I had the feeling I would be seeing him all the time. That hasn't been the case.

"I thought life would slow down once the kids were out of the house," Kevin says, "But the truth is, Shel and I like to keep busy." He winks. "You know what they say? A rolling stone gathers no moss." He looks down at his Green Bay Packers jersey and adds, "And look at that, no moss!"

The waitress comes over and Kevin orders an extra-large curd platter along with a pitcher of beer. When she leaves, he tells me I can drink whatever I want after, but the only way to enjoy curds properly is with an ale.

"I'm looking forward to it," I tell him truthfully. Even though I've never been a big beer drinker, my new neighbor seems like a man to be trusted with this experience.

Shelly takes her napkin off the table and puts it into her lap. "How's the hospital?"

"It's fine. Good, actually. Just a lot different from what I'm used to."

Kevin's gaze narrows like he's looking for a hidden meaning. "Hard to get used to, huh?"

"Yeah," I confirm. "The reason I left New York was because I was reaching the point of total burn out. Which is not something I expected to happen by thirty-six."

"Our son is thirty-six!" Shelly says excitedly. "He owns a house painting company right here in Elk Lake."

"Collin," Kevin adds.

"How many kids do you have?" I ask them.

"Three." Shelly beats her husband to the punch. "Collin is the oldest. Then there's Chris. He's thirty-two, and Camille is twenty-eight. They all live in the area."

"That must be nice." I feel a momentary pang of guilt that by moving here, I've broken up my own family unit.

"It's the only way we'd want it," Kevin says. "Collin has three kids, so we get to see the grands grow up." Both of my neighbors are positively beaming.

"What about you?" Shelly wants to know. "Where does your family live?"

The waitress brings over a pitcher and pours the beer into three glasses. When she leaves, I tell my new friends, "My parents and sister are in New York City."

"They must have been sad to see you go," Kevin says.

I take a sip of my drink before answering, "I don't think they were thrilled." I hurry to change the subject away from my disappointing ways. "So, tell me, have you ever gone to Happy Snaps?"

Shelly claps her hands together loudly. "Finley takes our family photos for us. Do you know her? Isn't she lovely?"

I have no intention of mentioning my previous encounter with the photographer, so I simply reply, "She's going to take a headshot of me tomorrow for the hospital."

"Great girl," Kevin says. "She loves her work and it shows in the pictures she takes." I immediately feel guilty for being part of what must have been the worst day of her professional career.

"I'm looking forward to it," I tell them. Which isn't exactly the case, even though I am looking forward to seeing Finley again.

The waitress drops a platter of cheese curds on the table before asking, "Would you like to order your supper now?"

"We'll wait a bit," Kevin tells her, before looking at me. "You might like these so much you'll want another batch for your main course." I can't imagine that will be true, but I don't say as much.

Shelly picks up the first curd. "There are three standard sauces—honey mustard, ranch, and pepper jelly." She dips her bite into the pepper jelly and pops it into her mouth. The expression on her face is one of pure enjoyment. Picking up her beer, she takes a sip and swallows before telling me, "That's how it's done. The curd first and then the beer chaser."

Kevin and I follow suit. He dips his into the ranch, so I choose honey mustard. "Huh," I say after finishing my first bite. "It's kind of like mozzarella."

"These are tangier and less salty," Shelly assures me.

"Not as stretchy as mozzarella but, wait for it, they squeak." Kevin bites into one, relishing the sound.

I try both the ranch and pepper jelly before declaring, "I like them."

Kevin raises his glass and toasts, "Welcome to Wisconsin, Tommy! You're as good as a native now."

I'm not sure about that, but I do know I will always remember cheese curds fondly. I ask my companions, "What do you all do around here for fun?" I have yet to go anywhere other than the hospital or the grocery store, but I'm looking forward to venturing out.

"Oh, my goodness," Shelly says. "There's a lot." She itemizes, "In the winter you can go sledding, ice skating, skiing, or snowmobiling. In the summer, there's swimming at the lake and fishing. Golf, if that's more your bag."

"I love the fall," Keven adds. "Wait until you see the leaves change color here. It's perfection!"

"What about spring?" I inquire about the current season.

"It's kind of wet out right now," Shelly says while wrinkling her nose like spring isn't where it's at.

"You could go to the movies or bowling," Kevin suggests.

Shelly sighs. "The park district offers a pottery class."

"Darts at the pub," Kevin interjects.

I laugh. "It sounds like you're pretty much just waiting for summer at this point."

My new friends nod their heads in unison. "Pretty much," Shelly agrees.

The waitress comes back to check on us and takes our dinner order. While the curds were enjoyable, they're sitting in my stomach like a lead weight. That's why I opt for a salad. Kevin and Shelly both order burgers. My mother would be appalled that any of us are eating more. She'd be half-way home on her way to the Peloton in her closet to burn off the already-consumed cheese.

The evening flies by in a flurry of chatter. I like Kevin and Shelly very much. Living next door to them will be like having a second set of parents close by. When it's time to go, Kevin asks, "Where did you park?"

"I haven't gotten a car yet," I tell him.

"I was wondering about that. I haven't seen one in front of your house." Shelly confirms the stereotype that people in small towns are aware of everything.

"I might need to take a driving refresher course before I get one," I confess. "There's not much occasion to get behind the wheel in New York City."

"Kevin teaches drivers' ed in town," Shelly says excitedly. "He can help you."

"I sure can," her husband agrees. "I can do it without having you sign up, too. I wouldn't want you to have to pay."

I don't want to take advantage of him so I say, "I'm happy to do it officially and take the class." As long as I can fit it into my schedule. That's another thing about being an ER doctor. Shifts change from week to week so it's nearly impossible to have standing engagements, like taking classes.

"You wouldn't have to take a Wisconsin driving test at the DMV that way," Shelly offers. "Just show your certificate and your Wisconsin license is as good as yours."

After paying the check, I tell them, "I'll see when the next class starts and let you know."

My new friends give me a ride home and drop me off in my driveway. "Thank you for such a fun night," I tell them.

"Thank you for supper," Shelly says. "Have fun at Finley's tomorrow."

I'm not sure if having fun will be on the menu. In fact, I'm convinced it's going to be more awkward than anything. But it will be good to see her and put her mind at ease that there are no hard feelings about our first session.

"I'll see you both soon," I say before getting out of the car.

After walking to my front door, I put the key into the lock, feeling a new sense of optimism about life in Elk Lake. Sure, it's slower paced and absolutely nothing like Manhattan, but there are good people here who help to make it feel like it could be my new home.

Yet for some reason, it feels like a lot depends on how things go tomorrow.

CHAPTER ELEVEN

FINLEY

I had the hardest time falling asleep last night. I turned the light off at ten, like always, but I just couldn't turn my brain off. I finally picked up the romance novel Margaret gave me in hopes it would distract me from my thoughts. It did. I conked out somewhere around the fourth chapter only to have world-class nightmares.

I dreamed that Thomas Culpepper showed up for his reshoot looking like a real pirate—full-on with a scraggly beard and a pegged leg. I told him he had to shave and put on a nice shirt, but he refused.

He wielded the hook that replaced his left hand as though he was intent on running me through. "Avast ye, matey! It's time to walk the plank!"

I was more annoyed than afraid. I was not going to disappoint Constance again. "Put that away," I yelled at him, while handing him a shirt.

Pirate Thomas was not interested in doing what he was told. Instead, he jumped on the furniture and demanded, "Where's the treasure, lass? If you tell me, I won't have to kill ye!"

The weird thing is that even though I knew this was a stupid dream, I couldn't force myself to wake up. So, I sat down and waited for Thomas to expend all his pirate energy and get on board with the mission at hand. Which never happened.

Instead, an entire crew of buccaneers showed up in my studio, and they all demanded to have their pictures taken. It was the longest, most exhausting night of my life. When my alarm finally rang, it was all I could do to not roll over and go back to sleep.

Being that I have a full day before Thomas comes in, I drag myself out of bed and start what I'm sure will be an all-day task of caffeinating. I get dressed in a pair of jeans and my second-fuzziest sweater—I don't want to wear my softest because I don't have any confidence today will go well and I don't want to taint it with bad juju.

At the bakery, I order my daily latte with three shots of espresso instead of one. Then I get a chocolate croissant in hopes it will make my mood better.

My morning is spent taking class pictures for the Little Sunshine Preschool class. The kids are full of energy and it's like herding a bunch of baby bunnies hopped up on sugar. While it was challenging, I wind up having so much fun that my bad mood disappears entirely. The day also flies by, and six hours are gone before I know it.

I've grown accustomed to the fact that time does not flow for me like it does for others—I cite the whole nose drawing event from college. An hour can feel like a day, and twelve hours can feel like a minute. The whole "timeline" thing isn't a concept my brain gets.

Once the kids and their parents leave, I hurry and eat the lunch I brought from home. When I'm finished, I crawl under a blanket on a bed I use for boudoir shots. I need a power nap if I'm going to get through Thomas's reshoot.

Here's the thing about me and naps: unlike my nighttime sleep, where ninety-five percent of the time I know I'm dreaming, naps always feel more like an alternate reality. You know, like I'm still fully awake, just visiting the dimension next to ours. That's the only way I can make sense of what happens next.

In my dream, I open my eyes, and Thomas is standing over me. He gazes at me with what I can only describe as longing. "Finley," he croons with a voice as silky as my favorite hair ties from childhood. He's once again in full pirate regalia, but this time he looks like a swashbuckler from one of Margaret's novels.

"Thomas?" I ask sounding unsure. "Is it you?"

"Aye, lass." He kneels at the side of the bed until our eyes are on the same level. "I've come to take you with me. Get up and pack so we don't miss the tide."

"Where are we going?" I'm both nervous and excited at the prospect of being whisked away by this devilishly handsome man.

"Wherever the water takes us," he says cryptically. "But we're being pursued so we have to go now." He suddenly jumps to his feet. "Hurry!"

Sitting up, I ask, "But what about the picture we have to take for Constance?" *Don't you just love when enough reality slips into your dreams to confuse them?*

"I don't know who this Constance is." His voice is rough like a bag of freshly cracked walnut shells. "If you don't want to be hung alongside me, you'd best move."

I stare at him, trying valiantly to make heads or tails out of what's going on. I want to go with him, because you know, Pirate Thomas is a total babe. But then again, I know I have to take his picture, so Constance won't tell everyone in Elk Lake what a bad photographer I am.

"I can't go." I choke out the words disappointedly.

"If you don't, you'll never see me again." Pirate Thomas sounds devastated at the prospect.

"I can't let Constance down another time."

He pulls at my arm. "Finley … Finley …"

"No, Thomas!" I shout at him. "I can't run away with you! I have a job to do."

"Finley?" Something in his tone changes, but I don't let him finish whatever he's going to say.

Instead, I cover my eyes so he can't tell I'm about to cry. "Life isn't fair," I say. "Our love cannot take priority over this job."

"Excuse me?"

"You heard me," I say bravely. "Our love cannot prevail. Not this time." I wistfully add, "Maybe in the next book …"

I wipe away the lone tear that has escaped its confines and open my eyes to say goodbye to my pirate love. But guess what? When I do, Pirate Thomas is nowhere to be seen. Instead, Dr. Thomas Culpepper is standing over me, looking like he's ready to call for reinforcements.

"Thomas?" I ask while trying to figure out how much of my dream he might have overheard.

"Finley?" he replies. "Are you okay?"

"Um, yes." I sit up and fling my legs over the side of the bed, nearly kicking him in the knee in the process. "When did you get here?"

"A few minutes ago." He turns his head slightly and side-eyes me like he might still make a run for it. Shoot, I'm guessing he heard stuff.

"Ah, yes, well … I was taking a small nap. I didn't sleep well last night."

"And you were dreaming about pirates?"

There is only one way out of what is sure to be the worst embarrassment I've ever suffered. Bald. Face. Lying. "I wasn't dreaming about pirates." I glance up and stare at him challengingly. "I was dreaming about … tornados …"

"Tornados?"

"Yes." Avoiding his gaze, I stand up and straighten out my clothes. Then I run my fingers through my hair and ask, "Are you ready?"

He looks as confused as I was hoping to make him. *Mission accomplished.*

"I guess. Do you want to start with hair and makeup?"

Red hot embarrassment fills my entire body as I remember the last time I did his hair and makeup. His silky soft follicles slipping through my fingers ... the sensation of baby oil on his rock-hard chest ... I start to feel woozy and have to remind myself to breathe. I inhale slowly to the count of seven before assuring him, "We don't have to do hair and makeup today."

"Don't you want me to get into character?" he asks, once again referencing our last photo shoot.

Imagining him in his pirate regalia makes my heart rate pick up speed, which forces yet another ragged inhalation. This time, I exhale to a full count of seven. "I'm sure you'll look fine," I say. "It's just a headshot."

I can tell he wants to ask me what happened at our last meeting, but I can never talk about that horrible day again. Instead, I point at his shirt. "Are you wearing that?"

"I brought a couple different things if you want to see them."

"No, that's fine." I point to a dull gray backdrop. "Go sit on that stool. I'll be with you in a minute."

Thomas looks unsure but ultimately does as I've instructed.

Meanwhile, I hurry through the bathroom door and close it. Turning on the faucet, I pick up a hand towel and run it under the cold water. Then I dab it across my face to bring my temperature down. It does nothing to calm me. If anything, the roughness of the cloth against my skin agitates me even more.

When I come out of the bathroom, Thomas asks, "How long do you think this will take?"

If I put my mind to it, I could be done in ten minutes, but I can't rush him out that quickly. If he tells Constance, she'll think she overpaid me for sure. "Maybe an hour," I answer, making sure not to look him directly in the eye.

After flipping on the studio lights, I grab my camera before turning back to Thomas and asking, "Would you like me to play some music?" *That ought to fill any awkward silences nicely.*

I'm reaching for my phone when he says, "No, thanks. I'm good."

Shoot.

"Well, then." I lift the camera to my face. "Pretend you're a doctor."

"I *am* a doctor." His smile is soft and sweet and it's all I can do not to walk up to him and go ahead and run my fingers through his hair again.

The temptation to touch him persists so I count to five slowly until I can trust myself not to do it. I snap a good thirty pictures of Thomas, and his smile never falters. Which is perplexing given our previous session. Those expressions ranged from looking like he had contracted food poisoning to suffering from severe intestinal distress.

"Take a break," I tell him before walking over to my laptop station. I sit down on the stool in front of it and check out the photos. I turn around and tell Thomas, "They all look good. We can try it with your doctor coat on, if you'd like."

He stands up and moves toward the hanging rack. I pretend to be busy clicking around the computer while he puts on his coat. Unfortunately, the pirate shots pop up on the screen as he approaches me. He stops dead in his tracks when he notices what I'm looking at. "Those were pretty awful, weren't they?"

Crud, now I have to say something. But what? Opening my mouth, I try to come up with something semi-intelligible. Not surprisingly, that's not what comes out …

CHAPTER TWELVE

THOMAS

Seeing Finley this afternoon is even more uncomfortable than I thought it would be. I mean, I knew it wouldn't be easy, but even so, I was prepared to persevere and get the job done. Then I got here and woke her from a dream she was having about "Pirate Thomas," and my plan fell apart.

Finley is not your average bear. She's completely unexpected and adorable. Imagine making someone dress up like a pirate when they were there to have a business picture taken. The whole thing is too funny to believe. That's why when I see her looking at those very images, I have to say something. "Those are pretty awful, huh?" I ask.

I expect her to laugh with me, but she doesn't. Instead, she demands, "Why didn't you tell me you weren't here to have pirate pictures taken?"

"I did," I tell her. "Repeatedly."

Her indignation turns to embarrassment in a split second. "It's just that I thought Constance was talking about Margaret Rogers." She sounds so disappointed, I want to console her.

"It was an honest mistake," I say. "Really, it could have happened to anyone."

Her mood shifts back to angry. "No, it couldn't have," she snaps. "Any normal person would have figured out there had been a misunderstanding."

"Misunderstandings happen all the time," I tell her. "That must mean there aren't many normal people out there." I walk back to the set and sit down on my stool.

Finley eventually picks up her camera and joins me. "Why are you trying to make me feel better. You should be mad."

"What's the point?" I shrug. "And now, just think, I have all these amazing pirate pictures of myself that I didn't before. I'm thinking of using one on my Christmas card."

"Did you look at them closely?" She doesn't seem to get the joke.

I snort laugh. "I was teasing."

Finley's head bobs up and down three times. "You're a terrible model."

I figure that now is as good a time as any to tell her the truth. "I did it on purpose."

"Sure you did." The accompanying eye roll makes it clear she doesn't believe me. She really does think I'm a lousy model.

"I didn't want those pictures to be used in a calendar, and you told me that's what Constance was going to use them for *if* they were any good."

"I'm sure she wouldn't have used them if you asked her not to. What kind of girlfriend exploits her boyfriend?"

Boyfriend? "I'm not Constance's boyfriend," I tell her.

The camera shakes in her hand. "Oh?"

"She's my boss," I clarify.

Suddenly Finley turns around and bends over. Her entire body heaves and her shoulders start to shake convulsively. Is she crying? I get up from my perch and walk over to her. "Finley, it's okay. Really, there was no harm done." That's when I realize I've gotten it all wrong. She isn't crying, she's laughing.

"Your *boss*?" she demands between hiccups of merriment.

"Yup. My boss."

Tears are pouring out of Finley's eyes as she gasps, "I took pirate photos of you and ... and ... sent them to your *boss*?"

"You did," I tell her. "But that's not the worst part."

She stands up and stares at me with a look of trepidation. "What's the worst part?"

"My boss now knows what a horrible pirate I am."

Finley practically spits during her next bout of laughter. Her amusement is so contagious, I join her. "Can you imagine the look on Constance's face when you emailed those to her?"

"She must have thought it was some kind of pitiful prank." She hiccups again. "Can you imagine pulling a trick like that on someone? Who would do something that awful?"

"My family is known for pulling out all the stops on April Fool's Day," I tell her. "We get really competitive about it." She looks surprised, which confirms that most people don't take it as far as the Culpepper clan.

"What was the worst prank they ever played on you?" she asks.

An image immediately pops into my head. "We were going on vacation one spring, and my mom told me we were leaving the morning of April first. She said all pranks were called off that year because we'd be traveling and she didn't need the extra stress."

"And that was a lie?" Finley's eyes opening widely in what can only be construed as fear for my tweenage self.

"Oh, we went away. Just not like to Hawaii like we were supposed to."

"Oh, dear." I appreciate her sympathetic tone. "Where did you go?"

"Cleveland."

Finley exhales loudly. "No."

"Yes," I confirm.

"Cleveland? As in Cleveland, Ohio?"

"My dad had a medical conference. He and my mom concocted the story about Hawaii."

"Thomas, that's not a prank, that's just mean."

"It is and it isn't," I tell her. Then I explain, "We actually went to Hawaii two weeks later."

"Still." Her expression makes it clear she's appalled on my behalf. "What did you do in Cleveland?"

"We swam in the hotel pool, a lot," I tell her. "My mom took us to the Rock and Roll Hall of Fame and to the house where they filmed *A Christmas Story*. I wore Hawaiian shirts the whole time."

Finley's eyes fill with moisture and I'm not sure if she's going to laugh again or cry. I'm not sure she knows either. "Did you ever forgive them?"

"Two weeks later when we landed in Kauai," I assure her. "But I never forgot."

Her posture relaxes. "Have you ever gotten even?"

"I've tried," I tell her. "But nothing I've ever done has come close to that practical joke. They truly are the masters."

A determined look comes to Finley's eyes. "You have to get even."

"Twenty-five years later?" I ask. "There must be a statute of limitations on that kind of thing."

She shakes her head which causes her sleek blonde bob to sway back and forth. I'm busy wondering if it's a soft as it looks when she replies, "Not on something that diabolical."

"My mom and dad are in their sixties," I tell her. "I don't want to do anything shocking enough that I'd give one of them a heart attack."

"You don't have to fill their house with boa constrictors or boobytrap their front door with a bucket of red paint." *What kind of pranks is Finley used to pulling?*

"I would never do anything like that," I assure her.

A thought suddenly pops into my head and before I can censor it, I blurt out, "I could move back home and tell them my relocation was the prank. Neither of them was happy I left New York."

Finley's frown causes her eyebrows to nearly touch. "Move home? Why would you do that?"

"I'm not sure this was the right move for me," I confess. "Don't get me wrong, there are parts of being here that I really like, but it's also very foreign-feeling."

"It was the pirate pictures, wasn't it?" Her shoulders sag in defeat. "I'm truly sorry about those, Thomas."

"If anything," I tell her, "That was the highpoint of being in Elk Lake. I can assure you I would never have had that experience back home."

"Maybe *I* should move there," she teases. "It sounds like they might need me." Her green eyes sparkle mischievously.

"You'd have more business than you'd know what to do with," I tell her. I'm not sure that's really the case, but then again, I'm not sure it isn't. People in New York City are known for being quite adventurous and what better undertaking than playacting?

Finley stands up and stretches her arms above her head before walking back to the set. I follow behind and take my place in the spotlight. "I could never live in a big city," she says. "Too much noise."

"You get used to it," I tell her. "I've lived there my whole life, and I barely hear it anymore." That's the truth, too. The silence of Elk Lake is way more disconcerting than the noise of the city.

"*I* wouldn't get used to it," she assures me.

For some reason, I feel the need to challenge her. "I bet you would."

"No, Thomas, I wouldn't." She sounds so certain, I decide to let it go.

Finley approaches me and touches my face with her pointer finger. She turns my chin toward the light. "Where are you from?" I ask her.

"Central Illinois." After a beat, she adds, "Small farming town."

"Are your parents farmers?" She shakes her head, but doesn't offer any other information. So, I ask, "Is your family still there?"

Her chin bobs up and down three times, which I'm starting to think is her standard.

"Do you ever think of going back?"

Finley's eyes narrow like the very thought haunts her. "I will *never* live there again." Emphasis on the *never*.

"Why is that?"

She lets her camera drop again. Then she approaches me slowly. When she's within reach, she stops and adjusts one of the lights. "I'm going to need you to stop talking, Thomas."

"But I want to know …"

"Now," she orders. Except for small demands on her part—chin up, turn to the right, smolder more!—the rest of our session is silent. While that can be a rattling experience with some people, it's actually quite pleasant with Finley. It's rare to find someone you can be comfortable around without the need for constant chatter.

The only problem is I want to know more about her. Finley is having an odd effect on me. I feel like I've known her my whole life, which is not a usual reaction I have to people. I suddenly wonder what makes her tick. What are her likes and dislikes? What are her favorite foods, books, and television shows?

That's when it hits me. I like Finley Harper a lot. Her uniqueness makes her a thousand times more appealing to me than other women. Although, she's currently not letting me talk, so I'm not sure how to go about asking her out on a date.

If I ask her when she's in a bad mood, she'll say no. But how will I get the opportunity to spend enough time with her to catch her at the right time?

That's when the most surprising idea pops into my head.

CHAPTER THIRTEEN

FINLEY

"I'm sorry, what did you say?" I stop taking pictures of Thomas and stare at him like he just morphed into a reptile. *I must have heard him wrong.*

His smile is positively blinding as he repeats, "I'd like to book a couple more sessions with you."

"Why?" I've done nothing but make this man uncomfortable. Why would he want to spend one more minute with me than he has to?

"I'd like to have some real pirate shots taken. Maybe throw in a snooty duke, and I don't know ..." He shrugs before adding, "How do you feel about cowboys?"

I feel like I'm in one of my napping dimensions. "I love cowboys," I tell him, all the while envisioning him in a pair of chaps. Goose bumps pop up on both of my arms. *Breathe, Finley.*

Thomas stands up and walks over toward me. Then he reaches out and rests his hands on my shoulders. An honest to God electric charge shoots through me that I'm pretty sure is about to make me start levitating. "It just occurred to me how I can get even with my parents for that awful prank they pulled on me as a kid."

My synapses have stopped firing, and I have no idea what he's talking about. "What does having fantasy pictures taken have to do with getting even with your parents?"

Thomas turns around and takes a giant step backward. Then he faces me again. "I'm going to make one of those calendars you thought Constance wanted."

"What? Why?" I'm having a strange out-of-body experience that I can't seem to wake up from.

"I'll give it to my parents for April Fool's Day and tell them I've taken a hiatus from being a doctor to become a model." Thomas practically lights up like a thousand lightbulbs have turned on under his skin. "What do you think about that?"

"I think ... I think ..." I'm thinking but I'm not processing. I eventually say, "I think it's genius. But they might actually have a heart attack. I mean, who gives up being a doctor to dress up like a pirate for a living?"

"That's clearly the prank part," he tells me. With a very satisfied grin, he adds, "This is the best idea I've had in a long time. Are you in?"

"Yes. Of course. I'll do it." I have an expansion to pay for, after all. But I'll have to spend time with Thomas looking like a pirate, which makes me worry I'll behave badly. And if not badly, then certainly oddly.

"Should we start today?" he wants to know.

I look at the clock and discover it's already four thirty. Even though I *could* start now, I'm not mentally prepared. I need to consider stuff like how I'm going to do this without acting like a total groupie. I need to plan. "I'm sorry," I tell him. "I'm busy tonight. We'll have to do it another time."

He looks disappointed, which I decide to take as a compliment. Even though he's not doing this to spend time with me, we will technically be spending time together. I'm positively giddy at the prospect.

"Can I look through your costumes before I go?" he asks. "That way I can see what I might need to buy."

"Oh, you don't have to buy anything," I assure him. "I have a lot." I gesture toward a rack against the back wall. "It's all over there. Go ahead and look."

As he leaves the set to go look at the outfits, my mind starts to reel. *Can I really do this? Can I spend time with Thomas dressed as a pirate/duke/cowboy and not throw myself at him?* I'm afraid this might stretch the bounds of my professionalism. But even so, I really want to see how he looks as a cowboy...

I sit down in front of my laptop and look through the pictures we just took. Unlike our last session, these are all acceptable. In fact, they're boring enough that Constance will probably do backflips of excitement.

Thomas walks over to me with a police officer's uniform draped over his arm. "How about this one?"

"That's a popular one," I tell him. I immediately cross my arms to stop myself from stretching out my wrists for him to handcuff me and drag me off to jail. "There's also a firefighter if you're interested." *Oh, gosh. I'm done for now. Why did I tell him about that?*

"How many sessions should we set up?" Thomas wants to know.

"It depends on how many costume changes you want." I'm hoping he says a hundred, but it would be better for my sanity if he kept the number down.

"There are twelve months in a year, so it stands to reason I would need twelve different looks." He really sounds excited about this, which both pleases me and assures me that I'm going to have to take some personal time to recuperate when it's all over.

"Then we should do four sessions with three looks each. But it's already March, so we'll have to move fast."

The energy radiating off Thomas is intense. In fact, the

atmosphere is practically vibrating with it. "Let me grab my phone and check my schedule."

I watch as he strides across the room. I realize there's no way I can act normal around him for the amount of time we're going to have to spend together. I should tell him I've changed my mind, but I don't. Thomas dressed as a cowboy is something I now need to see before I die, and this is my opportunity.

Four sessions mean that Thomas and I will spend a minimum of sixteen hours together. Almost a thousand minutes with him dressed up as every woman's fantasy. Nearly sixty thousand seconds of me trying not to run my fingers through his soft hair. It's going to be excruciating, and yet, I can't wait.

Once he leaves, I hurriedly tidy the space up before going home. The important plans I used as an excuse for not starting his revenge plan consist of ordering Chinese food and organizing my sock drawer. I do this according to color and texture.

I buy these buttery soft packs of socks from the nearby warehouse store by the dozens. I've discovered that if I wash them in warm water and use fabric softener, they'll stay supremely soft for fourteen washes. After that, they're just nicely soft. At twenty-four washes, they're just boring old socks, and I donate them to a shelter. Tonight is the big night when several pairs will be coming out of their twenty-fourth drying cycle, which means new socks for me!

I'm sure most people would think this is outrageous, which is why I don't talk about it publicly.

Even though I feel pretty secure about who I currently am, I've still spent my life feeling like everyone but me got a "how to" manual when they arrived on the planet. I imagine it explains how to do everything from getting dressed in the morning to comporting yourself in all manner of situations. Being that I am without such a coveted tome, I've had to watch how everyone else acts. That way I can mimic them, and no one will know I arrived without an instruction book.

"Normal" people do a lot of stuff that doesn't make sense to me. Yet, with so many of them behaving the same way, there must have been entire chapters explaining the minutia of being human. For instance, why can't women put on mascara without opening their mouths? In every locker room, public bathroom, and dorm room I've ever been in, hordes of woman paint their eyelashes with their mouths wide open like they're hoping to catch flies.

Most people yawn with their eyes closed. I do not. I yawn with my eyes open, which I understand makes me look like a ravenous lion about to devour anyone in my path. Instinctual behavior that is inherent to most is not to me. But I want to fit in, so I copy them.

Conversely, I'm also compelled to complete rituals that don't seem to be part of everyone else's wheelhouse. When I turn on lights, I tap the switch three times. Five times when I turn them off. I don't just close a door, I have to yank on it to make sure it's firmly shut. Three times. I count stairs ascending and descending, even if they're the same steps I went up yesterday or the day before. I know what the number is going to be but I can't accept it unless I verify it every time. Plus, if I count them, it stops me from worrying about falling up (or down) them.

I don't like my foods to touch each other on my plate. I start at the twelve o'clock position and work my way clockwise around the food servings. I'm okay when the ingredients are mixed together in a soup or casserole, but if the elements are served separately, like meat loaf, mashed potatoes, and peas, those peas had better not start rolling out of their territory.

My mom tells me the food one is normal, and that a lot of people have it, but I've not witnessed that. The truth is, I think my mom has a touch of the 'tism herself. Not that she'd ever go through the steps to be diagnosed at this point in her life. She's carved out her place and seems pretty happy with it.

Once my kung pao shrimp is ordered, I go to my front closet and retrieve the box of socks I have at the ready. Some people prep for the end of the world by stockpiling rice and dried beans.

Not me; I buy socks. I don't fear starvation as much as I fear unhappy feet.

I carry the box to the couch before sitting down to perform one of my most favorite tasks. I pick up the pack of dark grays and blacks first. As I caress the silky fibers, my entire body unclenches and releases stress I didn't consciously know I was carrying. I like the dark ones just fine, but for some reason, I think the cream-colored socks are softer. I spend even more time petting those.

Several minutes later, I move onto the baby pink socks. They are the softest and bring me the most joy. Which is why I save them for last. Always end things on a high note, am I right?

You might be wondering why I don't just buy pink and not bother with secondary colors, but even I know I can't wear pink with everything. For instance, what if I wear a bright orange sweater—not that I ever would because I don't like bright orange. But if I did, the cream-colored socks would be a better combination. When I wear black clothes, I like to match them with black socks. Also, there's something about knowing that all my socks aren't the softest that makes the pink days even more prized. It's the anticipation of it all.

When the buzzer rings, alerting me that my supper has arrived, I hurry to reorganize the box of spare socks and return them to the front closet. Then I open the door and wait for my food.

As Flip, the delivery boy, walks up the stairs, he smiles and waves. "Kung pao again?"

"Kung pao always," I assure him. I'm sure he's not surprised when I ask, "Three fortune cookies?"

He shrugs. "I didn't pack the bag."

After handing him a five-dollar tip, I open the brown paper sack in front of him and look inside. Shoot, there are four cookies, not three. I know they do this because I'm a regular customer and they're trying to make me happy. They don't understand that four cookies makes me anxious.

"How many?" Flip asks.

"Four," I grumble.

He knows the drill. When I stretch the bag out to him, he pulls one out and takes it back. He's learned to never open it in front of me though because I can't remain calm if I've given away a good fortune. Not that fortune cookies ever have bad news, but what if he took the best one?

Once he has his cookie, Flip tells me, "Have a good night, Finley."

"You, too," I reply before shutting the door and pulling at the handle three times.

Being autistic may sound like a lot of work, but luckily at this point in my journey, most of my compulsions are automatic. It's when a new impulse hits me that it can be overwhelming. Happily, it's been a while since I've felt the need to add additional stuff to my routine, which makes me hopeful I might be past that little segue into neurodivergence.

For some reason, the silkiness of Thomas's hair springs to mind, and I start to worry that touching it will become a new compulsion. I try to think about something else, so I don't manifest this. Blue cheese … butterflies … lemon scented floor wax … tacos … Thomas's hair … Thomas's hair … Thomas's hair.

Uh-oh.

This wouldn't be such a big deal if I knew I wasn't going to see him again. I'm not so far gone that I'd stalk him just to touch his hair. But I am going to have to see him a minimum of four more times—probably more so he can pick up his prints when we're all done.

How in the world am I going to keep my hands off him?

CHAPTER FOURTEEN

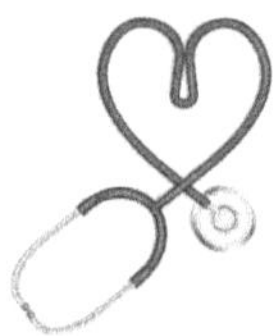

THOMAS

I may not have found the courage to ask Finley out on a date, but I did come up with a brilliant way to get even with my mom and dad for that awful prank they played on me and my sister all those years ago. While I don't particularly want to dress up and pretend to be a bunch of glamorized he-men, I can't wait to see my parents' reaction when I hand them a calendar. The trick will be getting them here so I can give it to them in person.

As driven as I am to get revenge, I'll also get to spend more time with Elk Lake's most adorable photographer. Finley didn't seem as excited as I thought she'd be at the prospect of seeing me in a pirate costume again, but I suppose I can see why. The last pictures were *that* bad.

Picking up my phone, I start a group text to my parents and sister. Vivie is going to love this idea, and I plan on giving her a heads up later on. Privately.

ME

I've got some big news I want to share but I need to do it in person. I'd like to fly you all out here in a couple of weeks.

MOM

No. Come home.

DAD

What news?

VIVIE

I'm in!

ME

Mom, I can't come home. I can't miss work this soon after starting.

MOM

Well, I can't go there. I'm allergic to Wisconsin.

ME

You'll be sorry.

MOM

Why?

ME

It's a secret.

MOM

Are you seven?

ME

This is going to make you happy, Mom. Trust me.

DAD

Did you meet someone?

MOM

Is that what this is about? A woman? How special can she be? You've only been there two weeks.

VIVIE

Did you meet someone, Tommy? I can't wait to meet her.

ME

I'm not telling you all on the phone. I want to do it in person.

I hurry to check the calendar and discover April first is on a Wednesday this year. Even though we haven't pulled April Fool's Day pranks on each other in several years, I don't want to do anything to tip them off. I hurry to type:

ME

Can you come out on Sunday March, 29th? You could stay until the following Saturday or Sunday.

MOM

I'm not going to spend a whole week in Wisconsin, Thomas.

DAD

My calendar is free. I don't have another speaking engagement until the middle of April.

VIVIE

I'll be there.

ME

I'll book the tickets and send you the itinerary.

MOM

I have book club on April first.

DAD

You can miss it this month, Morgan.

MOM

I can't miss it, Jason. I picked the book.

VIVIE

What book is more important than Thomas, Mom?

MOM

It's a book about Watergate. I saw the author interviewed and she claims to have never-released information.

ME

While Watergate was shocking in its time, Mother, that scandal is child's play compared to what politicians do now.

MOM

It involves aliens. You know how I feel about them.

VIVIE

Like you want them to come and take you back to your home planet?

Vivie adds seven laughing face emojis to her last question. Our mother was in Arizona for a spa week nearly thirty years ago, when the Phoenix Light UFO sighting happened. It was purportedly the largest sighting in the history of the world, witnessed by tens of thousands of people. Our mom claims to be one of them.

It's not that I don't believe in life on other planets, I just have a hard time believing more intelligent life would bother visiting us. And if they can get here, there's no doubt they're more intelligent.

Mom, on the other hand, is sure the *otherworldlies* are watching and are ready to intervene when we screw things up too badly. When she saw the Phoenix lights, she claimed to have experienced a sensation of peace, like never before. Which, if you ask me, is not a normal reaction to seeing the outline of the football field-sized spaceship in the sky. Either way, she's been all about the aliens ever since.

MOM

Laugh if you want, Vivienne, but Kurt Russell saw them, too. He was the pilot who first called the sighting in.

VIVIE

Well, then, that makes it totally credible.

MOM

The universe is big, Vivienne. Don't doubt what's out there.

DAD

The aliens can find your mother in Wisconsin. We'll be there, Tommy.

My parents have a great partnership, and as a rule, neither of them tells the other what to do. Having said that, when something is important to one of them, the other always goes along for the ride. My dad has just declared the importance of coming to see me. That's why I'm not surprised by my mom's response.

MOM

Fine. But I won't be eating any cheese.

ME

You might be sorry. They have something called cheese curds here that are surprisingly good.

MOM

I know what cheese curds are, Thomas. I've been to Canada.

On that note, I sign off with my family. Texting with them makes me sad we won't be having supper together on Sunday. But the good news is they'll be in Wisconsin soon, and I'll still get my fix.

Before heading off to bed, I quickly check my other texts. Other than two from my colleagues in New York, there's one from Constance.

CONSTANCE

I emailed you the information about our Spring Fling. Please let me know as soon as you can if we will be attending together.

ME

Thank you for sending the information. I won't be able to go with you, but I will look forward to seeing you there.

Not.

Constance reads the message but doesn't answer right away. Instead, the ellipses come and go several times like she's trying to figure out how to respond. She ultimately winds up with:

CONSTANCE

Take your time deciding but let me know a week in advance.

She clearly doesn't want to take no for an answer, but I am not going to change my mind. Instead of telling her that, I put my phone away.

There's a lot to recommend life in Elk Lake. There's Finley and her odd fetish for pirates. Even though she kept up an emotional shield today, I feel like I got to know her better. And I like what I see.

Then there's Kevin and Shelly next door. It's nice having neighbors who stop to chat with you. There's comfort in knowing people are looking out for you. Also, I'm looking forward to learning how to drive with more finesse, and I figure Elk Lake is a much better place to practice my skills than New York City. I set a reminder on my phone to check the timing of the next session.

Another bonus: my job is a lot less stressful here. Almost to the point of putting me to sleep at times. One day, our biggest emergencies were an infected splinter and a twisted ankle.

In addition to the negative impact of workplace boredom, I don't like being pursued by my boss. It's weird and uncomfortable. Constance does it with such entitlement, I briefly wonder if this is how women have felt since the dawn of time. It makes me ashamed to be a man.

After climbing into bed, my mind once again wanders back to

Finley. If things go well between us during our sessions, maybe I'll invite her to the Spring Fling. I don't want to ask her before then because I don't want our time together to be uncomfortable if it turns out she doesn't like me that way.

Having said that, I get the feeling she might. That dream she claimed to have about tornados surprisingly included a character named "Pirate Thomas." I fall asleep with a smile on my face.

So far, Finley Harper is the biggest draw for my staying in Elk Lake, and I'm really looking forward to seeing her again. Now that we've accomplished the original assignment Constance hired her for, we can get busy having some real fun.

CHAPTER FIFTEEN

FINLEY

I was scrolling through social media before going to bed last night and saw an advertisement for my dream car—a 1990 white Ford Mustang convertible with tan interior. I've loved that car since I first saw it in a vintage romcom movie when I was a teenager.

I used to daydream about driving it around my little town. I'd wave to the locals, but not as me, Finley Harper, small-town girl on the spectrum. No. I was Miss Illinois, blowing through town on her state-wide tour. Sometimes I'd stop and chat with the people.

In one of these fantasies, Penny Freeport—our senior year prom queen and my biggest tormentor—gasps in disbelief, "Finley Harper, is that you?"

I pull over and smile at her smugly while acting like I'm trying to remember who she is. "Yes, I'm Finley Harper," I tell her while adjusting the giant rhinestone crown on my head. "And you are …"

Staring in complete awe, she answers, "Penny. Penny Freeport. You know, from Mr. Hinkleman's geometry class?"

I loathed Mr. Hinkleman's geometry class. My failure there is what led me to being tested. Had I managed a mere two percentage points higher and gotten a D, I might have never known I was different from my peers. But as much as I hated geometry, I hated Penny even more.

"Penny Freeport ..." I tap my chin five times before remembering. "Oh." With a look of pure condescension, I ask, "Do you still live in town?"

This is where she pats her giant pregnant belly and tells me, "I married Jacob Smart. We're pregnant with our second." Their first came shortly after high school graduation. Two months to be exact.

"Jacob Smart?" Even though I spent hours upon hours fantasizing about running my fingers through his thick, wavy, black hair, I pretend I don't know him either. *Apparently, I've always had a thing for hair.*

"Sadly, that name doesn't ring a bell," I tell her in my most bored tone before glancing at my watch. "I need to run. I'm flying to Paris tonight for my date with Wills." That was before his wedding to Princess Catherine, of course. Once the two of them got hitched I lost my best revenge fantasy material. I'm no homewrecker, even in the land of make believe.

Jumping back into my convertible, I peel back out onto Main Street and leave Penny in a cloud of dust and disdain.

Now, someone in Elk Lake is selling my fantasy ride at a very reasonable price. While I won't be able to reenact my favorite fantasy—you know, because I'm not actually Miss Illinois—getting my hands on that car would still be sweet. There's only one problem: I don't drive.

That's why when I woke up this morning, I went online and contacted our local driving school. I've wanted to get behind the wheel for years, but for the same amount of time I've been worried I'd get overstimulated and wind up careening off a cliff. Not that there are any cliffs in Illinois or Wisconsin, but I've never wanted to risk it. Until now. Now my dream car is for sale.

It turns out if I take a six-week class and find someone to take me out to practice for fifty hours, I can be a licensed Wisconsin driver. *Take that, all you sixteen-year-olds who think you're so special with your "Please be patient, new driver" bumper stickers.*

This morning, I'm taking pictures of Allie and Margie. They want them, so when the baby grows up, they can show him or her that both its mothers were always present. If you ask me, the whole arrangement is amazing.

When Allie agreed to adopt Margie's baby, she made it clear she wanted Margie to be part of their baby's life. She didn't want her child to question their place in the world and ever feel like they weren't wanted. The amount of love that little person is going to grow up with is positively staggering.

After getting dressed, I put on a brand-new pair of pink socks. I allow myself a full five minutes to relish the feel of them against my skin before putting on shoes. The confinement of the shoe constricts the fibers, making the whole experience moderately less gratifying.

When I walk into Rosemary's for my morning latte, Faith greets me with a grin. "I talked to Teddy last night about doing a photoshoot for our anniversary and he's up for it."

"Excellent. What kind of look do you think you want to do?" Both Faith and her husband are gorgeous and would look amazing no matter who they dressed up as.

"Teddy wants to go with Princess Leia and Luke from *Star Wars.*"

She doesn't look very excited at the prospect, and rightly so since Luke and Leia are siblings. I tell her, "Why don't we do that one for him and then you can pick one that you'd like."

With a dreamy look on her face, she tells me, "I'd like to recreate our look from the summer when we were kids and had our first kiss."

Taking the latte she hands me, I reply, "I thought you guys only met a few years ago."

"We did, really." She explains, "Teddy used to visit his grandparents here when he was a kid. I used to see him down at the beach, but I never talked to him." She pauses to sigh. "He was older and way hotter than anyone I ever thought would bother with me."

Girl, I feel you.

Faith continues, "The last time I saw him, he kissed me the night before he went back to Arizona. After that, he didn't come back to town until a few summers ago."

"That was pretty forward, kissing you and then leaving town." Why couldn't something like that have happened to me? My first kiss didn't come until college. *College.* I'm guessing that's probably because in addition to being a late bloomer, once I was diagnosed, I lost all confidence and subsequently all appeal to the opposite sex. *Autism, the gift that keeps on giving.*

Faith's eyes appear to glaze over in memory. "It was like one of those perfect teenage love stories. It just took a long time for us to get our happily ever after." She puts a sticky bun in a bag and hands it to me.

"You're going to make me fat," I tell her. Although, I still take the bag. I don't fear fat like the average woman. In fact, I figure if I get chunky, I'll just be softer, and that *is* my favorite thing in the world. So really, there is no downside.

Faith pushes her glasses up. "You look fabulous, Finley. And what better way to start the day than with a sticky bun?"

She's got me there. New socks *and* a sticky bun practically make this the best morning I've had all month.

After walking out of Rosemary's, I stand for a minute and appreciate the beauty of Main Street. Most shops aren't open yet, so it's still fairly deserted. There's something about Elk Lake, Wisconsin, that makes me think of Stars Hollow in that old show, *Gilmore Girls.* It's so deliciously quaint, you just want to climb into your TV set and live there. Lucky for me, I already do.

I walk to Happy Snaps slowly while counting my steps—twenty-three from Rosemary's to my shop. Occasionally, it's twenty-four, which means I have to go back to the bakery and get it right. The good news is that I never make the same mistake twice in a row so I don't get caught in a horrible loop of walking to and from the bakery all day long.

Unlocking the door, I step inside and tap the light switch three times before turning it on. I love my shop, and its location on the corner. Windows facing two directions means twice the light, and twice the shadows. Even though I shoot in the back with stage lights, I still love the look of sunshine as it dapples on everything it touches.

Once I flip the *closed* sign to *open*, I walk behind the counter and open the drawer where I keep the wet wipes and plastic silverware. I pull out a knife and fork before carefully removing the sticky bun from its bag. While I love the taste of the caramelly-covered sweet roll, I do not like sticky things.

I savor the first bite, letting the explosion of cinnamon and pecan fill my mouth. Whoever invented these is my hero. I'm halfway through the roll when Allie and Margie walk in. "Good morning!" I call out with my mouth still half-full.

"What are you eating?" my friend demands.

"Sticky bun," I mumble.

"From Rosemary's?" Margie asks.

When I nod my head in the affirmative, she turns and walks back out onto the street. "Get me one, too!" Allie calls after her.

When my friend turns her attention back to me, I ask her, "How are you two doing?"

She tucks a strand of auburn hair back behind her ear. "If I wasn't adopting Margie's baby, I'd want to adopt Margie. That girl really has it all together, you know?"

"Aside from the teenage pregnancy part, you mean?" I've never known of a teenager who was excited to find out they had a baby onboard.

Allie drops her duffel bag on the floor before sitting down on one of the chairs by the window. "Obviously, that wasn't part of her plan, but she's dealing with it so maturely, it's mind-boggling."

"I'm envious of you," I tell my friend. "Your whole life is coming together."

"It took long enough," she scoffs before adding, "Don't worry, Fin, your life is moving along just fine."

"I suspect that's true," I tell her. "But I would like to meet someone and have my own love story."

"You will."

"How can you be sure?"

She tips her head to the side while staring at me. "Any man would be lucky to have you."

While I wholeheartedly agree with her, there's still a tiny niggling doubt left over from my more fragile days. "What if every man I meet thinks I'm too strange to date?"

"Then they aren't the right men for you. Seriously, girl. You're just a little different. And different is good." She assures me, "You're too good of a person not to have your dreams come true."

Walking out from behind the counter, I sit down next to her. "Good people don't always get the ending they deserve." I'm not being down on myself as much as I'm just speaking the truth.

She pats my arm. "You will, Finley. I believe that from the bottom of my heart."

"I'm strange," I remind her. "You said so yourself."

Plain-speaking can sometimes be misinterpreted as self-deprecation. That's why I'm not surprised when Allie seems to feel the need to comfort me. "I said you were quirky, not strange."

"Same thing, though, right?"

"No," she says sharply. "Quirky is endearing and cute. Strange is eating your boogers on the city bus."

"Ew."

"You see?" She smiles smugly. "Big difference."

I decide to tell Allie the news that's occupying most of my waking moments. "Thomas Culpepper has booked four more sessions with me."

She looks adequately surprised by this information. "The doctor/pirate?"

"One and the same," I tell her.

"Why does he need four more sessions?"

I explain to her how he plans on pulling the prank of all pranks on his parents. To which she says, "Interesting ..."

"You sound like you don't believe that's the reason."

Allie kicks her legs out in front of her and leans forward, resting her elbows on her knees. "That might be part of it, but what if he's also doing it to spend more time with you?"

"Why would he want to do that?" Prickles of embarrassment stab at the base of my neck. I cannot believe he came to me for a head shot and I made him take his shirt off.

My friend waggles her eyebrows suggestively. "Maybe he likes you."

"Maybe he feels sorry for me," I more accurately predict.

"Why would he feel sorry for you?"

"Because I mucked up his first shoot so badly." I explain, "He probably thinks I'm a couple of cookies short of a dozen and he's trying to make me feel better."

"Even if that's true," Allie says, "He's willing to spend a lot of money to do so, which means ..." She flashes jazz hands in front of her. "He likes you!"

I let that sink in for a minute. Could she be right? Could Thomas Culpepper really be interested in me? A chill of awareness radiates from my head throughout my body.

Could I be that lucky?

CHAPTER SIXTEEN

THOMAS

This afternoon is my first session with Finley, and while I'm excited to see her again, I'm a little less than thrilled to be dressing up. Having said that, revenge against my parents is going to be so sweet, the pain of pretending will be more than worth it.

So far this morning, I've seen one little girl who fell off her bike and broke her wrist, one woman with a second-degree oil burn—darn those homemade hash browns—and a man with kidney stones. By Elk Lake standards, that means it's been a busy start to the day.

While I'm washing my hands after my last patient, I hear my name called over the intercom. "Dr. Culpepper, please pick up line one. Dr. Culpepper to line one," the voice repeats.

I walk over to the closest telephone hanging on the wall. Picking up the receiver, I say, "This is Dr. Culpepper."

"Thomas." The voice of my boss sends chills of dread through me.

"Constance, what can I do for you?"

"I was wondering if you were free for lunch today." *Is she serious?*

Yet, she's still my boss, so I don't feel comfortable telling her to take the hint already. "What is this about?" I ask. If it's business, I'll have to see her. If it's personal, I'll make sure I have other plans.

Her tone is borderline flirty. "I wanted to discuss the auction for our Spring Fling."

"I'm not participating with that part of the event, Constance. What does that have to do with me?" I ask warily.

"We're asking all the staff to donate something we can raffle or to help find donations. The money we raise this year will be used to repaint the pediatric wing. We want to make it bright and cheerful for the kids."

That's obviously a great cause. As such, I tell her, "I'd be happy to make a monetary donation, but I don't have anything to auction off."

"How about your time?" she asks, her voice dripping in innuendo.

I have a feeling I know where she's going with this, but I'm going to need her to spell her intentions out. "What do you mean by *my time*?"

"You could auction off a date or something," she practically purrs. "We can discuss it at lunch."

"I'm sorry, Constance. I can't have lunch with you today. I'm meeting my lady friend." I hurry to remind her, "Which also means I'm not going to go on a date with someone else, even if it is for charity. I will, however, be happy to write you a check to put toward painting."

"I suppose if that's all you can do …" Are you kidding me? How can a person in a professional situation, let alone my boss, actually sound *pouty* about my refusing a date?

"If there's nothing else," I interrupt her, "I'm still on duty."

"That's all for now, Thomas." This sounds like a threat. Like she's going to track me down every chance she gets. Which I wouldn't put past her.

Instead of responding, I merely hang up the phone.

One of the nurses walks by me. Becky is in her fifties and looks like one of those friendly moms from a sitcom. "You look like you just ate a bad burrito," she tells me. Reaching out to touch my forehead with her hand, she asks, "You okay? You're not coming down with anything, are you?"

I don't want to gossip, but I also want to find out as much about Constance as I can. It's in my best interest to know if she has the potential of turning into a serial stalker. "What do you know about Constance Brucker?" I ask Becky.

Her brown eyes open widely in surprise. "What do you want to know?"

"Is she ... you know ..." *Psycho?* A bunny boiler? But I don't ask that. Instead, I go with, "A good person to work for?"

"I don't have a lot of exposure to her," Becky says. "But I get the feeling that that's what you're asking." She takes my arm and leads me to an empty bay. Then she pulls the curtain around us and asks, "What's going on, Thomas? You can trust me."

I hem and haw before clearing my throat. As I have no one else to ask, I finally confess, "She wants to go out on a date with me."

Becky rolls her eyes and groans, "Yuck." She follows that up with, "I mean, oh. How do you feel about that?"

I don't want to come right out and bag on the woman, so I say, "I don't think it's a good idea for me to date my boss."

Her chin bobs up and down. "That's what Dr. Monroe told her."

"Who's that?" Not only haven't I worked with a Dr. Monroe yet, but his headshot is not on our wall of fame.

"Bill Monroe. You were hired to take his place," she tells me.

"Did he leave because of Constance?" I realize I'm jumping right into gossip territory here, but this is information I need to have.

Becky exhales loudly. "He claims he had a family emergency and had to move back to Rhode Island to be near his parents."

"But you don't believe that."

She shakes her head. "I don't. Because Dr. Monroe was hired

to replace Dr. Greg Post, who was also a single, good-looking man."

"And he left because?" I ask.

"Because he filed and won a sexual harassment suit against Constance." Becky confides, "Most men probably wouldn't do that, but Dr. Post did."

"Why is Constance still working here if someone won a lawsuit against her? I'd think there would be cause to fire her over that."

"I don't think there's any getting rid of her." She shares, "Her family founded the hospital over a hundred years ago. Your best bet would be to find someone else to date. That way, Constance would have to accept she doesn't have a chance."

An image of Finley pops into my head. Sweet, blonde Finley with big green eyes and the camera hanging around her neck. "There is someone I'm interested in," I tell her.

Becky's eyes sparkle with curiosity, but she doesn't ask who that might be. Instead, she says, "If I were you, I'd ask her out ASAP. Send the message to Constance that you're not on the market."

I've been telling our boss that very thing, but she won't listen. "Thanks for the advice, Becky," I tell her. "I'll definitely keep that in mind."

With those parting words, I head toward the doctors' lounge to make sure the afternoon doctor is here. I wouldn't want Elk Lake to have its first real emergency and not have anyone on hand to take care of them.

The quaint bell above the door at Happy Snaps rings, announcing my arrival.

I hear Finley's disembodied voice call out, "I'm in the back, Thomas."

Walking through the doorway leading to the studio, I ask, "What if it wasn't me? What if I were an ax murderer?"

Her eyes peer over the top of her computer, where she's probably reviewing someone else's pictures. "If you were an ax murderer, I'd hit you over the head with a baseball bat before calling the cops."

"Do you even have a baseball bat here?" I challenge her.

She leans down and stealthily picks up something beside her. She raises a baseball bat over her head.

"I'm glad you take your security seriously," I tell her.

Putting the bat back down, she replies, "Elk Lake is a small town, but that doesn't mean there aren't bad people everywhere."

"Have you ever met any?" I ask her. As far as I'm concerned, Elk Lake is the most mild-mannered town on the planet.

She shakes her head. "I haven't, but as a female business owner, I like to be prepared." She adds, "I grew up on *Law and Order*, you know." Taking a breath, she asks, "Now, which costume should we start with?"

I inwardly grimace at the thought of playacting. "You pick," I tell her.

"Why don't we start with a policeman?" Her eyes sparkle in such a way I can't help but wonder if that's her favorite. She points to the clothing rack against the wall. "I have a few different sizes, but I can always pin it if the fit is off."

I smile in response and walk toward the men's costumes. Then I rifle through them and pull out a uniform that looks like it's about my size. I take it into the bathroom to change. The pants are a bit snug but not too bad. The problem is with the shirt. It seems to be a much smaller size than the pants and it doesn't have any buttons.

I'm in here long enough that Finley knocks on the door. "You okay in there?"

"I'm … um … fine?"

"Your voice raised at the end like a question. What's wrong?" Apparently, it doesn't take a psychic to know I'm lying.

I open the door so she can see. "The buttons fell off this shirt. Also, I think I need a bigger size."

Finley starts laughing. "Thomas, you're here to have fantasy photos taken." Her eyes run down the length of my body before she mumbles, "This is how the uniform is supposed to look."

"It feels unnatural," I tell her. "I mean, how am I supposed to arrest a perp like this?"

"Arrest a perp, huh?" She giggles again.

"You're not the only one who watched *Law and Order*," I tell her.

"Good," she says. "Then you know what to do." I follow her as she turns and walks toward a lighted set. She's placed a streetlamp in front of a sweep of a city street. The whole scene looks impressively authentic.

I stand there awkwardly and watch as she walks over to the prop table. She picks up a pair of handcuffs and a billy club and brings them over to me. "Which do you want to start with?" I take the handcuffs.

As she walks off set and picks up her camera, I ask, "Aren't you going to … you know …" I gesture toward my bare chest. "Put baby oil on me?" I finally mutter.

Finley's gaze drops to my feet and she visibly swallows. "I usually save that for the pirate and fireman. You don't want all the photos to look the same, do you?"

"I hadn't really thought about it," I tell her. Although, for some reason I'm semi-disappointed not to be getting the full treatment. "What about hair and makeup?" I ask.

Both of her hands form into fists before they open and clench again. "I want to take a couple of shots first and see how they look. If needed, we can adjust your character from there."

An image from our first photo shoot pops into my mind. "In other words, you want to make sure I know what I'm doing."

Her supple pink lips form into a slow smile. "Something like that," she says. "Now, channel your inner lawman and show me what you've got."

As uncomfortable as this is for me, I'm determined not to disappoint Finley. I try to imagine how Dwayne "The Rock" Johnson would handle this assignment. Standing as tall as my six feet two inches allows, I throw my shoulders back and flex my muscles for effect. Then I narrow my gaze into what I hope looks like a fierce expression of virility.

I'm convinced I must look like the most impressive cop on the planet but then Finley gasps, "What are you doing?"

CHAPTER SEVENTEEN

FINLEY

What in the world is Thomas doing? This cannot be the same sorry pirate I took pictures of last week.

I realize I must have asked this question out loud when his face morphs into an expression of concern. "I'm pretending I'm The Rock. Am I doing it wrong?"

"No." In fact, he's doing it so very right I'm having a hard time catching my breath. I knew Thomas was built from our first shoot, but there's something about the way this uniform fits him that's making the lens on my camera steam up. "You're doing fine," I tell him, downplaying the staggering reality of the situation. *Swoon! Gasp! Attack of the vapors! He's doing great!*

"What's wrong then?" He clearly doesn't believe me.

"Nothing. Seriously." I put the camera up to my face and start taking pictures. "Just move around a bit," I tell him. "Change your pose, but do it subtly."

Thomas is such a natural at pretending to be a sexy policeman, I'm about to beg him to arrest me. In fact, if he was a real cop, I'd be tempted to commit a crime just to get his attention. After ten minutes, I tell him, "Take a break." Then I practically sprint toward my bottle of cold water. I might have to pour it over my head to bring my temperature down.

Thomas walks toward me and peers over my shoulder to get a look at the computer monitor where his pictures have popped up. "Hey, these are good!" He sounds pleased with himself.

"They are." I make sure to keep my back to him and emotion out of my voice. My face still feels like it's on fire and I don't want him to see what his image is doing to me.

"Who knew I was such a good model?" He's clearly as surprised as I am. And who wouldn't be, given our first disastrous session together?

"You're doing much better," I assure him without coming right out and praising him.

"I'm amazing," he declares confidently.

I inhale slowly and count to seven before facing him. "Should we try it with the billy club now?"

"Let's do it." He sounds like he's really enjoying himself, which is the point of these pictures. I just didn't think he'd take to it so readily. Those cross-eyed pirate shots were seriously so bad I didn't think he had it in him.

Thomas picks up the billy club and heads back to the set. He widens his legs in an imposing stance and grips the wooden stick like he's heading into a street fight. *Holy crow. The room starts to spin like I've had one too many sips of beer.*

I take another several more shots before declaring, "I think the police officer is a wrap."

Officer Culpepper practically skips off set before asking, "What now?"

"You call it," I tell him. "Go find another outfit and we'll take it from there."

As my client walks toward the costume rack, I release a ragged breath. I'm so discombobulated I forget to count. I have never reacted to a model the way I'm reacting to Thomas and it's very disconcerting.

Now that I know he's not dating Constance, I'm starting to have some impure thoughts. Which to be honest is making my job a lot harder. I remind myself once again that *I'm a professional.* and I have to behave as such. Having said that, once I finish Thomas's job, all bets are off.

Thomas comes out of the bathroom a few minutes later dressed in tight ripped jeans. He's bare-chested except for a cropped, bright orange vest. The hard hat gives it away. He's a construction worker. *Is there any outfit he doesn't look amazing in?*

"Wow, look at you," I say.

"Good? Bad?" He sounds nervous.

"Fine," I tell him.

"Just, fine?"

I gesture to the hair and makeup station. "If you're working construction, you'll need a tan. Let's get some bronzer on you." I rapidly cross the room like my pants are on fire and I'm searching for a lake to jump into.

Thomas follows me and sits down on the tall revolving chair.

I stare at him hoping it looks like I'm trying to formulate a plan. In reality, I'm inwardly lecturing myself to keep my hands off him. Picking up a large blush brush, I swipe it across a palette of bronzer and then start dabbing at his face.

After several applications, I stand back and look. *Perfect.* "Stand up," I tell him. Once he complies, I make long sweeping brush strokes across his arms to add that sun-kissed touch. His skin shivers in response.

"The brush feels great, doesn't it?" I ask. "It's the softest synthetic sable I've been able to find."

He exhales a jagged breath. "Yeah, it's nice."

The air fills with thick sexual tension, which is not normal during a shoot. Probably because I film couples and all their tension is for each other. I'm the outsider entrusted with capturing them on film. I hurry up and finish Thomas's tan before picking up a spray bottle full of water. Then I lead him to another backdrop.

I gesture for him to stand next to the "Men at Work" sign and position his feet behind the fake manhole cover on the floor. Then I mist him with the water bottle.

He jolts when the cold water hits him. "What are you doing?"

"Construction workers sweat," I tell him. "A nice sheen will do wonders for this look."

"The water is freezing," he complains.

I give him a conspiratorial look. "We've been through this."

He practically growls in response. "Right. You want certain parts of me to stand at attention."

"Exactly."

My model exudes blatant masculinity as he flexes his way through the next twenty minutes of shooting. He does this so well, I pick up the spray bottle and turn it on myself in hopes of once again reducing my heat level.

"Are you coming out here to join me?" Thomas teases.

"I am not. The camera lights are really putting out heat," I assure him, even though we both see they are pointed at him and far away from me. Then I say, "I think we're done with this one." Turning away, I walk over to my laptop to see what I've captured. One look and I consider getting a defibrillator to have on hand for our future sessions.

I don't know what kind of doctor Thomas is, but he could have a real future as a model. He's gone from making me look like I don't know what I'm doing to practically becoming Annie Leibovitz.

I feel the hot air of his breath on my neck right before I hear him say, "These are incredible!"

I don't know why I don't let him have this win, but I don't. "They're good."

My subject sighs like a heroine in a Jane Austen book before saying, "They're great and you know it, Finley."

"You're doing much better," I assure him.

I turn around to discover Thomas is practically standing on

top of me. I try to take a step back, but I run into my computer stand. "I know we started off badly," he says. "But that's all behind us. I think we should be friends. What do you say?"

"Friends?" I don't want to be this man's friend. I want to be his girlfriend, the banana to his split, his baby mama, his ... I could go on and on, but *I am a professional.*

Still invading my personal bubble, Thomas replies, "Why not be friends? I'm new in town and don't know very many people. I think you'd be a nice friend to have." He thrusts his hand out in front of him to seal the deal. "What do you say?"

Instead of accepting his offer, I tentatively tell him, "I suppose I could be your friend."

He looks slightly hurt that I'm not more exuberant. Then he says, "As my only female friend in town, how would you feel about doing me a huge favor?"

Ah, it wasn't just friendship he was after. There's a catch. I take a giant step to the left, hoping to release myself from his gravitational pull. "It depends on the favor," I say. For instance, I'd be happy to tell him where to go to get a good pedicure or advise him on Elk Lake's minimal night life, but I'm not interested in feeding his cat if he has plans to go out of town.

"I need a girlfriend," he tells me bluntly.

"You want me to be your girlfriend?" *Yes!* I can't help but wonder why didn't he lead with that.

Thomas shakes that gorgeous head of his. "Constance has targeted me as a love interest, and I need to make sure she knows I'm not up for it."

Shoot. "Just tell her you don't want to date her."

"Believe me, I've tried. She refuses to take no for an answer." I've met the woman and I can definitely see her not backing down if she's set her sights on something. She's that scary.

I turn and take another three steps before stopping. I need to think. Being that I'm super bad at taking social cues, I need to figure out if Thomas might really want to date me and he's using this as an excuse, or if he's telling the truth about Constance. I'd be disappointed if it was what he claims it is—a ruse to throw his boss off the scent. But maybe I could still use it to my benefit. Maybe if Thomas gets to know me better, he'll learn to like me—eccentricities and all.

Unless he already likes me. Then spending more time with me might work against me. Having said that, if we're going to be a couple for real, we'll have to spend time together, right? My head starts to hurt.

I'm quiet for long enough that Thomas asks, "So, what do you say? Are you up for being my fake girlfriend?"

"And friend?" I add.

He smiles so enticingly, I'm ready to jump into his arms and beg him to love me. Luckily for my dignity, I control this impulse. "What would being your fake girlfriend entail?"

Relief washes over his chiseled features. "I need a date for the hospital Spring Fling."

"When is that?" I ask, disappointed that's all he's after.

"April eighth," he says. "It would just be a couple of hours of your time, and I'd be happy to compensate you."

I'm sure he didn't mean to offend me, but nonetheless, that's how I feel. "I'm not a paid escort, Thomas. If we're going to be friends then I would be happy to go on a fake date with you."

"*If* we're going to be friends?"

I start pacing back and forth, carefully counting my steps. Five each way with a half step pivot to change direction. "If you want to be friends for real that includes doing stuff together. You know, seeing movies, eating out …"

His eyes begin to twinkle like an animator stepped onto the scene to draw little stars around them. "But we'd be doing those things as friends?"

"My friend Allie and I do those things," I say before assuring him, "and we're not dating each other."

"Let's do it," he decides quickly. "I like you, Finley. You're different from other women that I know."

If he thinks what he's seen so far is different, he'd run for the hills if he got a glimpse inside my head.

"I like you too, Thomas." I walk toward him and stick my hand out this time. With a firm shake, I add, "I'm glad you moved to Elk Lake."

I'm just sad that he doesn't want me to be his real girlfriend.

CHAPTER EIGHTEEN

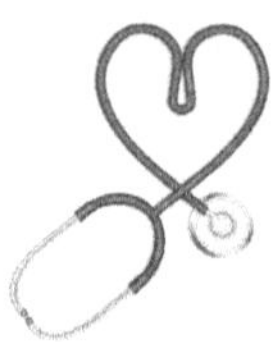

THOMAS

I don't know what to make of Finley. One minute she can barely stand being in the same room as me and the next, she's acting like I hurt her feelings. She appeared almost disappointed when I asked her to be my fake girlfriend. *Is it possible she wants to be my real girlfriend?* And if that's the case, then why is she prickly all the time? I suppose I won't learn the answer until we get to know each other better.

For my last shot of the day, Finley has decided I should be a duke. She walks to the costume rack and pulls out a pair of fitted trousers, riding boots, and yet another blousy white shirt. Actually, this one is more frilly than blousy. "Roll the sleeves up like it's been an exhausting day," she orders. "And leave the top four button undone."

"What have I been doing all day that's made me so tired?" I ask. I seriously have no idea what a duke does to wear himself out.

Finley shrugs her shoulders before tucking an errant strand of hair behind her ear. She repeats this gesture often and it's quite endearing. "I don't know. Just pretend that lording it over people has done you in."

I laugh out loud. "Lording it over people, huh?"

As Finley walks away, she says, "Margaret and Bob love the snooty duke theme. Margaret has loaned me several books in the genre but I haven't read them yet." She confides, "I don't think bodice rippers are my jam."

"They're not mine, either," I assure her. That comment makes her chuckle.

"I wouldn't think so," she says. "I think they're geared more toward women."

Instead of going into the bathroom, I stand behind the costume rack to change. I take off the ripped jeans and put on the duke's pants. "If they're geared toward women, why don't you like them?" I want to know.

She's quiet for a long beat before answering, "I feel like women are always second-class citizens in them. You know, they're being betrothed by their fathers or ordered around by societal dictates. That stuff makes me uncomfortable."

"I get that," I tell her. "But I think it has more to do with the fantasy of it all. You know, being forced into something and then discovering it's the best thing that's ever happened to you."

"I don't think real life is like *Bridgerton*," she says.

"What is *Bridgerton*?" I lean over to put a boot on and nearly lose my balance.

"It's a show on Netflix. The story comes from bodice ripper books that have been turned into a television show."

"And you don't like the show?"

"I haven't watched it," she says. "Allie says it's good though. She says if I can catch up to the current season, we could watch it together. I just haven't gotten around to starting it."

I don't know what comes over me, but I suggest, "Maybe we could watch it together. That's something friends would do, right?"

"I … um …"

Finley doesn't finish her sentence, so I add, "And we've decided we're friends, right?"

"Yes?" It's more of a question than a statement of fact.

I hurry to put on my duke shirt before stepping out from behind the costume rack. Finley takes one look at me and inhales sharply.

"What's wrong?" I ask. "Did I put this on backwards or something?" I didn't know if the laces on the pants went in the front or back.

Her silky blonde hair moves from side to side. "No. You look fine."

"Again with the fine," I tell her. "I thought I looked darn good."

Finley turns around and leads the way to another set. The background looks like a gentleman's library. There's an oriental rug on the floor and on top of that is a chaise lounge. Gesturing toward the little sofa, she says, "Recline on that and let's see how you look."

Instead of moving I stare at her blankly. I'm not quite seeing her vision.

In response, she sits down on the chaise and shows me what she wants. "You need to exude sexy entitlement. You know," she says, "Like it's just so hard and rewarding being you."

I snort under my breath. "You seem to have a good grasp on what this genre entails for someone who doesn't read it or watch it."

"I've seen all the renditions of the Jane Austen movies," she says matter of factly. "My mom was a huge *Masterpiece Theater* fan. She practically forced me to watch them with her."

"And?" I ask. "Did you enjoy them?"

"I did," she says almost against her will. "I like strong heroines who stand up for themselves. I just don't like all the obstacles in their paths." After a beat, she confesses, "I want to jump into the TV and yell at all those stupid men on their behalf."

"It's a good thing you were born in this time then," I tell her.

"It's a good thing for stupid men," she clarifies.

When she gets up, I sit down on the edge of the sofa with my legs spread wide open. Putting my elbows on my knees, I focus all my attention on Finley. Once I'm good and smoldering, I tell her, "All of the servants had the day off and I had to dress myself. Not only that, but I had to peel my own grapes." With a wink, I add, "I'm beat."

Finley snorts. "I think maybe this might be the look that comes most naturally to you."

"You're teasing, right?" Sometimes, I can't tell with her. She's got such a great poker face, I briefly wonder if she plays cards.

Without answering my question, Finley turns and walks off set before lifting her camera to her face.

I do my best to channel my inner spoiled nobility. Finley gives me positive feedback, but it's minimal. *Nice. Good. You've got it.* I finally break down and say, "I have to be doing better than I did during our first session."

She glares at me. "Nothing will ever be worse than that."

"And yet, you cheered me on then and told me how great I was doing. Why aren't you doing that now that I'm killing it?"

"I'm worried that overly positive reinforcement may make you a worse model." She concludes, "And I never want to see that cross-eyed pirate again."

I guess I can't blame her. But even so, I say, "I've already proven I'm a great cop, a sizzling construction worker, and a sexy duke. I think you can go ahead and tell me what an amazing model I am." I sit expectantly like a dog waiting for a treat.

Finley's expression turns from cool boredom to a smirk. "You're doing great, Thomas. Really. In fact, I'm proud of you."

"Are you making fun of me?" I just can't tell with her.

"I'm not." She walks right over to me and says, "You are an amazing model. I didn't tell you because, well …" She takes a deep breath before saying, "I'm still mad at you for those pirate shots. I spent days thinking I was the worst photographer in the world."

"You're a great photographer," I tell her enthusiastically. "Seriously, you saw the stuff we shot today. I can't wait to show my parents."

A brilliant smile appears on Finley's face and her cheeks flush. "Thank you, Thomas. That's very nice of you to say."

"You see how good a little praise feels?" I respond.

Her head bobs up and down several times. "You are a smoking hot cop, a sizzling construction worker, and the snootiest duke I've ever met. Nice work."

"Was that so hard?" I ask with a laugh.

"No, it wasn't."

I feel like we've finally surpassed our obstacles and we can start fresh. "How about if I take you out to dinner to celebrate our successful partnership?" I ask.

Finley, who has walked over to her laptop, suddenly stops moving. Hands in mid-air, she asks, "You want to have dinner with me?"

"Yeah, you know, to thank you for today." I give her my best "I'm a good guy" expression.

"You know I'm charging you for these pictures, right?"

"Of course you are, but I'm also celebrating the fact that I have a new friend and a fake girlfriend when I need one. Being that both of those people are you, I figured I owed you a little extra something."

Finley's eyes move from the left to the right like she's looking for the closest exit. But instead of running, she says, "You really do owe me. But you should know, I'm hungry. And being that we're friends and nothing more, I'm not going to eat delicately in front of you."

"I'm glad," I tell her. "I hate dining with women who don't know how to enjoy a good meal. My mom is always counting calories, and she feels guilty about enjoying her food. It makes me crazy."

"It must be a generational thing," Finley says. "My mom is pretty reserved when it comes to eating in front of other people."

She adds, "When she and my dad go out, she always asks for a doggy bag at the beginning of the meal. She puts half her food into it before she even starts."

"That's awful," I tell her.

Shutting the lid on her computer, Finley tells me, "I don't do that. In fact, if two different entrées sound good and I can't decide between them, I've been known to order both."

On my way to the costume rack to change, I ask, "Do you ever share bites with your friends?"

"It depends if they have something I want them to share with me." Ah, she's a tit for tat kind of lady. I can support that.

Stationing myself behind the screen of clothes, I tell her, "I'm always happy to share. And being that supper is on me, you can order as many entrees as you want."

"That's very noble of you."

"It's because I'm a duke," I tell her. "You know, noble by definition."

Finley laughs. "All right, Lord Culpepper, where are you taking me?"

"I don't know," I tell her. "I've only ever been to the diner. And while I'm happy to go back, I'm also game to venture out and try someplace new. Where do *you* think we should go?"

I can't see Finley, but I hear her mumbling to herself like she's weighing her options. After several moments, she says, "I love the beer battered fish and chips at the pub, but I also really love the patty melt at the diner. Then there's the lodge. I hear their restaurant is first class, but it's probably quite pricey. I'd feel bad making you buy me two entrees there."

"I have a good job," I tell her. "I'd be happy to buy you two expensive meals."

When I walk out from behind the costumes wearing my own clothes, I discover Finley standing by the doorway leading to the front of her shop. Her purse is slung over her shoulder and she appears ready to go. "I'm not opposed to letting you spend money on me, but let's go there another time. I'm starving and I don't want to have to go home and change clothes before we eat."

"So where are we headed?" I ask.

"My stomach is telling me patty melts at the diner," she replies. After we walk through the front of her shop, she turns the lights off and we head outside. As she stops to lock up, I ask, "It's nearby, right? I still don't know my way around town yet."

"Two blocks down," she says. "It's right across the street from my apartment building."

"Good," I tell her. "We're going to have to walk. I don't have a car yet."

She side-eyes me with interest. "You don't have a car?"

"I never needed one in New York City," I tell her.

"Do you know how to drive?" Oddly, she doesn't sound the least bit judgmental.

"I know how to drive *in theory*, but I don't get a lot of practice so I'm not very good at it. My neighbor teaches drivers' education in town and I'm thinking about taking a refresher class."

"No!" Now Finley sounds downright excited. "I'm going to start taking a driving class, too. I just signed up."

A cool breeze blows past us, making me wish I was wearing a heavier jacket. Even though New York City can get very cold, it somehow feels warmer than Elk Lake. It's probably the exhaust from all the traffic heating up the air.

"You don't drive?" I ask while jamming my hands in my pockets in hopes of warming them up.

Finley shakes her head but doesn't elaborate. Well, she didn't judge me, so I'm not going to judge her. Instead, I tell her, "Maybe we'll be in the same class. I just hope I can fit it around my schedule."

My new friend smiles at me like all barriers between us have been lowered. Which is a relief. Not only will Finley and I be shooting pictures together, but we can polish up our driving skills. If I can't convince her to like me as more than a friend spending that amount of time together, I don't deserve to be anything more than her fake boyfriend.

CHAPTER NINETEEN

FINLEY

The fact that Thomas doesn't drive very well makes me feel closer to him than anything else could. It's nice to know I'm not the only one who doesn't possess all the normal skills

It starts to pour down rain as we walk to the diner. Grabbing my new friend's arm, I pull him away from the curb, so we have rain protection from the awnings hanging over the buildings. "What's life like in New York?"

"Busy," he replies. "I was always on the move."

"But not here?"

He stops walking before turning to face me. "I don't know as many people here yet. I don't have as much draw on my time."

"You must have a lot of friends back home." Thomas is such a friendly and social guy, he's probably got plans every night.

"I have a good number," he says, but he pauses again like he's really thinking about the question. "I think maybe I just feel busier in New York because everything around me is busier. Does that make sense?"

"It's a stimulation thing," I tell him. "When there's a lot of outside stimuli, people can get overwhelmed."

As though I've just given him the key to understanding me, he asks, "Is that why you don't think you'd ever enjoy living in New York?"

I forgot I already told him that. "This might sound crazy, but big cities sort of squoosh my aura." The rain lightens up slightly, so I pull his arm to cross the street with me.

"Your aura ..." he repeats.

"Yeah, you know, the energy field around a person." I explain, "The body is just the vehicle. It's not us. And it's claustrophobic enough being stuck inside of it."

"So, what you're saying is that big cities squoosh your soul."

I love that he understands this. "That's exactly what I'm saying."

We walk into a rather crowded diner. "Is this too busy for you?" Thomas asks.

I shake my head. "It would be if the street was crowded with people and I'd already been bombarded with other energies. But I'm calm going in, so I'll be fine." I'm surprised I confess this as readily as I do.

Thomas takes my answer in stride and doesn't comment. We approach the hostess stand and by the time it's our turn, there's only one table left in the restaurant. It's a booth in the front window.

The hostess says, "You're lucky this one just opened up."

"It's very nice," Thomas tells her. While he takes his coat off, his gaze is diverted to something across the room. He looks disturbed.

"You okay?" I ask him.

Thomas offers a flimsy wave before turning toward me. "I need you to start the fake girlfriend angle tonight. Now, in fact. My boss is sitting over there."

"Constance?!" I half gasp and screech at the same time. Suddenly my aura is beyond squooshed, it's nearly snuffed out. "Maybe we should go."

He shakes his head. "No way. I need her to see us together. Hopefully, that way, she'll stop hounding me."

"Yes," I say, "but I don't want to talk to her. She's mean. She made me feel like a fool."

"So, get even." Instead of sitting across the table from me like a normal person, he scoots in next to me. Which is both crowded and lovely. His shoulders are so broad, they touch mine, and I instinctively lean in toward him.

"Get even how?" I manage to croak.

He tips his head toward mine like we're full-on canoodling, and whispers, "Show her you have the man she wants."

Stabbing hot awareness fills my body. It's like I've just been attacked by a colony of fire ants. "Conceited," I tell him. But he's right. I wouldn't mind showing Constance up. "Would you like me to crawl onto your lap?" I tease.

Thomas's face turns red in what might be embarrassment, or it might be returned interest. I can't tell. "I don't think you need to do that. Just hang on my every word like I'm the most fascinating man you've ever met."

"You'd like that, wouldn't you?" I laugh.

He leans closer to me and exhales into my ear, "I really would." His hot breath causes goose bumps to pop up all over my body. Talk about overstimulation. For a person who strives to keep balance, I'm failing.

"Can I get you something to drink?" Neither Thomas nor I heard the waitress approach, and we both jump at the intrusion into our little bubble.

"What would you like?" Thomas asks me.

I smile up at the waitress. "I'll have a diet cola, please. With three slices of lemon." I'll only use two, but two isn't one of my preferred numbers, so I order up.

"I'll have a glass of red wine," Thomas tells her. Turning to me, he asks, "Unless you'd like to share a bottle?"

My ability to pretend I'm normal ceases to exist when I drink alcohol. I'm not sure Thomas is ready for the real me yet. So, I tell him, "No thanks, I'm good."

When the waitress walks away, I inadvertently make eye contact with Constance. *Shoot.* She's glaring at me like she wants to rip all the hair off my head, one excruciating clump at a time. Forcing myself to turn away, I tell Thomas, "Your boss looks like she's ready to commit murder."

"You or me?" he wants to know.

"I think she'll start with me. But you might be next if you don't let her have her wicked way with you."

"Her behavior is very unprofessional," he grumbles.

I don't know why, but that comment rubs me the wrong way. "I'm sorry she's making you uneasy, but you are aware this is how men have treated women in the workplace since women were allowed to work outside of the home."

Thomas doesn't look the least bit offended by my comment. In fact, he agrees. "Every one of those men should have been reprimanded or fired, depending on the extent of his behavior."

My hackles retreat. "That's a very refreshing attitude."

"Have you ever been on the receiving end of workplace misconduct?" he wants to know.

"I work for myself so, not really. I'm a pretty great boss."

"You must have had a boss somewhere along the line …" he prompts.

An irritatingly cocky face pops into my head. "The problem with Dillion wasn't sexual harassment," I tell him. "He was into guys. His problem was that he didn't like me, and he made sure to let me know it as often as he could."

"Where did you and Dillion work?" he wants to know.

"At the faculty gym at our university. We handed out locks and towels, did laundry, that kind of thing."

Thomas gazes into my eyes with laser-like intent. "How did he treat you that made you think he didn't like you?"

"He used to throw the sweaty towels at me." I make a face like I'm going to throw up.

Thomas looks appropriately horrified. "Did you ever complain?"

"I complained to him, but that seemed to make things worse."

"Why didn't you go to his superior?" he wants to know.

"I would have, but I didn't know who that was. Don't worry, though. I got even the day I quit."

My dinner companion shoots me such an adorably expectant look, I'm tempted to go ahead and crawl onto his lap. "I brought a fudge brownie into work with me," I tell him. I love this memory so much, I take a deep breath to savor the recollection before sharing, "I rubbed it into a towel and then I screamed and threw it at Dillion. It looked like, *you know*." I don't bother spelling it out because the brain only conjures one thing when it sees ground-in brown stuff on a towel.

Thomas's face lights up in such a way I can tell he appreciates this story as much as I do. "What did he do?"

"He yelled and threw the towel right back at me. Then he fired me. But I told him it was too late to fire me because I quit. Then I opened the towel and licked the brownie remains. I thought Dillion was going to faint."

Thomas laughs out loud. "Licking the brownie was very childish." He says the last like it's the highest compliment.

"Thank you," I say proudly.

The waitress drops our drinks. I take the wrapper off my straw before inserting it into the soda at the perfect forty-five-degree angle. Only then do I squeeze in two of the lemon slices before taking a sip.

"Are you ready to order?" she asks.

I get the patty melt and Thomas orders the tacos. "Do you need a second entrée?" Thomas challenges me like he doesn't believe I'll get one.

Smiling up at the waitress, I tell her, "I'd like the meatloaf, too, please. What does that come with?"

Instead of looking surprised by my gluttony, she looks

delighted. After all, a bigger check means a bigger tip. "It comes with a baked potato and peas."

I love peas, but they're also my nemesis due to their rollability. "Can I get the peas in a bowl on the side?" I ask. She nods her head and walks away.

"Why not get something else if you don't like peas?" Thomas asks.

"I love peas," I assure him.

"Then why on the side?"

There's no getting out of telling him now. "I don't like them rolling all over my plate."

"Ah," he laughs. "You don't want them touching your other food." Before I can ask if he has the same predilection, he says, "My sister is the same way."

"What else doesn't your sister like?" I wonder if maybe she might be on the spectrum, too. That would actually be great for me because then Thomas would be used to people with differences.

"She doesn't like root beer," he says. "She says it tastes like medicine. And she thinks mint chocolate tastes like toothpaste."

I like root beer and mint chocolate, so I'm going to need something more. "Anything else?"

Thomas thinks for a moment before answering, "Humidity?"

Clearly he's not going to give me what I want. Which would be a deep-rooted hatred of whistling, a revulsion to nut chewers, an almost homicidal reaction to bubble gum poppers ... The list goes on and on. I finally ask, "Is your sister older or younger?"

He smiles fondly as though he's imagining her face. "Vivie is four years younger than me. She's an artist."

"An artist?" I ask. "Like a working artist or a hobby?"

"Working artist," he says. "She has paintings hanging all over the city."

"Wow, that's impressive. It's hard to become known in that field."

"She's kind of a prodigy," Thomas tells me proudly. "She

painted a piece in junior high school that won an award. It got some media attention, and one of the big bank buildings on Wall Street saw it. They wanted to buy it for their lobby, but my parents wouldn't let Vivie sell it."

"That's amazing!" I say excitedly.

"They hired Vivie to paint another one for them. She's been doing commission work since, but she also creates and shows her own collections."

"Thomas," I tell him, "that's truly incredible. I've never known anyone like that."

"My sister is one of a kind. You'd like her."

Before I can reply, we both hear the very stern voice of the woman responsible for us sitting on the same side of the booth. "Thomas. *Ms. Harper*." Yay. It's Constance. She says my name like she's cursing me to the depths of hell. My blood positively runs cold.

Thomas turns his head around so fast he almost bangs into my nose. "Constance, how are you?"

Her left eyebrow raises up at the same time the left side of her mouth does. She's full-on sneering at us. "You're dating Finley Harper?" she demands. She makes it sound like I'm the human version of chopped liver. And not pricey pâte, either.

"Blissfully," he tells her. "Is that a problem?" I can practically feel the anger radiating off Thomas. Instead of a mic drop, his question feels more like a gauntlet drop. Like he's marched onto the battlefield and won't leave without a victory. Although, I'm afraid he's stepped on a land mine and we're all going to get blown to smithereens as soon as he lifts his foot. That woman is unhinged.

Instead of answering his question, Constance demands, "Where did you meet her?"

"We met through you," Thomas tells her.

Constance shakes her head vigorously. "But you didn't work well together ..."

I decide it's time to enter the fray. "We do now. And honestly, we owe our happiness to you, Constance."

Steam is practically rising from her ears. I have never enjoyed putting someone in their place as much as I currently am. "I didn't get you together," Constance growls. "I hired you to take Thomas's picture and you bungled the job horribly."

"I retook those pictures," I tell her. "And they look fantastic. I'll be sending them to you tomorrow."

"We're very grateful to you," Thomas tells her.

The look on his boss's face causes me to scan the table for sharp objects to hide. She looks like she wants to take our happiness and crumple it up before grinding it under her booted heel. It goes without saying that dousing it in gasoline and setting it on fire would be the inevitable ending.

"I'd like to see you in my office tomorrow, Thomas. Nine a.m.," Constance says before turning around and practically marching out the front door.

As soon as she's gone, I tell Thomas, "I think you're in trouble."

He looks visibly shaken. "What could she possibly do to me?"

"I don't know," I say. "But whatever it is, I don't think you're going to like it."

CHAPTER TWENTY

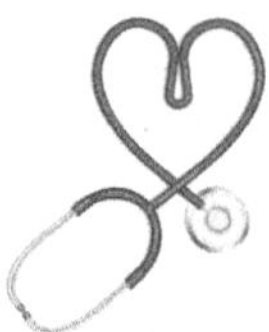

THOMAS

Even with Constance doing her best to intimidate us, Finley and I are having a wonderful evening together. In fact, my boss gave us a mutual enemy which seems to have brought us closer together.

Once our food arrives, I tell my new friend, "There's no way you're ever going to be able to eat all of that." Her eyes brighten at the challenge. "Never say never." Then she glances at the baked potato and grimaces.

"Don't you like baked potatoes?"

She shakes her head. "It's in foil."

"That's probably how they cooked it." While this makes sense to me, it still looks like a problem for her.

"Would you mind taking the foil off for me?" Finley asks.

"Off your potato?" She nods her head, so I reach out to remove the sheet of aluminum. As I do this, she turns away and sticks her fingers in her ears. Once I've accomplished the task, I crumple the foil and tuck it under the side of my plate. "All done," I tell her.

Finley turns around, looking relieved. "Thank you." As she doesn't say anything else, I assume she doesn't want to explain what that was all about. "Want a bite of my taco?" I ask her.

She studies my plate before saying, "I really don't."

"You don't like tacos?" I ask. *Who doesn't like tacos?*

"I like all the ingredients," she says. "I just don't like them together."

Finley has some definite opinions about food, but I guess we all do. For instance, I like both hot chocolate and marshmallows, but I don't like marshmallows *in* my hot chocolate.

We turn our attention to our meals, and don't talk a lot beyond the basics. Once again, the silence isn't strange so much as it's pleasantly unusual. I hate when people feel the need to talk just to avoid quiet. But for some reason, that seems to be the standard.

I polish off my tacos and declare them the best food I've eaten in Elk Lake. Finley eats a surprising amount, but she doesn't finish both of her meals. Instead, the waitress brings her a to-go container. As she drops it on the table, she says, "I don't have a small container for the peas, but I brought you a piece of foil so you can keep them separate."

Finley looks panicky, so I hurry to intervene. Looking up at the waitress, I ask her, "Do you have a paper coffee cup instead?"

When she nods her head, I pick up the foil and hand it back to her. "We won't need this."

When the waitress is gone, Finley lowers her head to avoid eye contact. "Thank you." Her voice is barely above a whisper. I know she feels overly observed, and not in a good way.

Once Finley packs her food, I ask, "Should we order dessert?"

"I would love to," she replies, "but I don't have a spare centimeter of space left in my stomach."

"We could order it to go, and you could take it home for breakfast."

Instead of commenting on dessert, Finley tells me, "I don't like the sound foil makes, and I don't like how it feels against my skin."

"What does that have to do with dessert?" I ask her.

"Nothing, but I could tell you wanted to ask me what was

going on. I figured after buying me this delicious meal, you had a right to know."

"I don't like plastic wrap," I confess. Her gaze narrows like she's trying to figure out if I'm making fun of her. So, I explain, "I can never find the seam and once I do, if I don't pull it evenly, it rips and then I only get the tiniest sliver and then the whole roll is destroyed."

"Huh." I can tell she doesn't share my annoyance with plastic wrap, but she doesn't say anything disparaging. Instead, she jokes, "You know we'll never be able to get married now."

"How's that?"

She shrugs her shoulders before saying, "I can't stand foil and you can't stand plastic wrap. What would we do with our leftovers?"

Pointing to the Styrofoam container on the table, I tell her, "We could order those by the gross."

She makes a face. "Those are bad for the environment."

"We can get those little cardboard boxes that Chinese food comes in," I decide.

Shaking her head, she tells me, "We'd never know what was inside of them. I like to see what I have when I open the refrigerator."

"Tupperware," I suggest.

Finley screws up her mouth like she's really thinking about this, but then she decrees, "You're not supposed to microwave plastic. Chemicals leach out into the food."

"We could transfer the food to a glass plate before microwaving it ..."

With a giant sigh, Finley replies, "That would be a lot of dirty dishes."

"It's like you don't even want to marry me," I practically shout, which causes the table next to us to turn and stare. I offer a brief wave, and tell them, "Don't worry, I'm not going to let her say no."

They smile awkwardly before turning back to their own

conversation. Meanwhile, Finley jokes, "You'd better not propose for real in the diner. I want something more memorable."

Finley Harper is nothing short of delightful. She's witty, clever, and she knows how to enjoy a good meal.

Picking up her to-go container, I scoot out of the booth and stand up. Then I reach out to help her. "Even though I'm sorely tempted," I tell her, "I'm probably going to wait until after we've gone on more than one fake date to propose to you."

Taking my hand, she slides across the booth seat and stands up so that we're practically eye-to-eye. Actually, we're more chin to eye. Finley's probably around five ten. She looks up slightly and holds my gaze before saying, "Chicken."

I want to wrap my arms around her and kiss her with every ounce of emotion she's making me feel. But that would probably scare her away. Instead of acting on impulse, I tell her, "I usually wait until the twentieth fake date to propose."

"I'm sorry," she says with pity.

"For what?"

"That all those women said no to you. That had to be rough."

Looking down, I realize I'm still holding Finley's hand. Instead of letting it go, I gently pull her toward the door. Once we're out on the street, I lean down and tell her, "I've never made it to the twentieth fake date. I suppose we'll just have to see if we last that long."

Finley's face flushes red but she maintains eye contact. "I suppose we will." Then she adds, "But if I say yes, we're either going to have to get divorced before our ten-year anniversary or we'll have to skip the tenth year and go straight to the eleventh."

This woman completely baffles me, and I'm thoroughly enjoying it. "Are you going to tell me why?"

Finley is standing so close to me I could easily lean down and kiss her. But before I can decide if that would be prudent, she takes a big step backward. Then she turns around and runs across the street before calling out, "The tenth year is the aluminum year!" Pointing to the building behind her, she adds, "I live here.

Thanks for supper!" Then she turns and walks through the door to the left of the yarn shop.

I walk home seven blocks in the rain, barely registering the discomfort. I've had a great night, and I owe that to one slightly left of center, eccentric photographer. From the moment I met Finley, I knew she was something special, and every interaction has cemented that belief.

By the time I turn up my street, I'm soaking wet. When I get to my house, I notice Kevin is getting out of his car. "Hey, neighbor," I call out to him. I still can't bring myself to call him Pickles.

"Tommy," he returns my greeting. "What are you doing walking on a night like tonight?"

"I still haven't gotten a car," I say while striding toward the property line, so we don't have to keep shouting.

Kevin is covered from head to toe in a bright yellow raincoat, full-on with matching pants and hat. He looks like a duck. "What kind of car are you looking for? I'll keep my eyes open for you."

"Something basic and used," I tell him before explaining, "I'm not sure how long I'll be living in Elk Lake, and I don't want to invest in anything else until I know for sure." Even though Finley and I had a fun night together, that's not enough reason to relocate permanently. Especially, as I still work for Constance.

"I have a friend selling an old Mustang," he tells me. "It's a convertible. It'll be fun in the summer."

"Hard top or soft top?" I ask.

"Soft top," he says. "The '90 Stang didn't have a hardtop option. But don't worry, he recently replaced it, so it's in good shape."

I suppose that would be fine. If I do decide to put down roots here, I'll simply get another car and save the Mustang for summers. "When do you think I can go look at it?" I ask.

"I'll call him tomorrow and tell him I have a live one," he says with a smile. "Text me and I'll drive you over sometime in the afternoon."

"I'd hate to put you out," I tell him.

"He lives ten miles outside of town," Kevin says with a grin.

"In that case, how about if I hire you to drive me?"

My neighbor shakes his head. "You can take me to the pub for a beer if you decide to buy."

I extend my hand for a shake. "You've got yourself a deal, Kevin."

"Pickles," he reminds me.

"Pickles." I nod my head. My neighbor is a character, and I'm lucky to have him in my life. Not only does he offer food recommendations, but he's helping me find a car before giving me lessons on how to drive better.

Now, if only I can settle things with Constance, maybe Elk Lake stands a chance of becoming my long-term home.

CHAPTER TWENTY-ONE

FINLEY

I barely slept a wink last night. Instead of nodding off to Dreamland, I kept thinking about Thomas. He's such a great guy. The thing is, I'm not sure if all the flirtatious banter was really flirting or if he's just being friendly. I'm guessing most people would be able to figure it out. Yet, as a neuro-sparkly person, I'm left wondering.

When my eyes finally pop open, after what I'm sure is only an hour of sleep, I reach over to my nightstand and grab my phone. I pick it up and call my mom.

"Finny!" She says delightedly before adding, "Hellooooo!"

"Hey, Mom. How are you doing?"

"I am flummoxed." My mother tends to use words that make her sound like she's closer to two hundred years old than the sixty she's nearing.

"What's got you confused?" I ask.

"I have a chicken in the sink and I'm not quite sure what to do with her."

"Are you defrosting it for supper?" I ask.

"Oh, no. She's alive and well," she says. I hear some splashing in the background.

"You have a live chicken in the sink," I repeat, hoping that doing so will bring some clarity.

"Bernadette," she says before explaining, "In my thirty years of owning chickens, I have never had one who behaves as oddly as she has been acting."

"What's she doing?"

"I know for certain Bernie is at the top of the pecking order, but she's been isolating herself lately, and she's been very noisy. Like she's protesting her life. But as you know, my girls live a very good life."

This is true. My mother takes care of her chickens better than most people care for their children. Their coop is practically a miniature palace, full-on with a tiny crystal chandelier hanging from the ceiling.

"Anything else?" I ask. I've not studied chicken behavior as deeply as my mom, but I did grow up with them. It's not beyond possible I might have some insight.

"She hasn't been laying like the other girls. But she's five. She might just be in henapause."

"Henapause?" This is not a term I've heard her use before.

"Menopause for chickens," she explains. "But I'm also worried she might be eggbound."

"Have you ever had an eggbound chicken?" I rack my brain for memories from when I lived at home, and I'm coming up dry. Even so, I know what the term means—a chicken with a stuck egg.

"I have not," she says. *Splash. Splash. Squawk.* "But I'm soaking Bernie just in case."

"And that's the cure for being eggbound?" I ask.

"The internet says maybe, so I'm trying it."

"Good luck," I tell her, thinking now might not be the best time for a heart to heart. Having a live chicken in the sink seems like an all-encompassing task.

"Why are you calling, dear?" my mom asks.

"I, um … I guess I just wanted to ask you some questions. But we can talk later if now is a bad time."

"So long as you don't want to know about ornery hens," she says. "I'm at my wits' end with this one."

"I wanted to ask about my childhood. You know, pre-diagnosis."

"I'm all ears," she says.

The squawking and splashing suddenly stop, which causes me to ask, "Did you drown her?"

"Huh, will you look at that." My mom sounds perplexed.

"What happened?"

"This funny little girl has settled right down, and she appears to be enjoying herself." Before I can comment one way or the other, she adds, "Now, what do you want to know?"

I roll over on my side before pulling the duvet up over my head. Having created my perfect cave, I ask, "Did you think I was particularly odd in my early childhood?"

"No more than any other kid," she says.

My mom has always been on my side. She's been my champion when faced with bullies and teachers alike. She's got my back to the point where I'm not sure if her perception can be trusted. "When was the first time you noticed I was different?" I want to know.

"Aside from the running thing?"

"Yes, Mom. Aside from that." I've seen old videos of myself, and my stride was pretty horrifying.

She exhales loudly before making noises that sound like a staccato grunting—this is her thinking sound. "I suppose in preschool. You didn't seem to relate to the other kids the same way they related to each other."

A shiver of alarm shoots through me. Preschool is early. "How was I different?"

"You used to watch your classmates play like you couldn't figure out what they were doing." She's quick to explain, "Not like you were too stupid to understand, more like you thought they were beneath you."

"Beneath me? Was I a snob?" I can't imagine such a thing, as I spent most of childhood in pursuit of being liked.

"Not at all, Finny. You were and are one of the sweetest people I've ever known. It was more like they confused you. Like they were babies and you were an adult."

"Yet we were all four and five," I say for accuracy.

"You've always been very mature for your age, dear. An old soul in a new body."

While her comment is disguised as a compliment, I'm not sure there isn't more to it. "Do you think the other kids hated me?"

I count a full five seconds before she answers. *Five.* Which is a lot. "I don't think they understood you, honey. I don't think they had enough on the ball to actively dislike you."

Oh. My. God. "Was I a freak?" I ask, full of panic.

"You were and are my special, beautiful girl," she tells me.

Nothing about this conversation is making me feel better. In fact, I'm now starting to question everything I thought I knew about my life pre-diagnosis. "I didn't eat paste, did I?" I'm only half-teasing.

"Oh, Finny, don't be silly. Of course you weren't a paste-eater. You did occasionally eat dirt, though."

"Excuse me?" I'm tempted to hang up and go back to sleep and maybe wake up in a dimension where I'm normal.

"You liked its scent," my mom tells me. "You used to say that it smelled alive and sweet."

I'm sure it was alive. Alive with bugs and God knows what else. "I hope you stopped me."

"It never hurt you, so what was the point? You didn't do it forever." She sounds so accepting that I can't quite decide which one of us is more troubled.

Cutting to the chase, I ask, "In your opinion, Mom, do you think kids mostly liked me, or not?"

"I think nice kids liked you, and those lousy good-for-nothing bullies did not. But keep in mind, they're probably all in prison now."

"I highly doubt that," I tell her. "They're probably making six figures, lording it over their minions, while vacationing in Europe every summer."

"Not Joelle Stinger," she says.

Now she's got my full attention. Whipping the comforter off my head, I sit up and ask, "What's she up to?"

"About three hundred and fifty pounds, as close as I can tell."

"*What*?" I am not a sizest, but Joelle always was. She would tell other girls their jeans were getting tight, and then she'd make mooing sounds at them. She is the last person in this world I would have ever thought would grow out of single digit sizes.

"She's a manager at Cow Patty," my mom says. "I guess her metabolism paired with her diet has caught up to her."

Joelle Stinger is the manager at our old high school hangout. Don't get me started on the name *"Cow Patty."* For some reason, no one found it odd until after they left town. "Is she still married to Jacob Smart?" I ask. In high school, he fully supported her meanness. As such, I can only imagine what he thinks of her now.

"Sure is. That boy has moved to the plus-size section himself. *And* he lost his hair. All except for about four strands, which he combs over the top of his head like a horrible scarf."

"Really?" I don't want to be the kind of person who takes pleasure in someone else's misery, but apparently I'm not as evolved as I would have hoped. This news is making my day.

"Yep," my mom says. "He's a big, bald fatty."

A laugh escapes my mouth. Even though I've just discovered I was a dirt eater (not previously known to me) and not universally liked (totally known), finding out my bullies aren't fairing as well as I thought they would helps restore balance to my world.

I throw my legs over the side of the mattress and relish the cool air on them. Then I ask my mom, "Do you think people thought I was undatable?" I largely ask this because no one in my hometown ever asked me out on a date. Zero people. Including the nympho who asked everyone to be his girlfriend, even the principal.

Instead of answering my question directly, my mom says, "I don't think boys in this town were smart enough to realize what a treasure you were." These passive/aggressive compliments are driving me insane.

Before I can express this, my mom asks, "Are you dating a nice boy now? Is that what this call is all about?"

"I have a new friend," I tell her truthfully. "But we're only fake dating."

"What does that mean, fake dating? Either you're dating or you're not." My mom is pretty literal herself and I once again wonder where she lands on the spectrum.

"His boss is pursuing him, and he needs an out. I'm his beard."

"Is he gay?" she wants to know. "Because if so, he should just tell her that. She'd have to understand."

"Thomas is not gay," I assure her. An image of him as a bronzed construction worker pops into my head and I feel my temperature rise. "He is very, very, *not* gay."

"You like him," my mom speculates.

I don't see any reason to lie to her. "I think he's amazing. He's funny, handsome, personable …"

"What's the problem then? Saddle up that stallion and go for a ride!"

She can't possibly mean that the way it sounds. "The problem is that I'm not sure how he perceives me."

"What do you mean, 'how he perceives' you?"

"I mean, does he think I'm weird? Does he feel sorry for me? Does he see me as a woman or you know, just a friend?" I hate that I'm regressing into my insecurities, but I like Thomas enough that I can't help but worry.

I hear my mom humming lowly in the background, so I ask, "Are you even listening to me?"

She practically whispers her response. "I was just singing to

Bernie and she fell asleep."

"The chicken fell asleep in a sink full of water?" Something like this could only happen to my mother.

"She probably thinks she's at a spa," she croons in a sing-songy voice.

I don't even know how to respond to that, so I repeat, "How do I know how Thomas perceives me? And before you suggest I come right out and ask him, I'm not going to do that. I'd send him running for sure if I were that forward."

"Then spend time with him and see what happens. Men really aren't that complicated, dear. They're very simple creatures with very simple motivations."

"What are those motivations?" Because as obvious as she thinks they are, I don't exactly speak the same language.

My mom snorts, "To get you in the sack, Finny. That's pretty much all that's going on in their heads for the first few years of being in a relationship." I'm not about to ask if that's how it was with my dad because … *ew*.

When I don't respond to her immediately, she asks, "Have I answered your questions?"

"Yes?" But like always with my mom, I feel more confused now than when we started talking.

"Is that a yes with a question mark or a period?"

Instead of answering, I ask, "Did you ever wish I was like other kids? You know, did you feel bad that I didn't fit in?"

"God, no. Children are annoying by nature. I've never been annoyed by you, dear."

My eyes tear up for multiple reasons. The first being that if I had to be born special, thank goodness I had parents who were equipped to handle it. The other being a bit of sadness that I was probably the cause of much parental concern.

I've grown to truly like who I am, but being different can mean being misunderstood and often ostracized. People want to be around those they find predictable. Which is something I am not.

"I love you, Mom," I say into the phone. "Thank you for everything you've done for me."

"Honey, you sound like you're getting ready to jump off the roof of a skyscraper. You're not depressed, are you?"

"No. I'm just a little melancholy." *Another turn of the last century word my mother loves.* "It's been a long time since I've liked a man the way I think I might like Thomas and it's scaring me."

"Don't obsess about it too much, Finny. Just let things happen. Life is a ride and the more you think about it, the less you enjoy it."

"I threw up on the tilt-oh-whirl at the county fair," I remind her.

She snorts. "Life can be nauseating, but also a lot of fun. Have fun, Finny. You're not as different from everyone else as you think." Says the woman who's probably even spicier than I am. Although, I still appreciate her advice.

"I'll do my best," I tell her.

"You should come home for a visit soon," she says. "I can show you how much Bernie likes her bath."

Watching my mother bathe her chicken is not the tempting offer she thinks it is. But seeing her and my dad is very appealing. "I'll let you know soon."

What I'd like to do is surprise them by showing up in town in my very own car with me behind the wheel. Which means I need to get up and make a call to see if my dream car is still available.

CHAPTER TWENTY-TWO

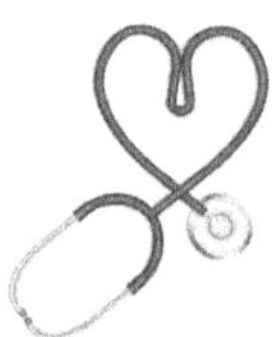

THOMAS

I want to meet with Constance this morning about as much as I want to take an ice plunge in Antarctica. Newsflash: I hate bathing in water that's not hot enough to make soup.

At nine o'clock on the nose, I walk into the administrative offices and let the woman at the reception desk know who I'm there to see. *Is it me or is that pity in her eyes?*

I sit on one of the double-wide chairs in the waiting room, eyeing the outdated magazines. While reading headlines about dramatic celebrity weight loss, it occurs to me I should just leave. What's Constance going to do? Hunt me down to tell me I can't date Finley?

As I stand up to go, my boss walks out of her office. Constance is wearing a black cocktail dress with rhinestone embellishments. If the sparkles aren't enough to scream "inappropriate work attire," then the short length and plunging neckline do the trick.

"Constance." I'm not even trying to keep the censure out of my tone.

"Thomas," she gushes as she takes a step toward me. "You

caught me trying on dresses for the Spring Fling!" She throws her hands into the air like she's just released fistfuls of confetti.

I don't believe I caught her doing anything she didn't want me to. So, I tell her, "You set the time, not me." I'm guessing she thought wearing an alluring dress would get me to see her as a dating prospect. If that was her plan, it didn't work.

"I suppose time just got away from me." She giggles like she's half-drunk.

"I have a full day ahead of me, Constance," I tell her. "What is it you'd like to talk to me about?"

Her face morphs into an expression of shock. "Oh." She waves at me to follow her back into her lair. Which I reluctantly do.

Once inside, I see several large bags scattered around from various stores. Constance has clearly been busy. She forces a laugh that comes out sounding like the cry of a wounded animal. "I bought way too many things, but I really want to look great for this year's fling."

"Why am I here?" I ask bluntly.

Again, she doesn't seem to expect my directness. "I guess I just … you know …" She walks over to her desk and rifles around it for a moment before picking up an envelope made of heavy card stock. She tries to hand it to me but I don't take it. "I wanted to give you a copy of the invitation."

She can't be serious. "You emailed me the information, Constance. I don't need a physical copy."

She hurriedly opens the flap and pulls out the invite. "But they're so pretty this year." Once again, she jabs it in my direction.

I should just take it and leave, but I don't. Instead, I stand totally still while narrowing my gaze like I'm peering at her under a microscope. Then I tell her, "I'm not going to the Spring Fling with you, Constance. I'm going with Finley."

"*If* you're still dating." She raises a blonde eyebrow in challenge. Constance really is an attractive woman—pretty, even—but her manipulative ways coupled with her entitlement make her downright loathsome.

"Even if I'm not dating Finley," I tell her, "I will not go with you. I don't date people I work with." This is a lie, but I'm not above telling a falsehood to shut this down.

Constance exhales loudly enough to show irritation. "Don't tell me you've never dated another doctor or pretty little nurse, Thomas. I refuse to believe that." The way she says "pretty little nurse" makes me feel dirty. Constance should show support to the medical community, but instead, she's disparaging them.

"I don't really care what you think, Constance. I don't mean to be rude, but I do not like feeling hunted." Her mouth hangs open at being spoken to so plainly. "I took the job in Elk Lake because I wanted a change of pace. I did not take it because I wanted to date you."

My boss glares at me with an expression akin to hatred, which is rather unnerving. "I didn't hire you because I wanted to date you, Thomas," she practically spits. *Liar.*

"Then why have you been pursuing me?" I ask. "You've been bent on getting me to go to this dance with you even though I've told you on several occasions I'm already spoken for."

Constance looks mad enough that if she had telekinetic powers I'd probably be on my way out the window. "I asked you to help you," she says condescendingly. "I was doing you a favor."

"A favor …" I repeat her words in shock. This woman is doing me no favors.

With her hands positioned angrily on her hips, she says, "I wanted to introduce you around. You know, help you get to know some more people in town."

I don't believe her for a minute, as she could do that regardless of who my date was. She's simply scrambling to try to get out of an embarrassing situation. At lease, I hope she's embarrassed. "While I appreciate your intent," I tell her. "I once again respectfully decline your offer. Now if that will be all, I need to get going."

I turn around to leave, but Constance stops me. "That isn't all,

Thomas." I turn back to face her in time to hear, "I'm going to have to make some changes to your schedule. You're going to take over the night shift starting next week. Dr. Ramirez is going to be taking some time off." The expression on her face is so superior, it's clear she thinks she's won.

"Dr. Ramirez is going on maternity leave," I tell her. "You mentioned that when I was hired. But you also told me Dr. Hammond was going to move to nights, and that I would take Dr. Hammond's place during the day."

"Is that what I said?" She's obviously trying to get even with me for not wanting to date her and I'm tempted to tell her what to do with her job. The problem is, I signed a contract and it didn't specify what shifts I would work. I only had Constance's word on that.

While I could accuse her of sexual harassment to get out of my contract, I don't have any real evidence yet. Of course, after today, I plan on going home and starting a journal of all things said and retribution executed.

"You clearly told me I would be working a day shift," I assure Constance.

"Well, Thomas ..."—she glares at me like I just ran over her cat—"things change. And they're going to change starting Monday. Please check your revised schedule and report for work accordingly."

I worked the night shift for four years when I was starting out and the whole time I felt like a vampire. It was dark when I went to the hospital and dark when I came home. I rarely saw the sun, and I missed it. Now, years after paying my dues, I'm being cast back into the shadows. I am not pleased.

With any luck, I'll have enough on Constance to file a formal complaint soon, but in the meantime, I'll have to play along with her little game. "If that's all," I tell her.

"That's all," she says dismissively before turning her attention back to her desk.

Instead of saying goodbye, I bolt out of her office like I'm trying to escape a horrible smell. Finley is right, male bosses have not always treated their female employees respectfully. And while I've known this, I've not experienced what they've had to endure. Before now, that is. It's sobering to get this kind of insight.

On the way to the lounge, I run into Edward Hall, a doctor I met last week. He's a gregarious middle-aged man, who smiles when he sees me. "Dr. Culpepper, how are you enjoying life in our little town?"

"I haven't seen much of it yet," I tell him. "But so far, so good." Better to sound happy to be here than to openly complain.

"I predict you're going to love it. Anytime you'd like a tour, you let me know and I'll be happy to show you some hotspots."

"Hotspots? Like nightclubs?" Dr. Hall does not strike me as a man who parties.

He releases a bark of laughter. "There are no nightclubs in Elk Lake, at least that I know of."

"What hotspots, then?"

"Fishing spots, son. I know all the best ones. Bass, pike, bluegill, walleye, and of course the mighty crappie!"

"Crappie?" This day is getting odder by the minute.

Smacking his lip together, he says, "Mild, sweet, flakey. You can't beat the crappie, Thomas."

"I'm not much of a fisherman," I tell him. "In fact, I've never been." And if I had, I feel that on principle I would have avoided trying to catch a crappie.

"Never been fishing?" Edward's posture jolts like he was just on the receiving end of a cattle prod. "Well, then, we're going to have to fix that. What mornings are you free? We should really get an early start. Five a.m. is best."

"I'm going to have to let you know," I tell him. "It appears I'll be covering for Dr. Ramirez at nights for a while."

He looks confused. "Didn't I hear that Dr. Hammond was going to be doing that?"

I shrug in response. "That was my understanding, too, but it seems there have been some changes."

Edward claps me on the shoulder. "You let me know if you ever want to get out of the ER game and go into private practice. I can give you some tips."

"Don't you work here at the hospital?" I ask. I haven't been here long enough to get to know everyone on staff, but I see him here regularly, so I just assumed.

He shakes his head. "No, sir. I only stop in to see my patients who've been admitted. I like to make them feel like a friend is looking out for them."

This is enormously kind of Edward. Traditionally, once a patient is admitted to the hospital, they're under the care of a hospitalist and not their primary care doctor. "Your patients are lucky to have you," I tell him.

"In private practice you get to form bonds with people." He smiles brightly. "Honestly, it's my favorite part of what we do. I like to feel like I'm part of my patient's daily lives."

"That's a refreshing attitude," I reply. Looking at the clock behind him, I add, "I'm running late though. I'd better be off."

As I turn to walk away, he says, "Let me know when your schedule changes back and we'll set up a time to catch some fish."

"Will do," I tell him. And while I've never particularly longed to fish for my own food, I expect I would enjoy spending time with Edward out on a boat somewhere. After all, the whole point of moving to Elk Lake was so I could experience a slower pace of life.

But first, I have to figure out how to shake Constance.

CHAPTER TWENTY-THREE

FINLEY

Along with my penchant for hyper-focusing—where twelve hours can feel like twelve minutes—there comes the flip-side to that phenomenon. For instance, I haven't seen Thomas in two days, but it's felt more like two weeks. No exaggeration. And I've thought about him nearly constantly. *What is he doing right now? What is he wearing? Does he smell like oranges and cloves?*

My dating history makes me nervous about my chances of attracting Thomas as a real boyfriend, but that doesn't mean it couldn't happen. Just because other men couldn't see what an amazing partner I'd be doesn't mean Thomas is similarly handicapped. Having said that, he didn't text me after our supper out, so he might not even think of me as a friend yet.

I fluff the blanket around Tanya Jackson's baby girl, Cherie. Then I make googly noises at her to get her to smile, which she does. "Only six weeks old, and already a pro!" I announce.

"She's pretty special," Tanya says. Her brown eyes are drooping like she hasn't had much sleep lately.

"Is she your first?" I ask. Tanya is a new client, and I don't know much about her yet.

"She's my fourth," she tells me. "I thought Mike and I were done, but this little girl had other plans."

Four? No wonder she looks worn out. "How old are your other kids?"

"Eighteen, twelve, and nine," she tells me. I try not to act surprised by the wide age gap but apparently fail. "I had my first in high school," she explains. "His dad isn't in the picture."

"My good friend is adopting a baby whose birth mother is graduating this year," I tell her. Allie and Margie have been very open with their story, so I don't worry I'm talking out of turn.

"That's probably a good thing," she says. "It's hard having a little one when you're still a kid yourself." She adds, "My parents helped out a lot, but I still missed being carefree like my friends."

Tanya's hair is styled in a high ponytail that makes her look younger than her years. According to the age of her oldest, I calculate her to be somewhere in her mid-thirties.

"I hope I get to be a mom someday," I tell her. For some reason I feel the need to add, "But I'm not even dating anyone …"

My client says, "I know people say there's nothing wrong with being a single parent, but take it from me, it's a lot easier when you do it with a partner."

"That would be the only way I'd want to do it." I snap several quick-fire photos of Cherie before telling Tanya, "I think we've got it. I should have the proofs ready for you in a couple of days."

She wraps her baby up in the fuzziest looking blanket I've ever seen. I can't help myself; I reach out to touch it. "Wow," I tell her. "If they made clothes out of that material, I'd buy a full wardrobe in it."

She laughs. "If I could wrap myself up in a king-sized version of this I'd fall asleep and never wake up." Picking up the baby, she adds, "Thanks, Finley. I'm excited to see what you got today." Then she walks out of the studio.

Babies are magical and unless you get a colicky one, they're the best models out there. Even if they have a gas bubble and make a face like they've just eaten bad cheese, everyone loves them. They simply can't do wrong.

I'm cleaning up the set when my phone rings. I don't recognize the number. "Hello?" I drop the basket full of fake pink roses next to my editing stand.

"Finley, it's Thomas." His voice feels like warm sunshine and causes a fluttering in the pit of my stomach.

Being that it's been two months since I've heard from him (Fine! *Two days*), I try to act nonchalant. "I'm sorry, who?"

"Thomas Culpepper."

Sitting on my stool, I reply, "Oh, Thomas, yes. How can I help you?"

He pauses like I've just been rude to him. Which is pretty much how I intended to come off. I'm not very good at pretending I'm feeling something different than I am. "Are you mad at me?" he wants to know.

"Why would I be mad at you?" *Say the words, Thomas, and I might forgive you.* Tell me you're sorry you didn't call after our dinner together *last year*. Even though it wasn't a real date, and you aren't obligated, *say the words.*

"I just wanted to see if you'd like to go on a drive with me." He sounds like a man walking through an active mine field, unsure where to step.

"When did you get a car?" I ask in shock. *Who decides they want a car and gets one right away without proper consideration?* I have to think about a large purchase, and weigh the pros and cons. I have to imagine myself using said purchase before seeing if it feels right. Only then can I pull the trigger. It took me three months to settle on a couch before buying one.

"I bought one yesterday," he tells me. "My neighbor Kevin knows a guy, and he took me out to see him." He adds, "It's not great, but it'll do until I can decide if I'm going to stay in Elk Lake."

"I *would* like to go on a drive with you," I tell him. "But you said you're not a very good driver."

"I'm getting better," he tells me. "Also, I have my license, so I'm allowed on the road." After a beat, he adds, "What do you say? Can I pick you up?"

"So long as we stay in town and don't go on any busy streets," I tell him, still unsure of his ability to keep us safe.

"You have a deal," he says.

"How about in an hour?" I ask. That should give me enough time to get everything straightened up and ready for tomorrow's shoots—which include three more looks for Thomas's revenge calendar that we're making for his parents.

"I can do that," he says. "But if you get done early, come on out. I'm parked in front of your store."

I practically run to the front room and look out the window. Once I see him, I release a hellish scream. Thomas is standing by my dream car with a huge smile on his face. His expression shifts to one of concern when he witnesses my distress.

Running to the door of my shop, he opens it and asks, "Are you okay? Are you hurt?"

"*That's* your car?" Tears well up in my eyes before I can stop them.

"Do you hate it?" he asks, sounding confused.

That's when I burst out crying like my grandmother just died. "Hate it? *Hate it?*" I repeat between sobs. "I don't hate it, I love it!"

The look on Thomas's face makes it clear he will never love me. Honestly, I can't blame him. I'm acting like a real fool here.

"If you love it, why are you crying?" He says the words slowly like he's trying to keep me calm so I don't do anything rash. Like hit him over the head with my baseball bat before stealing his car. That I would have to push because I don't know how to drive.

"*I* was going to buy that car! I saw it listed on social media, and I thought it was my sign to get my license. That's *my* car," I tell him forcefully. I can tell Thomas feels bad, but I don't care.

"I'm sorry," he finally says. "I needed a car and this one seemed like a good place to start."

My face is dripping with sadness. "I don't want to go on a ride with you anymore," I tell him.

"Really?" He sounds disappointed enough that I briefly consider he might be starting to care for me.

But even if that's the case, he bought *my* car, and now I can't learn how to drive. Instead of assuring him I'm serious, I turn and practically run into the back room. My whole day is ruined.

Rather than taking the hint and leaving, Thomas follows me. Once I'm sitting on my stool, I turn it around and stare at him. His jeans fit him like a second skin, but instead of looking like a rock-star wannabe, he looks like a rugged manly man. His sweater is a super-soft looking navy sweater—I wonder if it's cashmere—and he's wearing a dark leather bomber jacket. His wavy brown hair is practically screaming for me to run my hands through it. But I'm mad at him so I'm not going to.

Neither one of us says anything for several moments, and it's super awkward.

Thomas finally announces, "If I knew you planned on buying the car, I never would have. You should have told me."

"Why would I tell you?" I demand.

"Then how was I to know?" Darn it, he's right. I'm punishing him for something he couldn't have knowledge of. I really hate it when I'm wrong.

"How does it drive?" I ask him.

"Okay, I guess. I mean, it's old. It's not as smooth as a newer car."

"That shouldn't matter," I tell him. His questioning look has me explaining, "Harlow Gibson drove a car like that in that old movie, *Rocky Love Falls*."

Again with the confused look. "And that's why you want it?"

With a snort, I tell him, "Of course that's why."

"I'm not tracking here, Finley." Thomas shoves his hands in his coat pockets and steps toward me.

"Harlow Gibson played a character who wanted to get even

with the girls who bullied her in high school. She drove back to her hometown in that kind of car." *See? It all makes sense now …*

"Did they all want a car like that?" He's clearly not on my wavelength.

"No." I explain, "She won the title of Miss Nevada and went home wearing her tiara. That's how she got her revenge."

"What did the car have to do with it?"

"She was riding in *that* car, Thomas! How aren't you getting this?" I know I'm not explaining it well, and maybe this isn't even something that makes sense to a neurotypical. I mean, how would *I* know? I'm not one.

Thomas inhales deeply before asking, "How about if I sell you the car when I leave town?"

"What do you mean when you leave town? Are you leaving because of Constance?"

"She's putting me on the nightshift as a payback for my not being interested in her romantically. I can't work with a person like her."

"So, you're giving up on Elk Lake, just like that?"

He tips his head from side to side like he's going back and forth on his own pros and cons list. Which I respect. The pros and cons list really is the only way to make big life decisions.

"I need to gather evidence against Constance to break my contract," he says. "But if I can't do that, then I'll probably go back to New York when my current agreement ends."

While I really want to buy his car, I suddenly realize I want Thomas more. That must be why I blurt out, "You can't leave Elk Lake. I won't let you!"

He looks amused. "I'm not sure you can stop me."

I narrow my eyes and stare at him like I'm performing a Vulcan mind meld. I don't say the words out loud, but I still send the message, *Oh, yeah? Let's just see, shall we?*

CHAPTER TWENTY-FOUR

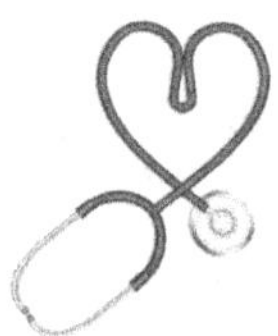

THOMAS

I feel bad telling Finley that I'm thinking about going back to New York. But except for spending time with her, I'm not really vibing here. Elk Lake feels more like a place you come and spend a couple of weeks during the summer. Not a place to live full-time.

I stare at her as she clicks away on her laptop. "So, how about that ride?" I ask.

"You still want to take me driving even though you're planning on leaving Elk Lake?"

I'm not quite sure what one thing has to do with the other. "Yes," I tell her. "It'll give you a chance to drive in your soon-to-be car."

That seems to be the right thing to say. "I still want to go on a drive," she says while standing up. She moves the basket of pink props at her feet. Then she turns in my direction and walks by me without saying another word.

Once we're outside, Finley locks the front door, and we proceed to the Mustang. I stop and open the passenger side door for her and wait until she gets in. Then I hurry around and join her.

As soon as I'm buckled, I turn to look at Finley. She's caressing the tan leather interior like it's a kitten—a kitten I suddenly wish was me. "What do you think?" I ask her unnecessarily. It's obvious she loves it.

"It's perfect," she tells me reverently. Opening the glove compartment, she looks inside and says, "I'll keep my sunglasses and snacks in there."

"What kind of snacks?" Maybe I'll go ahead and stock it for her.

"I like granola bars, and those little boxes of raisins. Maybe some cookies, too."

"Do you snack a lot when you're in a car?" I ask her teasingly.

Without seeming to get the joke, she responds, "How would I know? I'm never in a car."

"But you imagine yourself snacking in this one," I prompt.

She shifts in her seat. "I might get hungry. I like to be prepared."

Finley is the most unpredictable woman I've ever met. "Did the girl in the movie keep snacks in her glove box?"

Her complexion turns pink before she answers, "Why would that matter?"

I turn the key and start the car. "I was just wondering."

We sit for a moment in silence before Finley confesses, "She kept snacks in the glove compartment." I don't know why but I find her answer very charming.

"You really like that movie, huh?"

"I've seen it one hundred and fourteen times," she tells me.

My hand is on the gear shift and I'm about to put the car in drive, but her words stop me. "One hundred and fourteen times is a lot."

"I suppose it depends on what you're comparing it to." I can almost see the hamster wheel turning in her brain before she adds, "I find repetition comforting."

"Like how you're always petting your sweaters?" I ask.

She turns to me with a look of alarm. "Excuse me?"

I shrug. "I just assumed you liked soft things. And you know, touching them brings you joy."

Finley looks like she wants to cry again. But instead of doing that, she side-eyes me like she's trying to decide if she can trust me. "I do like soft things." Then she asks, "Is your sweater cashmere?"

"It is." The hand that was previously on her lap seemingly lifts of its own accord. "Would you like to touch it?" I ask her.

She shakes her head in such a way I can tell she's fighting a nod. Reaching out, I gently take her hand in mine. Then I slowly move it in the direction of my chest. I make sure to give her plenty of time to pull it back if she wants to. She doesn't.

Once her hand meets its target, Finley closes her eyes and exhales like she's experiencing pure bliss. Which I'm pretty sure I'm feeling as well. "May I rub it?" she asks so quietly I wonder if I imagined it.

I grunt in affirmation in case the inquiry was real. Then I sit in anticipation while I wait for her hand to move. When it finally does, I release a groan of pleasure. *Who knew having a woman touch your sweater could be such an erotic experience?*

"Was it expensive?"

"My sweater?"

"Yes," she says on a breathy exhale.

"It was a gift from my mother," I tell her. "So, I'm guessing it wasn't cheap."

"Do you know what brand it is?"

"I don't think I've noticed. But I can look and text it to you if you want."

"I would appreciate that." She hesitantly pulls her hand away from me and rests it back on her lap.

"Do you want to buy one for someone?"

Her chin bobs up and down. "I do."

"For your dad?"

Her profile makes her look like an elfin sprite. Her lips are lush, her eyelashes are long, and her nose has a slight upturn. Her head moves from side to side, but she doesn't look at me. All she says is, "No."

"Do you have a gentleman friend?" I ask with more than a tinge of jealousy. I don't know why I assumed Finley was single, because she might not be.

"I want to buy one for myself," she eventually says.

"I could loan you mine," I tell her, "but it would be big on you." The thought of Finley wearing my sweater fills me with a feeling of protectiveness. I like the sensation so much I'm about to take it off and hand it to her.

"I want to fill it with quilt batting and turn it into a pillow."

"A pillow?"

Her chin lifts and falls. "I'd keep it in bed with me and cuddle it."

That is probably the sexiest thing any woman has ever said to me. The vision of cuddling with Finley fills me with such contentment, it's all I can do not to turn to her and beg her to date me for real. The problem is that while I want to get closer to her, that would complicate my life more than it already is.

I've got to figure out my work situation before I let myself form personal connections, like having a girlfriend. If I can't have a happy working environment, there's no way I can stay in this town. I'm afraid that as long as Constance is my boss, I can't see myself being fully happy here.

I crack my window, hoping a blast of cold air will help me regain my senses. Putting the car into drive, I creep out of the parallel parking space I currently inhabit. "Where would you like to drive?" I ask Finley.

"How about around the lake?"

Heading in that direction, I ask, "Do you spend a lot of time there in the summer?"

"No."

I wonder why we're going there then. I tell her, "I spend as much time on the beach as I can,"

"In New York?"

"The Hamptons. My parents have a summer place there that we all use as an escape from the city."

"Oh." She doesn't sound pleased.

Looking for a little more insight, I ask, "Why don't you spend time at the lake?"

Finley waits so long to answer, it's clear she doesn't want to. She finally tells me, "I don't like sand."

"Really?" I don't know why that surprises me, but it does.

"Not everyone likes sand, Thomas." She sounds like a stern schoolteacher.

"Of course not," I tell her. "I just happen to love it. I love the feeling of it between my toes when I walk on the beach. I like how it holds both heat and cold. I like how crabs dig under it and make their homes." I could go on and on, but I don't.

In my periphery, I notice Finley's posture straighten into a stiff line. "How nice for you."

For some reason that causes me to laugh.

"Are you making fun of me?" She sounds mad.

"Not at all," I tell her. "Like you said, not everyone likes the same things."

"Then why are you laughing at me?"

"I'm not laughing at you. I'm laughing *with* you."

"I'm not laughing, Thomas." She says this so seriously, I know I've hurt her feelings. I just don't know how.

"I'm laughing at the fact that I pre-judged you," I tell her. "I guess I assumed you liked the same things I do."

"That doesn't make any sense." She inexplicably asks, "Do you like applesauce?"

"Not particularly," I tell her. "I do like apples though."

"I love applesauce." She says this like she's professing her feelings for more than pureed fruit.

"Good for you," I say while taking a right turn that leads us toward Elk Lake. As we near the road that wraps around the body of water, I ask, "Would you prefer I turn around and we drive through the woods?"

"No, thank you. Even though I don't like sand, I like looking at the lake. It's peaceful."

I'm so caught up in the oddness of this conversation I nearly run through a stop sign. As such, I wind up pressing the brake a little too hard and we stop with a jolt.

"You really aren't a very good driver," Finley announces.

"I haven't hit anyone yet," I tell her, like not killing pedestrians is a real accomplishment.

Instead of taking my comment lightheartedly, Finley confesses, "I'm afraid I would. That's one of the big reasons I haven't learned how to drive."

"Most people who drive cars never hit pedestrians," I say with authority. "I think you'll be fine."

She gives me a one-word answer. "Maybe."

"I won't be able to take drivers' ed with you," I tell her. "Constance is moving my schedule to nights starting next week. Which means I'll be sleeping during the day." I pull into a parking space with a great view of the lake.

That statement seems to shake my passenger. She reaches out and touches my arm. Taking a moment to pet the leather of my jacket, she asks, "Why would she do that?"

"She's doing it because she's mad I won't date her. I'll be working from eight at night until six in the morning. Which means I'll go to bed at eleven in the morning and sleep until six o'clock at night." Just the thought of returning to a nocturnal existence makes my skin crawl.

"Can she do that?" Finley seems as disturbed as I am.

"She can pretty much do anything she wants."

"Yes, but we still have to finish the calendar for your parents."

"I can do tomorrow's session," I tell her, "but would there be any way you could stay late for the other sessions? Either that, or maybe we can schedule them for my days off?"

"I guess." She sounds disappointed.

I'm disappointed, too. I like spending time with Finley and with us being on opposite schedules that's going to be hard to do.

We sit silently and watch the sunset. As the orange ball sinks into the lake, I ask, "Would you like to have supper with me tonight?"

My passenger is quiet for long enough, I'm convinced she's going to say no. But then she opens her mouth and surprises me.

CHAPTER TWENTY-FIVE

FINLEY

I can't believe Thomas is thinking about leaving Elk Lake. This town has been a dream come true for me. A dream that became sweeter when I met him. And now he wants to leave? I'm not pleased.

Also, I'm surprised Thomas wants to eat with me again. It's not that I don't want to go. I do. I just don't want to get more attached to him only to have him break my heart when he goes back to New York.

"Let's go to my studio and order in," I tell him. "They just cut the opening between my place and the shop next door. I have a lot of work to do to get it ready for use."

"Are you trying to get me to help you?" he asks suspiciously.

I could get addicted to that smile of his. Full lips and straight white teeth are near the top of my must-have list when it comes to a man. Other things include nice feet, properly clipped nails, and hair. I like a man with hair.

"You don't have to help," I tell him. "You could just sit there and eat while I do all the work." I raise one eyebrow and narrow my gaze to send a subliminal message: *You'd better not sit and watch me work without offering to help.*

I know he receives the message loud and clear when he laughs, "Nice guilt trip. You're going to be a great mother someday."

The sharp pain that stabs me to the left of my belly button makes me think I might have just spontaneously ovulated. I'm not sure I'd make a great mom, but I'm convinced Thomas would make a great dad. He's kind, funny, tall, gorgeous … Not that you have to be tall and gorgeous to be a good dad, but it certainly helps your spouse want to procreate with you. Especially, if that spouse is me. *Talk about getting ahead of myself …*

I force my brain not to start thinking about making babies with Thomas. Heck, we haven't even been on our first date yet. I don't count fake dates, or friendly get-togethers. Our first date will be official when/if Thomas asks me out and then kisses me at my doorstep when he brings me home. I'm old fashioned that way.

Thomas reaches out and snaps his fingers in front of my face to get my attention. "You in there, Finley?"

Just thinking about making babies with you. "I was just distracted by the beautiful sunset," I lie. "But yes, I'm here. Did you say something?"

"I said I'd be happy to help you out tonight. Are we painting? Ripping up carpet? What do you have in mind?"

"Fluffing feathers," I tell him.

The look he gives me is comical. "I'm sorry, what?"

"I just got a big box of ostrich feathers in and they arrived pretty smooshed," I explain. "They need to be fluffed before they can be used."

"How do you use ostrich feathers?" he asks, sounding totally baffled.

"I use the pink and baby blue for infant shots." Wiggling all ten of my fingers, I explain, "I fan them on the ground and then place the baby on top of them. People love that."

"Huh." He's clearly having a hard time envisioning this, so I make a mental note to show him some pictures.

"They also come in handy for the boudoir shots." I shrug my eyebrows at him suggestively. "Maybe you'd like a naughty maid photo for your calendar." Thomas audibly chokes when he hears that. I reach over and pound on his back.

"I'm not sure I can see myself in a little maid outfit," he says.

Giggling at the thought, I tell him, "We'd make you more of a manservant. You know, shirtless, carrying drinks on a silver tray."

"Where do the feathers come in?"

"I could make you a nice feather duster with them."

He looks alarmed. "I think I'll stick with the more basic shots."

I check the clock on the dashboard of my vintage dream ride and it's already six. "We'd better head back then. If I order supper now, we should be able to get some good work done."

"What should we get?" he asks before adding, "As you know, I've had the diner food twice but haven't tried anything else yet."

"It's Wednesday," I tell him.

"What does that have to do with dinner?" He slowly backs out of his parking space and doesn't stop until he hits the guardrail behind him.

"Don't ding my ride before I buy her from you," I scold.

"Sorry about that." Putting the car into drive, he says, "I'm used to having a backup camera in cars that I rent.."

"When do your lessons start?" I ask him.

"I don't know. Now that I'm moving to nights, I might have to see if the instructor can fit me in for private lessons." He glances at me briefly before asking, "What does Wednesday have to do with what you eat for dinner."

"Wednesday is pasta night," I tell him. "So I think we should order Italian."

Thomas pulls back onto the road slowly. "Sounds good to me. What's your favorite pasta dish?"

I really don't want to tell him, but if we're going to be eating together, he's going to find out. I inhale deeply hoping for a shot of courage. "I like angel hair pasta with butter."

"What kind of sauce?"

"Butter," I repeat.

"Butter as the sauce? You don't put any marinara on it? Or white wine and garlic? Alfredo?"

"Butter," I tell him for the third time.

"Cheese?" he asks.

"Plain," I tell him.

Thomas obviously thinks this is the most boring order in the world. "Do you like tomato sauce?"

"I like it on pizza."

"And no cheese?" Yeah, he's not impressed by my culinary prowess.

"I like extra cheese on pizza," I tell him. "And before you say I eat like a kid, I don't. I just really love buttery noodles." For some reason, I feel the need to add, "Butter is one of my food groups."

Thomas turns left on to Main Street. We're only five blocks from my shop now. "Butter falls into the dairy food group," he tells me.

I shake my head. "Butter is a separate group for me."

Thomas slows down about a block before he reaches the next stop sign. "How many groups do you have?"

"Twelve," I tell him.

"Finley, there are only five food groups." He itemizes them: "Dairy, fruit, vegetables, grains, and protein. How do you get twelve out of that?"

While I want him to get to know me, I really wish we'd had more time together before I had to share this with him. Lifting one finger I tell him, "Butter, fruit, vegetables, brownies, meat, cheese, milk, pizza, Chinese food, bread, and chocolate."

Thomas has been sitting at the stop sign for long enough that someone behind us honks. Lifting his foot off the brake, he gradually accelerates before pulling over to the side of the road and parking in front of Happy Snaps. Then he repeats, "There are only five food groups."

"That's like saying there are only seven continents," I tell him.

Thomas rams the gear shift into park. "There *are* only seven continents."

Shaking my head, I ask, "What about all the islands out there?"

"They're islands, not continents."

"But don't you think they feel bad not being included as continents?"

Thomas turns and stares at me with his mouth hanging open. "Islands aren't sentient. They don't have feelings. Plus, if you included all the islands as continents there would be thousands of them. You can't have thousands of continents."

He's really stressing over this, so I throw him a bone and lie. "I was joking about the continents."

"And the food groups?"

"Not joking about those. I feel like food groups should be individualized to the person. I have twelve food groups."

"That's not how it goes," he says.

"You can have five food groups if you want. That's totally your prerogative."

"What about other grains?" he wants to know. "Like oatmeal or rice?"

"They fall under bread," I tell him.

"Why not just lump them all together and call them grains then?" Poor Thomas, he's taking this pretty hard.

"I eat more bread than I do oatmeal or rice, so I like to name that category after it. It's only fair."

"Fair to whom?" His face turns bright red.

"To bread," I tell him. Then I suggest, "Why don't we go in. I didn't order our food while we were out so it's going to take longer now."

Thomas gets out of the car and hurries around to my side. I

open my own door, then I take his hand and let him help me out. "You are confounding," he tells me.

"I'm my own person," I assure him. "I like things the way I like them."

Thomas stops walking and turns to look at me. Then he asks, "How do you like your men?"

CHAPTER TWENTY-SIX

THOMAS

Finley is constantly throwing curveballs that make me wonder who in the world raised her. *Twelve food groups?* I've never heard anything that ridiculous.

I don't know what comes over me, but I ask her, "How do you like your men?"

She drops her gaze to my feet before telling me, "I like men who like me." She says this so quietly, I can tell I've hit a nerve.

"I meant, what's your type?" I'm obviously fishing for her to describe my physical attributes, but she doesn't.

"I like men who are kind and good. I like ones who talk to me and don't run away when they get to know me." She drops her chin until she's looking at me from under her eyelashes. "I like men who aren't afraid of me."

I think I've just found Finley's Achilles' heel. She's worried she'll be left when a love interest gets to know her. Meanwhile, the more I learn about her, the more intrigued I am. "Have you lost boyfriends because they didn't understand you?" I ask gently.

"I have." She doesn't elaborate.

"Do you want to tell me about them?"

"I do not," she says before taking the final steps to the front door. She puts her key into the lock and opens it.

I follow Finley inside, instinctively knowing things have changed between us. The atmosphere is thick with tension, and I don't want to go on without clearing the air.

"Finley," I say. "Please talk to me."

As she exhales, her shoulders slump until she looks like she's going to wilt to the floor. Without facing me, she says, "I really don't want to talk about this. You already think I'm weird enough."

"Is that what this is all about?" I ask before telling her, "I love weird people! My family is weird. My friends are weird. In my book, weirdness equals individuality and that's always a plus. Who wants to be like everyone else?"

She turns toward me and I immediately see tears in her eyes. "Most people want to be like everyone else."

"Why do you think that?" I take a step toward her and gently put my hands on her shoulders. "You're you and that's what makes you special."

"*Special,*" she spits the word out like it's a bad piece of meat.

"What's wrong with being special?" I ask her. "Everyone wants to be special."

"I'm going to tell you something, Thomas. And not because I want to, but because you're making me. But just so you know, I'm not very happy about it."

"What could you possibly tell me that warrants this kind of buildup?" I ask her.

Finley rolls her beautiful green eyes before flaring her nostrils in anger. "I'm on the spectrum. I'm autistic."

I can't help the laughter that explodes out of me. *That's* what she wanted to tell me? I stare into her very hurt looking eyes and declare, "I figured that out pretty quickly."

"You knew? How?"

"The foil, the peas, the sand …"

Tears are now free-falling down her face. I reach out to hug her, but she pushes me away. "You weren't supposed to know."

I'm not sure why she's upset with me. "Was it a secret?"

"Yes, it was a secret. It's always meant to be a secret!"

"Why?" I ask again.

"Because people don't like autistic people. They make fun of them."

My heart nearly breaks on the spot. Poor Finley. She must have been the recipient of some nasty treatment. "My sister is on the spectrum," I tell her. "Vivie is talented, funny, personable, and smart."

"Your sister?" She's staring at me like I just told her my sister was an alien.

"Yes," I assure her. "Which is probably why I recognized the signs in you. You have some similarities."

"Like what?"

"Vivie is also very creative and extremely touch oriented. She's not interested in soft things though. She likes rough textures. Rocks, wood chips, sandpaper …"

"Sandpaper?" Finley asks in horror, making it perfectly clear she's into soft and only soft. "Is your sister, you know …" she starts to ask but doesn't finish the question.

"Is she what?"

"Slower than normal," she finally says.

"As in running?"

"No, Thomas. I mean, does she have learning problems." She turns her head and focuses on the other side of the room.

"Vivie pretty much learns like everyone else, but some things take longer. For instance, math has always been a demon for her."

Spinning around so she's looking at me again, Finley shouts, "I'm horrible at math! It's the reason I was diagnosed." She hurries to add, "I failed geometry in high school."

I think the age of her diagnosis might be part of reason she's so upset about me learning she's autistic. "Finding out in high school had to be hard," I tell her. "Vivie was diagnosed in the second grade."

Finley walks toward a photo set at the back of the room. She sits down on a bed and picks up the furry throw lying across it. Petting it repeatedly, she confirms, "It was terrible. Not only did I flunk math, but everyone started treating me like I was mentally disabled."

"I'm sorry that happened to you. Are these people who had known you your whole life?"

Her head bobs up and down. "We lived in a small town. Almost everyone was normal." She squints her eyes briefly before saying, "Except Tucker Fox. He has fourteen fingers and six toes."

I sit down next to her and share, "Vivie had a special learning plan all along, but she was mainstreamed. Her classmates got used to the fact that she needed special things."

"Like what?"

"Noise cancelling headphones for tests," I tell her. "She was allowed to get up and walk around the school when she felt pent up. She only took two math classes in high school."

"Did people make fun of her?"

"Kids are kids," I say with a shrug. "There are always mean ones who like to prey on people's differences, but there are also nice ones. It doesn't matter if you're autistic, bad at sports, or you can't sing. There's always someone gunning for you."

"What were you bad at?" The skeptical look on her face suggests she thinks I'm blowing smoke.

"I couldn't get a basketball in a hoop to save my life," I tell her. "And before you say that's no big deal, then you've never been part of a friend group that played varsity basketball."

The first smile in a long while comes to Finley's mouth. "I actually have," she says. "I played varsity basketball. I played in college too."

"Are you serious?" When she nods her head, I tell her. "That's way more impressive than being good in math. WAY more."

"You're just saying that."

"I am not," I tell her. "You wouldn't believe how much crap I took from my friends."

This news seems to please her because her grin becomes positively radiant. "Do you think I'm stupid?" she asks.

"I think you're incredibly smart!" I assure her. "I mean, look at you." I make a broad sweeping gesture around her prop room. "You have your own successful business. So successful you've expanded."

"But I don't drive," she says, sounding down on herself.

"Some might say I don't either."

"True that." Finley laughs before adding, "But I have twelve food groups."

"Yeah, that's pretty nuts," I joke back. "But other than that, I think you're incredible."

Her eyes open wide and she gives three very slow blinks before asking, "You do?"

"I really do," I tell her. Then I lean toward her and do the one thing I shouldn't, especially because I'm not sure I'm staying in Elk Lake. I kiss Finley Harper.

It's not a grand, passionate expression of lust. Instead, it's sweet and gentle and so thoroughly moving I don't ever want to pull away from her. Ultimately, she's the one who retreats.

"That was nice, thank you."

"I should be thanking you," I tell her. "And it was more than nice. It was wonderful. Now, should we order supper?"

"You still want to stay?"

I want to find every person on the planet who ever made fun of Finley, and then I want to smack them upside the head. I hate that she feels vulnerable about being herself. In my eyes, she's darn near perfect.

In fact, I'm so wrapped up in my feelings, I suddenly tell her, "I'd like to take you out on a real date."

Her posture jolts ramrod straight. "But you might be leaving Elk Lake."

"That's true," I tell her. "But that won't be for months, if it happens."

"I can't live in New York," she tells me. "Not that you're asking me to, but why would we date if we didn't think it might go somewhere?"

"I don't know what the future holds for us, Finley. But I do know that if you and I are meant to be, things will work out. That's the way life is."

"But you still might leave," she repeats.

"I might. But at least you'd know that a possibility up front."

"One date," she decides. "I'll let you know after that how I feel about another."

I lean into her once again and lower my head toward hers. "That sounds fair," I tell her. And then I kiss her again. This time it's even sweeter than before.

CHAPTER TWENTY-SEVEN

FINLEY

When I woke up this morning there was no way I could have predicted how my day was going to turn out. Not only did Thomas buy the car I wanted for myself, but I told him I was on the spectrum. Then he asked me out on a real date and kissed me! I'm more optimistic than ever that he might just be my person.

After ordering our supper—buttered noodles for me, and linguini with puttanesca sauce for Thomas—I open a box full of ostrich feathers. I sit down cross-legged on the floor and start pulling them out of the box.

"First you take them out of the plastic sleeve," I tell him. "Then you need to ruffle them up." I illustrate by pinching the base of the feather and then sliding my hands up to the top. Finally, I shake it in the air seven times until it flumes to full capacity.

Thomas sits down across from me and follows my instructions. When he's successfully fluffed his first feather, he says, "These are really soft."

"They're my favorite," I tell him. "The best part is that they're humanely harvested." I explain, "Which means the ostriches aren't killed for their feathers."

"How do they get them?"

"They're sheared. This allows the feathers to regrow. Kind of like sheep."

"I never knew that." Thomas smiles at me sweetly before asking, "Isn't this something you'd enjoy doing on your own? There must be dirty jobs you'd rather I help with."

He's so thoughtful, my heart pings. Thomas is a wonderful man, and I'd like nothing more than to date him for real. It's just the thought of him leaving Elk Lake is really messing with me. Could the Universe be gunning for me so badly that it would bring someone like him into my life only to take him away?

"Why don't we do ostrich feathers until we eat?" I suggest. "And then we can head next door and look for a harder job."

"Sounds like a plan to me."

Thomas and I get a total of forty-eight feathers fluffed before our food arrives. When we hear the bell tinkle over the front door, he jumps to his feet and meets the delivery man. When I hear him ask for the price, I yell, "I'm buying dinner!"

"Too late," Thomas replies.

"But you're the one doing me the favor." I finally push myself off the floor and onto my feet before walking toward him.

As I take the bags from the delivery man, Thomas reminds me, "I bought your car out from under you. I owe you."

I like how he thinks. "You really do," I tell him. "But you're going to sell it to me, so …"

"I still owe you." He hands cash to the man from the restaurant and then leads the way toward a table that's part of a restaurant scene I used in one of yesterday's shots. The couple I filmed wanted to recreate their engagement. Talk about romantic.

I drop the food before walking over to the mini-fridge I keep stocked for clients. "You can have cola, diet cola, fruit punch, or sparkling orange-flavored water."

"Fruit punch? Does anyone even drink that stuff anymore?" He sounds appalled.

"They still sell it," I retort.

"I'll do the water."

I grab a bottle of water for him and a can of nice Hawaiian Punch for me. While I don't particularly love fruity drinks, based on the fact that not all fruits should be blended, for some reason I feel like I need to champion it. Thomas has already unpacked our food, and he's set the table with paper napkins and plastic silverware. The battery-operated candles are even turned on.

"Very romantic," I tell him softly.

"I aim to please," he says before taking the lids off our food.

Over supper I learn an array of things about my dinner companion. I'm surprised to find out that he's never been to Mexico, but he's traveled to Russia and Burma. He doesn't like bananas or honeydew melons, but he loves figs. He speaks French well enough to order dinner, but not to get directions to the bathroom. And he reads a lot of conspiracy thrillers.

I keep grilling him, so he doesn't have a chance to ask anything more about my life. He's already learned enough for one day.

When I only have a couple of bites left, I ask, "Would you like to try my buttered noodles?" I don't really want to share, but I sort of feel obligated. He did pay, after all.

"No, thank you. Would you like to try mine?"

I grimace. "Not even a little bit."

Once we're done eating, I clear the table and throw the empty containers into the garbage. Then I lead the way through the freshly cut doorway to show Thomas my new space. Turning on the lights, I ask, "What do you think?"

He looks around closely before deciding, "It's nice. What are you going to do with it?"

"My realtor suggested I put the beds in here so they're not off-putting to clientele looking for more standard pictures."

Thomas nods his head. "I can see that." Then he says, "The

walls and floors are in good shape. Are you planning on redecorating?"

"Not for a while," I tell him. "I need to make sure I can cover the additional expense first."

"Makes sense." Walking back toward the doorway leading into my main studio, he asks, "What do you say we move the beds in here tonight?"

Being that I can't move heavy mattresses on my own, I think it's a solid plan. In the end, we wind up relocating three beds, a chaise, and a claw-foot bathtub. By the time we're done, I'm wiped out.

Collapsing onto one of the beds, I declare, "I'm so tired, I could fall asleep right here."

Thomas laughs before pointing at the window. There are a couple of high school kids standing there with their faces pressed up against the glass. "If you slept here you'd have an audience," he says.

I sit up and wave at the lookie-loos before telling him, "I bought blackout drapes for the windows. They haven't come yet."

"Smart thinking." Thomas walks over to me and offers his hand. "What do you say I drive you home?"

"How about if we walk?"

He squints his eyes like he's trying to decide why I don't jump at the chance of getting back into my dream car. "You don't trust my driving yet, huh?"

Feigning an expression of shock, I tell him, "What? No. It's just such a beautiful night, and I love the fresh air."

Thomas looks out the window and declares, "It's pouring rain."

"Refreshing!" I exclaim.

"Finley ..."

I decide to tell him the truth. "Driving on a wet night is harder than driving during the day. You might not be ready for it yet."

"Why is that?"

"All the reflection from the lights on the puddles." I lead the way into my original shop and grab two umbrellas. Handing one to him, I say, "Come on, it'll be fun."

Thomas doesn't give me any more trouble. Instead, he walks outside ahead of me and opens his umbrella –a white golfing number that's probably five feet across. I sometimes use them on set to reflect light.

He immediately starts to dance around but then a gust of wind hits and nearly lifts him off his feet. He's practically blown into the middle of the street. Letting out a shout of surprise, Thomas starts to laugh. "Open yours up and join me," he calls out.

Instead of following orders, I lock the door of my shop before telling him, "Flying home is probably just as dangerous as driving with you."

"Where's your sense of adventure?" Now he's stomping in puddles under a streetlight.

"Your feet are going to get wet, and then you'll get sick." I sound like my grandmother.

"If I get sick, I won't have to go into work." He starts performing something of a jig.

"If you get sick, you won't be able to take me out on a date," I tell him.

That's all it takes for Thomas to quit fooling around and join me on the sidewalk. "My umbrella's big enough for both of us," he says before I can get mine open. "Just squeeze in next to me." He winks, letting me know he likes having me close. I like it, too.

Even though I'm currently pretty confident being myself, ever since my diagnosis, I've struggled with worrying about what other people think of me. My mom always said it was none of my business, but I couldn't imagine whose business it was more than mine.

She told me that if I go through life caring about the opinions of others, I'll give them power over me. Then she'd ask if I wanted to give Joelle Stinger power over me. Even though that's the last thing I wanted, it was hard to stop caring cold turkey.

In retrospect, I've probably lost out on some nice friendships because I kept other people at arm's length. My reasoning being that if they didn't know I was different, they would never learn the truth and then I wouldn't have to watch them change toward me.

I suddenly remember how I used to feel when I ran as a kid. Wild, carefree, completely believing that at any moment gravity would cease to exist and I would take flight. I have never felt anything quite that liberating. Then it hits me: that's exactly how I feel walking down the street with Thomas.

My soul feels like it's dancing around my body, lighter and freer than it's been in years. I know to the depths of my being that I cannot let him leave Elk Lake. I don't know how I'm going to keep him here, but I'm going to have to come up with a foolproof plan.

If I don't, my heart might never heal.

CHAPTER TWENTY-EIGHT

THOMAS

How is it that the best and worst things in my life are occurring at the same time? I love spending time with Finley. So much so, I've gone against my better judgment and asked her out on a real date. We had so much fun last night, I can hardly wait to wine and dine her for real.

Conversely, I've come to hate going into work. It's not that I've totally stopped enjoying my profession, it's just become a little dull. *What I wouldn't give for a flesh-eating bacteria or some mad cow disease.* Not that I'm wishing ill on people, I just want to use the skills I've spent my adult life honing. And then there's Constance. Just knowing she's somewhere in the hospital, plotting her revenge, makes being here very unpleasant.

Becky, the nice nurse that gave me the scoop on my boss's history as a predator, comes up to me and asks, "How are things going with *you know who*?"

I roll my eyes. "Did I tell you she put me on the nightshift?"

"That's awful but not surprising." She leans in and whispers, "You should complain to the board."

"I don't have any proof she's doing it to get back at me."

"They all know who Constance is," she tells me. "It's in your best interest to start an official paper trail. They might even be able to intervene and tell her to back off."

I hadn't considered that. If Constance has the history she's reputed to have, that might be all it takes to reinstate my regular schedule. "Thank you for suggesting this, Becky. I'll make an appointment with someone other than Constance today."

"Ask for Armie Bader," she says. "He was good friends with the doctor who sued her for sexual harassment."

"Good tip." Then I look at the clock and say, "I'm off in ten to meet my lady friend, so I'd better see if I can contact him now."

Becky suddenly looks very interested. "I know it's none of my business," she says, "but I don't suppose you'd tell me who you're dating."

"Are you going to spread the news around the hospital?" Good dish takes nanoseconds to travel in a hospital.

"I promise I won't," she says.

For some reason I believe her. "Her name is Finley."

"Not Finley Harper?" Becky's eyes open wide. It seems everyone in town knows her.

"The photographer," I say.

Becky reaches out and touches my arm. "That girl is a pure delight. She takes my grandbabies' first pictures, and they are all stunningly special. Be good to her, Thomas," she warns like I'll have her to deal with if I'm not.

Apparently, everyone loves Finley. I'm going to have to tell her so she can quit worrying about people finding out she's on the spectrum. I'm guessing she's the only one who cares about that.

It's not that I blame her. It's got to be tough being around so many different personalities without being able to fully understand motivations. I've gotten insights into this from observing my sister's world.

Vivie works alone in her art studio and only contends with the outside world when she shops or eats out. When she's feeling overstimulated, she orders her food—groceries as well as meals—

to be delivered. She says she doesn't miss having people around because they exhaust her.

I wonder if Finley feels the same way. Choosing a people-focused profession seems odd for someone on the spectrum, but I suppose it's called a spectrum for a reason. Autism encompasses a wide variety of symptoms that go far beyond the stereotypical ones.

I stop by the information booth and get the phone number for Armie Bader's office. Then I find a quiet corner and call. When his secretary asks for the reason I want to meet, I tell her plainly, "It's regarding a sexual harassment claim."

She immediately asks if she can put me on hold. Within seconds she's back on the line. "Dr. Bader can see you now, if you're free."

"I'm just getting off my shift. I can be there in five minutes," I tell her.

I text Finley quickly to let her know I might be a little late for our session, but I assure her it's for a good reason. Then I speed-walk to the other side of the building.

Unfortunately, Dr. Bader's office is in the same wing as Constance's. Even though I shouldn't be surprised when I run into her, I still rear back like a lion tamer trying to keep his charge from attacking.

"Dr. Culpepper." She sounds as surprised as I am. I wonder why she's suddenly decided to address me formally. Up until this point, she's only called me by my first name.

"Ms. Brucker," I say, mimicking her tone.

This seems to catch her off guard. "Are you here to see me?" Now she sounds hopeful.

"I'm not." I don't elaborate. Instead, I walk around her and announce myself to the person at the front desk. "I'm here to see Dr. Bader."

Constance sprints to my side. "Why do you need to see Armie?" she demands. *Good, she's nervous.*

"It's a private matter," I say while looking down at her panicked expression.

She swallows loudly. "Is it something *I* can help you with?" She suddenly seems very eager to please, which has not been her vibe up to this point. She has been much more interested in what I can do to make her happy.

"I don't think so," I tell her.

Before Constance has a chance to try to convince me, a short man in an argyle sweater vest walks out of one of the offices. "Dr. Culpepper?" When I nod in the affirmative, he stretches out his hand and introduces himself. "Armie Bader."

Taking his hand in a friendly grip, I tell him, "It's a pleasure to meet you."

Constance steps forward and addresses Dr. Bader. "I was just explaining to Dr. Culpepper I'd be happy to help him." She's clearly on edge that I've sought out someone on the board other than herself.

"And I told Ms. Brucker," I insert, "I really wanted to meet with you, instead."

Dr. Bader's gaze shifts between us before he tells Constance, "I've got this. But thank you for your interest." Even though she's been dismissed, she doesn't move.

Dr. Bader turns around and asks me to follow him. Once we are in the office, he closes the door. Then he crosses the room and sits down behind a large mahogany desk. "What can I do for you, Dr. Culpepper?"

"Thomas," I tell him.

He nods his head. "Call me Armie." He taps the top of his desk with a gold pen. "What's on your mind, Thomas?"

I sit on one of the winged-back chairs across from him. "I understand you were friends with Dr. Monroe."

His posture straightens noticeably. "Do you know Bill?"

"I don't," I tell him. "But I think he and I share a common complaint."

Armie releases a growl in the back of his throat before saying, "Go on."

"Constance Brucker seems to have taken a shine to me," I tell him.

"And?"

"I don't feel the same way about her." After a beat, I add, "She's making things uncomfortable."

Armie rolls his eyes. "What is she doing?"

"She asked me to be her date to the Spring Fling, and she doesn't want to take no for an answer." Armie gestures for me to keep talking. I tell him, "I explained to her that I have a lady friend. After declining her offer on three separate occasions, she's decided to put me on the night shift." I hurriedly add, "Which she made clear she would not do when I signed my contract."

He leans forward on his elbows. Entwining his fingers, he asks, "Is that contingency specifically noted in your contract?"

"It's not. I don't know why I didn't make sure it was, I suppose I just trusted Ms. Brucker."

Armie exhales loudly enough to express irritation. "I assume you know why Bill left." When I nod in the affirmative, he continues, "We learned a lot about the nuances of the law during that time."

"I imagine you did," I tell him.

He explains, "In order to prove sexual harassment, you need to have several instances that show a pattern." I nod again, so he concludes, "It sounds like you don't quite have that yet."

"Not quite, but I'm getting there." Then I tell him, "I will not be renewing my contract if this doesn't get cleared up. In fact, I might look into breaking it."

Armie nods his head. "I'll talk to the rest of the board and let them know what's going on. We'll issue Constance a warning."

"Thank you."

Looking concerned, he says, "We'd like to settle this without legal action."

"I would rather it not go that far, either," I tell him. "I just want to be able to come into work without having to deal with a vindictive boss."

Standing up, he says. "Thank you for bringing this to my attention. Please know we're on your side here."

I follow his lead and get up. "I appreciate your help, Armie. I'm not a litigious person by nature. I just want to be able to come to work in peace."

"I hope that's the outcome." Offering his hand again, he says, "Let me know if Constance gives you any more trouble. We all need to keep records in case this goes further."

As I walk out of Armie Bader's office, I can't help but wonder how many women have gone through similar situations. I imagine it's been much harder on them as they have historically been the primary recipient of sexual misconduct. And up until recent years, their claims have by and large been swept under the rug.

I can't help but feel that as a man I should just suck it up and take it. But I also want this kind of abuse to end for everyone. No one should have to go to their job and feel like they're working for the enemy.

As I walk out the door in the direction of the parking lot, my phone rings. When I see who it is, I merely turn it off and keep going.

CHAPTER TWENTY-NINE

FINLEY

Thomas kissed me last night. I roll over in bed and stretch like a lazy cat in a sunbeam. It has been two years since I've been kissed by a man. *Two years.* And trust me when I say that was nowhere near the sheer bliss of being kissed by Thomas. In fact, no kiss I've ever experienced can even touch it.

I'm not a person who believes in fate. Of course, that might be because I've had too much else on my plate. Namely, autism. For example, a neurotypical might have four tabs open in their brain at one time, but an atypical, like myself, probably has closer to fifty. And each one of those can have multiple subtabs. As such, my head is a very busy place that doesn't always allow pontification on peripheral topics. Like fate.

I live in a world where I'm considered an outsider because my brain doesn't work like everyone else's. Which makes me wonder why that same world would care about my destiny.

My reasoning may be flawed, and it may sound like victim mentality, but walk a mile in my shoes before you judge. In my opinion, if fate exists then it has been out to get me from the start.

It's only because of my strong resolve and belief that I'm a stellar person that I've come as far as I have.

Having said that, what if it's finally my turn for the Universe to be on my side? What are the chances Thomas left a fancy hospital in New York City to move to Elk Lake, Wisconsin? What are the chances I decided to come here myself? And while I'm at it, what are the odds he would be sent to me to have his picture taken? Which of course, I totally bungled, but that only meant we got to see each other more.

A lot of random occurrences had to take place for us to have spent the kind of time together that would lead to us kissing. A thoroughly dreamy, toe-curling, spine-tingling smooch that I want to experience every day, a dozen times a day, until I'm a hundred.

Leaning over, I pick up the phone and call my mom. As soon as I hear her voice, I ask, "How's Bernadette?"

"She laid an egg in the sink yesterday," my mom tells me proudly.

"Ah, so she was eggbound."

"Looks like it."

I hear squawking in the background. "Are you in the henhouse?"

"No, I'm in the kitchen."

"Do you have someone else in the sink?"

"Bernie again." My mom explains, "She really likes it."

"So, you're giving her daily baths now?" As if I needed any other reason to think my mom might not be normal.

"What else do I have going on?" Before I can answer, she tells me, "Your father is building the goats a teeter totter."

"What's that, now?" I snuggle under my down comforter to await what I am sure will be an astounding answer.

"He saw it on the TikTok," she tells me.

"Dad has TikTok?" *What is going on with my parents?*

"Jim, down at the feed store, showed it to him. The two of them spent three hours taking their pictures with those goofy filters. Dad is hooked."

"And the teeter totter?"

"He loves watching those clips about barnyard animals." She adds, "He's trying to get me to agree to start breeding hedge hogs, but I told him I wanted no part of it. Who has the time?"

I don't mention that she just professed to have all kinds of time. Instead, I say, "Bathing chickens will keep you busy."

"Just Bernie." Like this makes it an ordinary task.

"Mom," I decide to tell her why I've called. "I got kissed last night."

"Oh!" She sounds excited. "With the boy you're fake dating?" She makes Thomas sound like he's a teenager.

"Yes. He helped me move the beds from my old studio into the new space next door."

"You didn't happen to do anything else with those beds, did you?" She sounds particularly eager to hear the answer.

"We did not," I tell her primly.

"Too bad," she teases. At least I hope she's teasing.

"After kissing me, he asked me out on a date, and I said yes."

"I'm pleased to hear this, Finny. It's time you get out there and paint the town red."

"I don't understand …"

"It's an idiom, dear." As a more literal person, I don't usually track those things unless I've heard them several times before. This one is new.

"And it means …" I prompt.

"It means to have fun, party hard, get your groove on."

"Okay then. I guess I'm ready to paint the town red. But if it's okay with you, I might paint it pink instead. That's a better color for me."

"Paint it any color you want," my mom tells me. "Just paint it!"

"Thanks for your support, Mom."

"Always, Finny. I love you more than anything in the world."

I really did luck out when it came to the parent lottery. "I better get up and get going," I tell her. "I have a full day."

"Okay, honey. I'm going to get Bernie out of her bath and give her a blowout."

"You blow dry her?" I don't know why this is more surprising than bathing her, but it is.

"It's cold outside," she tells me. "I don't want her to get sick."

"I guess that makes sense." It really doesn't. Bernadette is a chicken. She's used to the elements, but I suppose my mom needs someone to nurture now that her own nest is empty.

"Let me know how the date goes," my mom requests before hanging up.

I roll back over, but instead of getting out of bed, I wonder what Thomas would think if he ever met my parents. I realize he had better be full-on in love with me before I let that happen or he might bolt.

I eventually get up, shower, and head out to work. I'm supposed to start drivers' ed over the weekend which means I'll have to try to get to the Department of Motor Vehicles today and take the test for my permit. I'm pretty sure I'll pass, even though I haven't studied for it yet. I mean, how hard can it be? I spend a lot of time reading street signs while walking everywhere. I already know a lot.

Once I get to the shop, I turn on all the lights and hurry to the back to get ready for my first appointment. Margaret and Bob are coming in this morning. They're venturing out of their bodice-ripping norm and going with a Tarzan and Jane theme. This required ordering vines that I've tied to a pipe hanging from the ceiling and palm fronds because Margaret thinks they might be more fun to use than loin cloths.

When they don't show up at ten, I check my messages. There's one from Margaret informing me that Bob tripped over a tree stump in the yard last night and broke his foot. While I'm bummed to not be using my creative juices this morning, I decide to use the time wisely and walk over to the DMV ahead of schedule.

It's cold and rainy out, but once I think about Thomas, I warm up like nobody's business. I'm positively toasty for the twenty minutes it takes me to get to my destination.

There's no line at the DMV, so I step forward and declare my mission. After paying the fee, I'm directed to a computer near the front desk to take my test.

I ace the first several questions because they're all about signs. But then things go south because they ask questions I'm not prepared for. Questions like, "What do you do if you're driving on a road behind a horse and buggy in a no-passing zone?"

I have never even seen a horse and buggy in real life, let alone on a Wisconsin highway. I walk away from my computer and return to the person who took my money. I'm about to ask him if I have an old test—you know, like a hundred years old—when he tells me, "If you talk to me, I'll have to fail you."

Why can't I ask him a question? It's not like I'm asking for the answers.

I stand there and stare at him, unsure of how to proceed, until he reminds me, "Skip any questions you don't know the answer to and come back to them if you have time."

While that should ease my concerns, it doesn't. I forgot I was being timed. I hurry back to the computer in a panic. Then I wind up reading and skipping every question because I can no longer focus. I want to scream, but I'm not even allowed to talk.

The computer screen in front of me eventually goes black before the words, "Out of time," appear. *Shoot.* There's no way I answered enough questions to pass. I go back to the desk and heatedly declare, "I was given an old test."

"No, you weren't."

I stare at the gruff-looking man who wouldn't let me air my complaint sooner. "I definitely was," I assure him. "I was asked what I'd do if there were a horse and buggy in the road."

He shrugs. "That's a legitimate question."

"I've never seen a horse and buggy on the road," I tell him. "We drive cars now." I say this like he's the idiot here.

"The Amish drive horse and buggies," he tells me. "And Wisconsin has the fourth largest community in the country."

While I know there's a significant Amish presence in the state, I suppose I never really thought about how they get around. I mean, I'm never out on country roads. *Darn it!*

The annoying DMV worker sneers at me. "May I suggest you take a booklet home and study it before you try again?"

I flash back to high school, which I might have mentioned was not the most pleasant time in my life. I have never tested well. Even if I studied my butt off and knew the material, there's something about knowing I'm being timed that makes it nearly impossible for me to concentrate.

I take the booklet handed to me and turn around to leave. Maybe this is my sign that I should forget about learning to drive. I don't go directly back to my shop. Instead, I walk for blocks and blocks, letting my disappointment soak in.

I must be gone longer than I thought because when I finally approach Happy Snaps, I see Thomas pull up to the curb in my dream car. He parks at a very odd angle. Honestly, he's such a bad driver that if he can pass a driving test, surely I can, too.

Not only do I feel better about my chances of getting behind the wheel, but I now get to spend the next few hours with Thomas.

I hope he goes for my suggestion about pretending to be a new character …

CHAPTER THIRTY

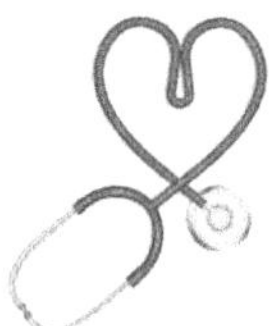

THOMAS

Spending time with Finley has turned out to be the best part of living in Elk Lake. Yes, the people are nice, and the cheese curds are good, but neither can compare to her. I've decided that as long as I'm here, I'm going to see her as much as I can. Luckily, I'll be doing that soon.

While I hope Armie does talk to Constance today, I don't anticipate her changing her evil horn-dog ways immediately. In fact, I'm preparing for retaliation of some sort. Although I don't know what else she can do to me. She's already scheduled me for the graveyard shift.

I hurry home to shower and shave before my session with Finley. I'm getting increasingly excited to pull this prank on my parents. And the photos are looking so good, they might actually believe I've decided to become a male model. I'm considering hiring a videographer to capture the moment for posterity. That way I can watch it on repeat.

Getting into my new car, I turn on the ignition before blasting the heat. Then I pull out of the driveway slowly and try to convince myself I'm getting better behind the wheel. I keep my speed a good ten mph under the limit, which results in my getting honked at twice. I briefly consider getting a bicycle, but then remind myself I've offered to help Finley with her driving, so I'd best persevere.

Finley is walking into Happy Snaps at the same time I am. Not only is she soaking wet, but she looks like she just lost her best friend. Hurrying to her side, I gently drape my arm over her shoulder. "Hey you, what's wrong?"

She looks up at me and tries to smile but instead of looking happy, she appears to be in pain. "I just failed the test to get my permit."

"I'm sorry," I tell her, knowing how much she wants this. Trying to make her feel better, I share, "I failed the actual driving part of my test twice before I finally passed."

She nods. "I can totally see that." *Ouch.*

"Should we study together?" I ask before waggling my eyebrows. "You know, after I become a cowboy?"

"A cowboy, a gladiator, and how do you feel about Tarzan?"

"Tarzan?" I think about it for a beat before deciding, "Why not?"

Once we're in the shop, Finley turns toward me but keeps her gaze lowered to the floor. "You're not looking at me," I tell her.

"Duh, I'm on the spectrum."

"Maybe so," I say, "but I've noticed you only seem to have difficulty making eye contact when you're nervous. What can you possibly have to be nervous about with me?"

She lifts her eyes slowly, coyly even, before commenting, "You kissed me last night."

"I did." With a self-satisfied grin, I tell her, "And I'm looking forward to doing it again." I lean toward her thinking now is as good a time as any.

When Finley sees me advance, she puts both hands up in front of her to keep me from getting closer. "We have work to do, and I need to make sure I keep my wits about me." Then she turns around and leads the way into the back of her shop.

As she sets the lights for the cowboy scene, I tell her, "I bet you're one of the only photographers left who doesn't use AI."

"I think AI is cheating," she says plainly. "There is enough organic intelligence on the planet without turning our autonomy over to computers."

"Creatively speaking, it's probably a lot cheaper though." I know she's worried about the expense of taking on the space next door.

"It lacks integrity," she tells me. "If everyone uses artificial intelligence before their own talents, it won't be long until there's no creativity left in this world."

She has a point. "China has already built a hospital that doesn't staff any people."

Her face morphs into an expression of horror. "No people? What about the doctors?"

"Robots," I tell her. "As are the nurses, the lab techs, even the cleaning staff."

"I don't want to live in a world like that," she says sadly.

Taking off my rain jacket, I commiserate, "I think it might be too late. China already has robots patrolling the border between them and Vietnam."

Finley adamantly declares, "I'll move home and live in my parents' basement before I give up my humanity."

"Me, too," I say in solidarity. "Although my parents live on the tenth floor and their basement is the parking garage, but I'm with you in spirit."

Shifting to a lighter subject, I ask, "Is the cowboy first?"

A faint blush crosses Finley's features. "Yes." She points to the costume rack. "Let me know if you need help buckling your chaps."

That sounds like a highly suggestive offer, but I don't tease her about it. Instead, I say, "I thought chaps snapped on."

"Some do, but I prefer the old-school ones. They look more

rugged." She averts her gaze again which makes me think she's envisioning me in my cowboy regalia.

In my changing corner, I take off my street clothes and start my transformation. Faded jeans come first, along with a pair of cowboy boots. Then comes the denim shirt. Once again, there doesn't seem to be enough fabric, and there are no buttons. As I step out into the open, Finley takes one look at me and glides across the floor like she's floating on air.

Once she's within arms' reach, she stops. "You look amazing!"

I happen to agree with her. "Thank you," I tell her cockily. "Do I get my chest greased up for this one?" I ask, hoping I'm lucky enough to get to feel Finley's hands on me.

She shakes her head slowly. "The cowboy gets a suntan and some dirt."

I look around, and ask, "Do you keep a bucket of dirt here somewhere?"

"I use eye shadow," she tells me. "It's stays on better." She tugs at my sleeve gently. "Come on over to hair and makeup."

"Do I get windblown cowboy hair?" Maybe she'll run her hands through my hair—a close second to the baby oil.

"You get a cowboy hat with this one." *Is it me or does she sound disappointed?*

Finley spends the next ten minutes brushing my face, neck, and chest with that incredibly soft brush of hers. When she's done, she steps back and simply stares. "Wow."

"Thank you," I tell her smugly. There's nothing quite like feeling appreciated by the woman you're interested in. And boy, am I interested in Finley.

She walks over to a shelf near the costumes and pulls down a dark brown cowboy hat. Then she grabs a rope off a hook on the wall. Leading the way to a backdrop of a field, she calls, "Over here, Cowboy Thomas."

I practically run to her side. "I like it when you call me Cowboy Thomas," I tell her in what I hope is a flirty manner.

"You look good in that costume." She winks and walks over to her camera table. Picking one up, she comes back and orders, "It's go time. I want you to flex your muscles and smolder like you've never smoldered before."

So far, this is my favorite look. Probably because every little boy dreams of being a cowboy at some point in his life, even a city boy who rarely gets his hands dirty.

Giving her my best John Wayne, Clint Eastwood, and Gary Cooper all wrapped into one, makes me feel like the manliest of men. "I might have to buy an outfit like this for my days off," I tell her. I'm only partially joking.

Finley stops snapping pictures long enough to say, "You can have this one. Wear it on our date."

Even though the air is heavy with tension, I can't help but laugh. "You want me to take you to the lodge looking like this?"

"Is that where we're going?" She sounds excited.

"You said it was the nicest place in town, and I think our first date warrants that, don't you?"

Her complexion tinges pink. "I do. And to answer your question, if you showed up looking like that, you'd ruin a lot of other dates. No woman with a pulse would be able to keep her eyes off you."

"In that case," I tell her, "I'll wear something else. After all, I only have eyes for you." *Cowboys have game.* I'm currently a thousand times smoother than I've ever been.

We spend another three hours shooting for my revenge calendar. We even manage to fit in a fourth look—a Scottish highland warrior. That one required having extensions added for a wilder look. The best part was that Finley had to run her fingers through my hair when she clipped the synthetic pieces in.

It's nearly five o'clock by the time we're done and I am worn out from pretending to be so many different people—modeling is harder than you'd think. Yet, I don't want my time with Finley to end. "I know we talked about having our first date tomorrow night, but what do you say we go out tonight, too?"

"We could, except I'm not ready to commit to two dates," she tells me bluntly.

"Okay. Why don't we go out tonight, and if you decide I warrant a second date, we can go out tomorrow night, too?" I cringe a little at the blatant hope in my voice.

"I'd have to go home and change," she says. Then she turns flirty. "Are you sure you don't want to put that cowboy costume back on?"

After assuring her I'd be more comfortable in my normal clothes, we agree that I'll pick her up in an hour and a half. She has decided that because it has stopped raining and the roads are dry, she'll be safe enough with me behind the wheel, and we probably won't die in a gruesome car accident. I've decided to take this as a vote of confidence.

Once I'm back at my house, I walk inside and look around. I've done nothing to make it feel like mine, yet. And at the rate I'm going, I'm not sure I will. The place came furnished, and as near as I can tell it was inhabited by someone's eighty-year-old grandmother. There are a lot of chintz and floral patterns. The pictures on the walls are illustrations of Victorian-era calendar girls.

I briefly toy with the idea of replacing the artwork—if you can call it that—with my modeling images. A maniacal burst of amusement fills the air when I envision my parents' reaction to them. This is seriously the most devious and entertaining prank I've ever played. And I owe it all to Finley. I could have never concocted such an outlandish concept without her misinterpretation of why Constance hired her.

With a smile on my face, I pick up my phone and call my sister. She answers around the twentieth ring, as is her norm. Vivie rarely keeps her phone on her and often loses it altogether. "Thomas." Her voice is breathy like she's just run a marathon.

"Hey, Viv," I say. "How are you doing?"

"I'm doing fine. How are you?"

"I'm great," I tell her. "Really good." I sound suspicious even to myself.

My sister immediately guesses, "So, there *is* a woman! I knew it."

"Her name is Finley," I tell her. "But don't tell Mom and Dad yet. I want to surprise them."

"Is she surprising?" Vivie is very literal, which I know goes hand-in-hand with being on the spectrum.

Sitting down on the living room couch, I tell her, "She's unlike anyone I've dated before."

"That must be refreshing," my sister says, sounding relieved. "Your regular type left a lot to be desired." She's not wrong.

"Finley isn't a slick city woman," I tell her. "She's from a small town in Illinois and she's a photographer."

"I love that she's artistic. That's definitely a step up for you."

"She's also on the spectrum," I tell her. "But you can't act like you know. I think she's a little sensitive about it."

"Why?" I'm not surprised my sister asks this question. She's very comfortable with who she is and she apologizes to no one.

"She found out in high school," I tell her. "I think it created an identity crisis for her."

"Bullies," my sister surmises the problem in one word. "I'm looking forward to meeting her."

"Also …" I decide to share part of my scheme with her. Jokes sometimes confuse Vivie, and I don't want her to think I'm really giving up being a doctor. But I do want her to enjoy the reveal, so I tell her, "I'm finally getting even with Mom and Dad for that trip to Cleveland."

"Really?" She sounds positively delighted. "What are you going to do? Kidnap them and drop them off on a deserted island to fend for themselves? Tell them you bought them tickets to swim with dolphins, but it's really sharks?"

"Nothing that extreme," I assure her.

"You should tell them you got three women pregnant at the same time. Mom will lose her mind."

"Yeah, not going to do that, either." Is it me or is my sister a bit more Machiavellian than I've ever noticed?

"You should ..."

Instead of hearing her out, I say, "I'm not going to tell you what I'm doing, but I wanted to give you some advance notice that it isn't real."

"Thank you, Tommy. I appreciate that." Vivie is not a huge fan of surprises. My parents knew that when they took us to Ohio instead of Hawaii, but my sister's therapist at the time thought it was a good idea to expand her boundaries. Our parents didn't seem to realize switching vacation destinations went beyond gentle pushing and bordered on childhood trauma. Having said that, I was more negatively affected than Vivie. Hence my desire for revenge.

"I'm already packed to come see you next weekend," my sister says. "I hope the weather is nice."

"Bring a raincoat," I tell her. "A heavy one." While she does some traveling, she doesn't do a lot, and she never does it alone. "Are you ready for the flight?" I ask.

"I have a tranquilizer, my headphones, and a new eye mask," she says. "I'm also bringing that scratchy wool blanket for the plane. I should be fine."

This has been Vivie's way of coping since we were kids, and she's gotten good at it over the years. "You're a real trooper," I tell her.

"That's nice of you to say." She pauses before adding, "I miss you, Tommy. And while I'd like for you to move back home, I'm happy you're living your life for you."

I don't want to get her hopes up by telling her I'm not totally happy here. Instead, I say, "I appreciate your support, Viv. It means the world to me."

"That's what family is for. You've always had my back, and I will always have yours."

I hang up with my sister feeling the warmth of being genuinely loved. Vivienne is a person completely without artifice.

Once she loves you, she will do anything for you. No questions asked. I'm guessing she and Finley are a lot alike in that way.

Speaking of Finley, I can't wait to see her tonight. I pick up the phone and call the lodge in hopes they can execute tomorrow night's plan tonight. Then I hurry to shower off all the body makeup I'm currently wearing. Once I'm all dried, I go to my closet and pick out my softest sweater.

I'm hoping Finley won't be able to keep her hands off me.

CHAPTER THIRTY-ONE

FINLEY

I haven't been to the lodge yet so I'm super excited. In fact, I rarely go anywhere that requires my dressing up. But tonight is a special occasion. I pull out the dress I wore to my cousin's wedding and hold it up to my body. Then I stare at my reflection in the mirror. It's the most appropriate thing I own, but it's not particularly soft, and I want to be comfy tonight.

I stand there in my towel for another five minutes trying to decide if sacrificing my comfort is worth the price of looking good. I decide it's not. I'm going to be nervous enough being on a real date with Thomas that I need to make sure everything else is as calming as possible.

I hang the dress back up and then close my eyes. Reaching out blindly, I touch various pieces of clothing. I feel around for the softest thing I can find, which—*surprise, surprise*—is my favorite sweater, the fuzzy pink one. Then I dive back in for something for my bottom half.

Skirts and pants are never as satisfying as sweaters and blouses, so I pull out the least rough thing I can find. Which turns out to be a dark green corduroy skirt. Laying it next to the pink sweater on my bed, I stand back and stare. I can't decide if it's an acceptable combination or if it's awful. One thing is clear—it's not the best.

I decide to put it on and see if it looks any better. Returning to the mirror I realize I look like a watermelon. But I like watermelon, so my immediate thought is that it's okay. But what if Thomas doesn't like watermelon? Could that be a deal breaker?

I'm driving myself crazy going back and forth about what to do when I glance at the clock and discover I only have ten minutes before he gets here. I rush to the bathroom and put on my makeup. Then I fluff my hair and spritz my wrists with my favorite perfume. It smells like grapefruit. I'm like a fruit salad which must be why I decide on earrings with cherries dangling from them. Apparently, I'm fully committed to this theme.

Looking out the front window, I see Thomas trying to parallel park between two cars. He's doing an awful job, so I grab my raincoat and head out the door.

Once I reach the street, I see my dream car positioned at such an extreme angle there's no way Thomas is ever going to park. I jump off the curb and knock on the passenger side window. He immediately unlocks the car for me to get in.

"Worried you're going to get highjacked?" I ask, making fun of his locked doors.

"Always," he assures me.

"This isn't New York City," I remind him.

"Maybe not, but you should never drive around with your doors unlocked. My grandmother did that once in North Carolina and a guy got in while she was waiting at a red light. He demanded she take him to the bank."

"What did your grandmother do?" I ask in shock.

"She put the car into park, turned off the ignition, and then got out in the middle of traffic. Then she waved down a passing police car," he tells me.

I redirect the heating vent so it's blowing right on me before saying, "You're making that up."

Shaking his head, he assures me, "I am not. My grandmother was nothing if not sassy. That must be where my mom gets it."

"What did the cop do with the guy?" I want to know.

"He ran his driver's license number." Thomas turns to me to give me a dramatic look. "He was wanted for bank robbery."

"No!" I smack his arm before alerting him, "You're about to hit a squirrel."

Thomas slams on the brakes so hard I probably would have shot through the windshield had we been going any faster. But it turns out an abrupt stop at ten miles an hour isn't that dangerous.

"Sorry about that," he says before slowly letting up on the brake.

"Did you grandmother live in a big city?"

"She did not. That's why you should always lock your doors when you're driving."

"I'll remember that," I tell him. "Although, I'm not convinced I'll be driving any time soon. I can't take drivers' ed without my permit."

"It's amazing there are so many children getting licenses every day." This sums up my own feelings quite accurately. Then he asks, "Did you even think about getting your license as a kid?"

I shake my head. "I'd just been diagnosed, and I thought that meant I wasn't smart enough."

"Did your parents encourage you?"

"They told me I could get it whenever I was ready, but they didn't push me." I explain, "Whatever confidence I'd had up to that point sort of vanished."

Thomas turns onto the road leading to the lodge. "You know there's nothing wrong with you, right?"

"I know that now," I tell him. "I'm on the spectrum, not mentally handicapped." Although perhaps I have seemed a little defensive about my diagnosis with him. I just really want Thomas to see me for me and not a label that's been thrust upon me.

He turns left into the wooded entrance that leads to the lodge.

"I've been thinking, what if people who are autistic are actually more evolved than everyone else?"

That's an interesting theory, and not one I've entertained before. But it might also be flawed. "There are people on the spectrum who cannot stand any sound or touch," I tell him. "They scream in agony when they're overly stimulated and that can happen very easily. How do you think they might be more evolved than other people?"

Thomas pulls into a distant parking spot—I'm guessing because he doesn't trust himself getting too close to other cars. He answers, "Maybe people like that are more spiritual creatures. You know, like they're wired to a higher frequency that doesn't resonate with the human body."

I don't hate that idea. In fact, I really kind of love it. But I want to know more. "What's the point of them coming into a human body then? Why wouldn't they just stay in spirit form where they're comfortable?"

"I'm sure there are a thousand reasons. How about if they're sent here to teach other people?"

"Teach them what?"

"Maybe to be more sympathetic?"

I think back to Joelle Stinger and realize that if Thomas is right, she missed a real opportunity with me. "Your theory is interesting," I eventually tell him. "But I can assure you that if given a say in the matter, I would have not signed on for this."

Thomas turns off the car before looking at me. "I'm guessing on the other side of the veil, when we're in spirit form, we're more inclined to make decisions based on the greater good."

"Like you becoming a doctor," I say.

"Maybe, but I made that decision here." He adds, "I've seen how my sister's life has impacted people and believe me when I say, she's made a real difference."

"Through her art."

He nods his head. "I would love for you to see it sometime. Her pieces are giant, like twelve feet by twelve feet. When you look at them, you feel like you've been transported into another time and place. Another dimension even."

"So, they're abstracts."

"Yes and no. There are dozens of smaller scenes within the bigger picture, but you have to really look to find them. You could stand in front of one of Vivie's pieces for hours and still not absorb all the detail within."

I'm getting cold so I wrap my arms around each other and tell him, "My pictures aren't that deep."

"You capture a lot of emotion," he says. "Your pictures are full of love and hope. They bring fantasy to people's lives. And we all need some of that."

"That's very nice of you to say," I tell Thomas. "But I'm getting cold and I'd like to go inside."

He jumps out of the car and runs around to open my door. I let him because unlike the other night, tonight we're on a real date. Thomas offers his hand to help me out, but he doesn't let go of it once I'm on my feet. Instead, he uses it to pull me closer to him.

As we walk into the lodge's vaulted entry, Thomas declares, "This is nice. Rustic, but elegant at the same time."

"Do you know who Trina Rockwell is?" I ask.

"Wasn't she a presenter on television?"

"She used to have a show called the *Midwestern Matchmaker*," I confirm. "They shot the last season in Elk Lake a couple of years ago and Trina never left. She and her boyfriend, Heath Fox, built this place." I add, "They're married now."

"I've definitely heard of Heath," Thomas says. "He's a renowned philanthropist."

We walk through the entrance and follow the signs to the restaurant. At the host stand, Thomas tells the hostess, "Thomas Culpepper, party of two."

Her eyes light up, "Oh yes, Dr. Culpepper. We have your table waiting." I don't know why, but she seems particularly excited by our arrival.

We follow the hostess into the dining room, which is once again elegantly rustic, as per Thomas's description. There are elk horn chandeliers hanging high overhead. The chairs are made of heavy wood, but the tables are covered with white linens that are already set with silverware and crystal wine glasses.

She leads us to a four-top right under one of the chandeliers. Two chairs have been taken away and the remaining two are positioned side by side instead of across from each other. Unlike the other tables, which only have small votive candles on them, ours has an honest to goodness candelabra with long candles. There's also a large vase with what must be two dozen long-stemmed white roses. My breath hitches.

"May I take your coat?" the hostess asks after putting our menus down on the table.

I slip out of my raincoat and hand it to her, then I sit down on the chair Thomas has pulled out for me. Once he joins me, I tell him, "I can't believe you did all this."

"Why can't you believe it?"

"Because ... because ... No one has ever done anything this thoughtful for me before."

"It's their loss then." The sincerity of his tone causes a shiver to radiate throughout my body.

"I love white roses," I tell him. "They're so pristine and pure looking."

"White roses traditionally stand for new beginnings." There's a glint in Thomas's eyes that makes me shiver. "And this *is* our first date."

"Yes, but if you're thinking about leaving Elk Lake, what's the point of having a second date?" It hurts to even ask that question, but not as much as it would hurt if I fell for the guy and he left me. There's no way I can live in a city like New York. I don't know how his sister manages it, but I know I never could.

"I thought we were trusting the right thing would happen between us," he says.

I raise my left eyebrow to show my skepticism. But instead of vocalizing it, I tell him, "Prove to me that it's the right thing to do."

CHAPTER THIRTY-TWO

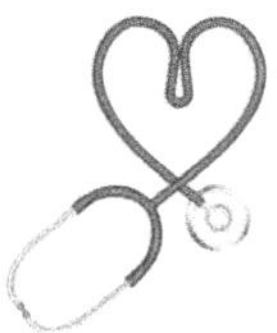

THOMAS

The candlelight glistens against the golden highlights of Finley's hair. She looks positively gorgeous tonight. "Let's pretend neither of us know what lies ahead and just enjoy tonight for what it is," I tell her. "Our first, of what I hope will be many, dates."

Finley removes her napkin from between her silverware and puts it on her lap. "I'll try."

The waiter comes over and greets us before asking, "May I bring you something from the bar to start?"

Picking up the wine list, I ask my date, "How about a glass of champagne? We are celebrating after all."

She nods her head slowly. "That sounds very nice, thank you."

I order a bottle and when the waiter leaves, I tell Finley, "If I hadn't met you, I'd already be on my way back to New York."

"I find that hard to believe," she says. I notice her looking at my sweater as she reaches out her hand and rests it on my forearm. Within moments she's petting me.

I want to tell her that I like it when she touches me, but I'm afraid if I draw attention to it, she might stop. So, instead, I say, "I'm not lying to you. Getting to know you has been the highlight of being here. You are a big part of my trying to make a go of life in Elk Lake."

She blushes delicately. "Thank you."

"Thank *you*."

Leaning toward me, she says, "You make me feel more special than any man ever has. I'm not sure I know how to process that."

"You deserve nothing but the best."

The waiter comes back and presents the bottle. Once it's opened and assessed, he pours our glasses while telling us the specials. Finley orders the halibut with roasted asparagus and fingerling potatoes. I get the prime rib with mashed potatoes.

I can tell Finley wants to tell the waiter something, but she seems hesitant. That's when I turn to our server and say, "I'd appreciate it if you could make sure the asparagus and potatoes on my date's plate aren't touching each other, or the fish, for that matter."

He looks at me like I'm a controlling lunatic, but at the same time I feel the pressure of Finley's hand as she squeezes my arm. "Thank you," she whispers.

When the waiter walks away, I smile at her. "Any time."

"Tell me more about your parents," Finley says.

I lean back in my chair which causes her hand to slip off my arm. *Darn it.* "My dad is a retired cardiologist. He worked at the same hospital I used to."

"What about your mom?"

"She stayed home and raised my sister and me," I tell her. "While other people had nannies shuttling their kids all around the city for various activities, my mom was determined to be our main caretaker. Her motivation increased when Vivie was diagnosed."

"My mom did the same," she says. "She also tended the garden, the chickens, and canned most of our food for the winter."

I try to imagine my mother gardening and I can't. Our farm fresh food came from the Union Square farmers' market, and our flowers came from the bodega on the corner. "That sounds like a wonderful way to grow up," I tell her.

"It was. I mean, it was all I knew. A lot of my friends had parents who both worked, and while they had more things—you know, vacations, and more clothes—I had a super strong relationship with my mom and dad. I wouldn't have traded that for anything."

"I hope I get to meet your parents someday," I tell her. "I'm looking forward to you meeting mine next week,"

She looks alarmed. "You want me to meet them?"

"I assumed you'd want to see the looks on their faces when I presented them with my calendar."

Finley smirks. "I *would* like to see that, but don't you think it's a little too soon for me to meet them?"

"No," I assure her. Then I tease, "We don't have to introduce you as my fiancée." Her cheeks turn pink, so I add, "You're the reason I'm finally getting back at them, after all."

She seems to relax after that. "We're going to have to finish up your pictures tomorrow if there's any hope of getting the calendar here on time."

"I'll pay to have it shipped overnight, if I have to," I assure her.

The rest of the meal is spent in enjoyable conversation. I share some of my most embarrassing stories, like the time I walked into a street sign when I heard someone call my name; and the time I was on my first date in high school, and I tripped and fell into Bethesda Fountain in Central Park.

I learn that Finley doesn't like hamsters or porcupines. She likes caramel syrup in her hot chocolate, but does not like actual caramel because it's too sticky.

Our meals are delicious and we both clean our plates. For dessert we share a pear galette and a lemon tart. Finley also orders a hot chocolate.

When all our dishes have been cleared, she leans back in her chair and declares, "That was the best meal I've ever had. I'm stuffed."

"It was my favorite in Elk Lake."

"What was your favorite meal ever?"

I don't even have to think about it. "It was a footlong hot dog, pink cotton candy, and a strawberry lemonade. I was ten and my parents took me and my sister to Coney Island."

Finley laughs. "I think maybe your favorite meal has gotten tangled up with your favorite memory."

"That's possible," I tell her. "Although I got pretty sick on Dino's Wonder Wheel. Which was not a great memory."

"What's that?" she wants to know.

"It's a gigantic Ferris wheel. The cars toward the middle slide back and forth while the whole thing spins around. It's the oldest ride at Coney Island," I tell her.

She looks a little green around the gills. "I'm not a huge fan of amusement parks."

"They're very stimulating," I tell her.

Finley's eyebrows knit together. "Does your sister like them?"

"She went for the food," I tell her. "She used to wear her noise canceling headphones, and she'd bring a blanket along. That way she could sit down and throw it over her head. You know, create a sort of sensory deprivation cave?"

"I like to make a cave out of my bedcovers," she says excitedly. "It feels like I'm in the middle of a soft hug."

Finley is nothing short of magnificent. I love finding out about her likes and dislikes. I even find her more peculiar quirks to be charming. Reaching over, I take her hand in mine. "You're a lot of fun to spend time with."

She lowers her eyes to her lap before slowly returning them to my gaze. "So are you."

"What do you say we get out of here and go sit in the main room next to the fireplace?" I ask. When I looked up the lodge online, the website header was a picture of rocking chairs in front of a roaring fire. I can't think of a better place for us to keep the evening going.

"That sounds very romantic," she says. She's blushing again, which is another thing I love about Finley. You know how she's feeling just by looking at her.

After paying the check, I ask the waiter if he would put the vase of flowers out in the lobby so we can collect them easily before we leave. I slip him an extra twenty for his kindness.

As we leave the restaurant, Finley says, "I hope there are chairs available for us."

"There will be," I assure her. I know this because after booking our table at the restaurant, I called the front desk and reserved the two best seats.

Walking into the great room is an enchanting experience. There are love seats and overstuffed chairs all around, creating intimate gathering spots. There's only one chandelier here and it's positively enormous. The flickering lights reflect around the room like a thousand fireflies in the sky, making it feel like you've walked into an enchanted forest.

The far wall consists of a giant vaulted picture window that looks out into the woods. There are several torches burning outside for effect. On the opposite end of the room is a giant stone fireplace that looks big enough to walk into. There are eight rocking chairs situated opposite it. Two of them are empty except for the "reserved" signs hanging over their backs.

"You've thought of everything," Finley says, looking enormously contented.

There's something about her that makes me want to impress her. In the past I've dated women who are nonchalant about everything. They act like they're bored because they've already done everything there is to do. Finley is refreshingly nothing like that.

"I wanted tonight to be special," I tell her while removing the signs.

As we sit down, she says, "I don't think I'll ever go on a date this good again."

"I feel like you've just issued a challenge," I tell her. She stares at me wide-eyed, so I tell her, "I don't want this to be your best date ever. I want you to go on much, much better ones."

Her eyes turn sad. "I'm guessing that's not going to happen. But even if no one ever treats me this nicely again, I will always remember what you did for me."

My heart physically aches at hearing this. "It sounds like you're saying you're not going to go out with me again."

Finley stares at me for the longest time before saying, "I'll go out with you again. I just don't know how many more times after that."

"Did I do something wrong?"

She shakes her head. "I don't think I'm enough to keep you in Elk Lake, Thomas. And when you go back to New York, I don't want you to break my heart."

I don't really know how to respond to that. I can't assure her I'm not going to leave. If my work situation doesn't get better, I won't be happy in my career. Yet I'm enjoying getting to know Finley so much that I'm starting to wonder if I could ever walk away from her.

"One date at a time," I remind her. Then I take her hand in mine and give it a squeeze. "Let's just enjoy each moment as it comes."

"I'll try," she tells me.

But something in her tone makes me nervous.

CHAPTER THIRTY-THREE

FINLEY

Thomas makes me feel like a heroine in a movie, like I've stepped into a romance so fabulous only a screenwriter could create it.

After he dropped me off last night, he walked me up to my apartment and gave me another toe-curling kiss that made me want to succumb to the fantasy of "what if." What if he stays in Elk Lake? What if we go on thirty more dates and fall in love? What if he asks me to marry him? What if we live happily-ever-after?

The problem with the "what if" game is that when you allow yourself to ask all the enticing questions, their counterparts always show up. What if Thomas leaves Elk Lake? What if he breaks my heart? What if I never meet another man who is as good, kind, and caring as he is? What if I die alone and miserable with nothing more than my memories to haunt me?

Even though Thomas and I have only officially been on one date, we've had three meals together and spent many hours shooting in my studio. While some people may think we barely know each other, I feel like I've known him for years. I know some of this has to do with my inability to accurately mark time, but I'm convinced most of it has to do with the quality of our connection.

I roll over in bed and throw a pillow over my head. Relishing the cool silk on my skin, I try to formulate a plan for how to date Thomas without letting myself fall for him. I mull this over for a very long time, but can't seem to figure out how to protect myself from heartache.

I'm tempted to call Allie and talk to her about it, but I'm afraid she'll tell me what she thinks I want to hear, which is, "Of course Thomas is going to stay and you're going to live happily-ever-after!"

I don't need anyone to blow smoke up my skirt. That's one of my mom's favorite sayings. She says it means to tell someone what they want to hear. On impulse, I pick up the phone and call her. "Hellooo, Finny!" She's always so happy to hear from me.

"Hey, Mom," I say glumly.

"You sound rough." Pulling no punches, she asks, "Was the date that bad?"

"Not bad. Good. Very good."

"Oooooh, is he still there?"

"No, Mother, he is not. Thomas dropped me off at my front door like a respectable gentleman."

"That's nice to hear," she says, contradicting the excitement of her previous question.

"He's a wonderful man." I tell her every little detail about our evening and she gushes appropriately.

"When are you going out again?" she asks.

"We're supposed to have another date tonight, but …" I let the remainder of the sentence dangle in the air.

"But, what?" she demands.

"I don't know if we should go out again. Thomas still isn't sure he's going to stay in Elk Lake, and I could really fall for this guy, Mom." I release a pathetic moan before adding, "I don't want him to break my heart."

"Remember what Alfred—Lord Tennyson—said." My mom

loves Tennyson to the point of ridiculousness. She quotes him all the time.

I know exactly which quote she's thinking about, but I'm not ready to agree with her. I intentionally guess wrong. "Knowledge comes but wisdom lingers?" I figure that's as close a one as I'm going to get to support what I'm feeling.

"You know which one I'm talking about, Finny." Then she says the words I dread hearing, "Tis better to have loved and lost than to have never loved at all."

I kick off my fuzzy socks and feel the cold sheets against my feet. Then I tell her, "If you've never loved, you don't know what you're missing. Therefore, you can't be sad to have lost it."

"Balderdash!" Ah, another one of her nineteenth century words. She continues, "If you've never loved, you will *always* know you've missed out on something big."

"But if you find out how great love is and then lose it, you'll mourn its loss forever," I tell her.

"Finny, life isn't for the faint of heart. You've already come through a lot and you've made a nice life for yourself. But there is so much more. I want you to experience all of it."

"I want that for myself, too, Mom. I'm just not sure I have the kind of courage it takes to go for it."

"Says the girl who's met every challenge life has thrown at her." I know she's trying to motivate me, but it's not working.

"I've struggled, Mom."

"Everyone struggles, Finny. *Everyone.* You're not special in that."

I hate feeling defeated because I've worked very hard not to be that person. It's just that I've never felt I've had as much to lose as I currently do. So, I tell her, "Other people have more options than I do."

"How do you figure?"

"They can live in places I can't. They can do things I can't. Don't pretend you don't know what I'm talking about."

"Honey, everyone has their stuff. At some point you've got to just throw it all against the wall. I promise, something will stick."

She's used this metaphor my whole life. It originates with old Italian women who used to throw cooked spaghetti against the wall to see if it was done. If it stuck, it was time to eat. It's not my favorite saying because, you know, sticky stuff. But Mom loves it.

I'm silent for a moment before telling her, "I'll think about it."

"While you're doing that, dear," she says, "Remind yourself why you called *me*. You knew what I was going to tell you. You knew I was going to encourage you to open yourself up to possibility." Before she hangs up, she adds, "I love you, honey. You've got this."

I suppose she might be right. The reason I called her instead of Allie is that my friend would have told me what I wanted to hear, regardless if she thought it might really happen. Girlfriends do that for each other, not because we want our friends to get hurt, but because we want them to enjoy the dream even if the dream might never come to fruition.

My mom, on the other hand, would never lie to me to protect my feelings. If she thought going for Thomas was going to be bad for me, she'd tell me. But that's not what she said. She said that even if it doesn't work out in the end, the experience might just be rewarding enough to make the journey worth my while. And it will never happen if I don't give it a chance.

I have a lot to think about.

I'm about to get out of bed and get ready for my shoot with Thomas today when my phone rings. Speak of the devil …

"Hello?" I say in my most seductive voice.

"Hello, yourself," he croons.

I feel a dipping sensation in the pit of my stomach like I just sped over a bump in the road at a hundred miles an hour. My dad used to call this experience "belly ticklers." While he never went too much over the speed limit, he went fast enough to give us a thrill.

"I had a wonderful time last night," I tell him.

"Me, too. But that's not why I'm calling." He sounds upset.

"Are you okay?" I ask, worried he's having doubts, too.

"We have two doctors out sick, which means that instead of having a day off, I need to pull a double. I won't be able to do our shoot or go on our date. I'm really sorry."

"I'm disappointed," I tell him. "But you have to do what you have to do."

"It looks like I might be living at the hospital for a few days," he says. "Would you mind going through the pictures we have, and cobble together enough looks for a calendar?"

"I'd be happy to," I tell him. "In fact, I'll go ahead and lay it out and put in the order. That way you don't have to worry about approving anything."

"You're the best, Finley. Thank you so much."

"Call me later, if you get a chance," I tell him.

"I will," he promises. Before hanging up, he says, "I can't wait to see you again."

I snuggle back under the covers. As my morning has just opened up, I don't need to rush into work. Maybe I'll study for my driving test. After that I'll think more about what my mom said. As much as I want to listen to her and just go for it, I'm still not sure that is going to be in my best interest.

I feel another pros and cons list coming on …

CHAPTER THIRTY-FOUR

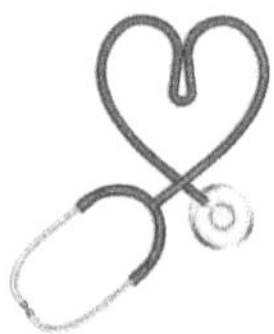

THOMAS

I feel terrible about lying to Finley; no one called in sick at work this morning. But something significant did happen, and I'm going to need time to figure out how I'm going to respond to it.

My alarm had just gone off, and I was about to get out of bed when my phone rang. I thought it might have been Finley, which is why I didn't bother looking at the caller ID before answering. It wasn't her though. It was the CEO of my old hospital.

As soon as I said hello in my sexiest voice—which I'm sure threw him for a loop—I heard, "Thomas, this is Randolph Collins. How are you doing out there in Wisconsin?" Wisconsin is said as though synonymous with the wilds of the Yukon Territory. Which in fairness to a New Yorker, it kind of feels that way.

Randolph Collins is the last person I expected to hear from, and it knocked me sideways for a moment. I told him I was fine, which of course is not the complete truth. But there was no way I was going to tell the CEO of my previous hospital that I might have made a mistake by leaving them.

The next words out of his mouth were a complete shock. "I'd like to make you an offer, Thomas." When I didn't respond right away, he went ahead and made me that offer. *Chief Medical Officer at my old stomping grounds.* It's a position I had hoped to get by the time I was fifty. And it was being presented to me fourteen years ahead of schedule.

I listened to Randolph's complete pitch, full-on with details of a sizable salary increase and enhanced benefits. I didn't say no. Instead, I told him I'd have to think about it. Which is what I'm currently doing.

Returning to New York means going back to an extremely hectic life. But the thing with being chief is that it's a largely administrative position. I'd still get to weigh in on treatments, but I wouldn't be seeing patients myself. I'd be the guy who made sure everything ran the way it was supposed to, from daily operations, quality patient care, and crisis management, to more mundane areas like the budget. I'd get to have all my fingers in the pie so there would be no chance of getting bored and even less risk of burning out by doing the same thing on repeat.

Had this offer been made before I left New York, I probably would have never moved to Wisconsin. But I did move, and then I met Finley.

It's outrageous to think I would turn down my dream job for a woman I've only been on one date with. Complete lunacy. But I don't feel like she's someone I just met. She feels like she's been in my life forever. Most accurately, she feels like someone who *should* be in my life forever.

The angel on my shoulder says, "There's no accounting for love, Thomas."

The devil on the other side shouts, "You don't love her! You've only been on one date. This is your dream job, man!"

Back to the angel: "Love is wonderful and mysterious, and it does not come around every day, Thomas."

The devil flipped her the bird in response.

I remember how I preached to Finley about taking things one step at a time. And while I still believe that in theory, the problem is that I now have more impetus than ever to go home.

Also, I gave her that spiel when I saw myself stuck here until my contract ended. But now, even if I can't break my contract with cause—i.e. proving that Constance is behaving unprofessionally—with the help of New York Presbyterian, I should still be able to get out of it.

I'm afraid seeing Finley today might keep me from making the right decision for my career. I like her so much that if I stayed here, I really could see us having a future together. The question is, would being with her be enough compensation to stay in an unfulfilling job?

I've got to talk to someone, but the person I feel closest to in town is the person at the very heart of my conundrum, Finley. Getting up, I put on my robe and slippers before walking downstairs and leaving the house. I tromp over to the neighbors' and knock on the door.

Shelly greets me with a smile. Then she looks me up and down before asking, "What do you need? Coffee? Creamer?" *Because why else would I show up in my pajamas?*

"Advice," I tell her.

"Kevin's already left," she says. "You want me to give it a try?"

"Sure," I tell her. Seeking the counsel of someone I don't know that well might seem imprudent, but who else do I have? I can't talk to anyone at my current hospital. I can't talk to my parents because they would both do backflips at the thought of my coming home. I might be able to discuss this with Vivie, but she also would love it if I moved back to New York.

So, here I am sitting at Shelly's kitchen table. Without asking, she pours me a cup of coffee. Then she hands me the mug and demands, "What's up?"

I spend the next twenty minutes telling her everything, including how I'm starting to feel about a certain beautiful photographer in town.

My neighbor purses her lips together tightly while tapping the tabletop like she's sending an urgent message in Morse code. She finally asks, "How was your dating life in New York?"

I make a so-so motion with my hand. "I went out, but I never met anyone I could see a future with."

"And you can see that with Finley?"

Reason rears its ugly head and forces me to say, "We've only been on one date."

"Don't try to get out of answering the question, Thomas. Yes or no are the only words I want to hear out of your mouth."

"One date, Shelly."

She shakes her head. "That doesn't matter. What's your gut telling you? Do you see yourself with gorgeous blond-haired, green-eyed babies whose mother won't let them chew gum because the snapping sound drives her crazy?"

I didn't know gum chewing annoyed Finley, but I'm not surprised. "I sense a story here," I tell her.

"Kevin was chewing gum during one of the grands' photo sessions and Finley kicked him out of the studio."

I would have loved to have seen that.

Shelly takes a swig from her coffee and then slams the mug down loudly. "Answer the question, Thomas. Do your future children look like Finley?"

"You're kind of scaring me, Shelly."

"People who are afraid are more apt to tell the truth." She says this like a CIA operative in the middle of waterboarding a spy from the enemy camp.

"Everything I say here is confidential, right?" I ask.

As she nods her head, the sharp peak of bedhead on top bobs with the force. "Of course," she says. "Neighbor to neighbor confidentiality."

In that case, I tell her, "I don't have a hard time envisioning my future children looking like Finley." I still feel the need to add, "But we've only officially been out once."

"Psh!" She waggles a finger at me. "Why don't you take the

job and continue to date Finley long distance? If things go well, she might be interested in moving to New York."

I shake my head. "She won't. She's already told me she'll never live in a big city."

"Crap." Shelly sounds as disappointed as I am.

"Are you sure you hate your job here?

"Pretty sure," I tell her. "I have a difficult boss and I'm bored."

Shelly stands up and starts to pace across the linoleum. Once she hits the far wall, she stops and reiterates, "On one hand, you've met a wonderful woman." She starts moving again and when she arrives at the opposite wall, she raises her other hand. "On the other hand, you've been offered your dream job back in New York."

Sitting back down, she asks, "Would you ever consider doing something else?"

"Shelly," I tell her, "It took eleven years and four hundred thousand dollars to get me to this point. I don't think a career shift is an option."

"I guess I can see that." She starts drumming her fingers on the table again. Then she stands up abruptly and announces, "I can't help you." Shaking her head, she adds, "I'm sorry, Thomas. This is something you need to figure out for yourself."

I slowly push myself back up to my feet. "I appreciate you hearing me out. Let me know if a solution comes to you."

"Will do," she says while walking me to the front door. "You want me to ask Kevin about it when he gets home?"

"Why not?" I say. Not that I think he'll have a solution, but at this point I've got nothing to lose.

I usually do my best thinking in the shower, which is why I go home and take the longest and hottest one of my life. I don't get any insights, which leads me to conclude this is an unsolvable problem.

As a last resort I drive down to the lake. Maybe a walk on the beach will bring miraculous insights. I park in the same spot Finley and I parked the other night. Then I hike a short distance until my feet hit the sand. Sitting on a rock, I take off my shoes and socks and let my toes sink into the cold depths.

Leaning my head back, I offer up a plea in case anyone in the Great Beyond is listening. "I could really use some help here." After uttering my prayer, my eyes pop open and look around half-expecting a bolt of lightning to slice through the sky, bringing the answer I need. Yeah, that doesn't happen.

Instead, I look out onto the lake and spot a boat heading toward shore. It's moving fast like it's on a mission. When it nears the dock, it slows down and I watch as the driver ties it off. Then two people get out and walk right toward me.

One of them raises his hand and calls out, "Thomas! We were just talking about you ..."

CHAPTER THIRTY-FIVE

FINLEY

I feel bad that Thomas has to work. What a champ though, doing a double on his day off. I suppose that's how it is for doctors. There are only so many of them, and when someone's sick, whoever is left must take over.

I kind of feel sorry for myself, too. I was really looking forward to seeing Thomas today. And I know he was excited about finishing our photo shoots. Instead of enjoying some free time at home, like I thought I might, I decide to go into work and get started on his calendar.

Once I arrive at Happy Snaps, I turn on the computer and immediately start a new file titled "Revenge." Then I drag Thomas's best shots into it. From there, I'll whittle them down according to which month they'll fit best.

Because we'll be a couple of looks shy, I'll have to double up. I figure I can run two or three duplicate photos through photoshop and make small adjustments. Like I can add a Santa hat to make it suitable for December, and I can add an Uncle Sam top hat to one for July.

I spend the better part of an hour putting together a fabulous layout that's as good as any professional calendar I've seen. I don't doubt it would sell like hotcakes on the open market, but as a revenge tool, it's a work of art. I'm immensely proud of the results and can't wait to show them off.

Being that I don't have any other appointments today, I decide to head over to Rosemary's to pick up some treats. I'll deliver them to the hospital to Thomas as a booby prize for having to go into work. Just the thought of seeing him sends a shiver up my spine.

I grab my purse and coat before locking up. Then I practically float down the street. Maybe my mom is right, and I should let myself fall in love without worrying how it will turn out. After all, there are no sure things in life. I could get hit by a bus right now. I briefly glance around to make sure I'm not in any imminent danger.

I walk into Rosemary's, full of excitement that I'm going to see the man who makes me feel all tingly just thinking about him. Faith waves when she spots me. "Good morning. You look pretty today."

I look down at my third favorite sweater. I've paired it with boring blue jeans and boots, but I'm wearing new soft pink socks, so my feet are happy. "Thank you," I tell her before declaring, "I need a bunch of your best goodies."

"How many do you want?" she wants to know.

"Maybe a dozen?" I reply. Then I tell her, "I'm taking them to a friend."

"Lucky friend," she says with a grin before assembling a collapsed box. She picks up individual pieces of parchment and starts selecting items from the case in front of her. When she's done, she asks, "Anything for you?"

I order a hot chocolate and a ginger scone. After paying, I retrieve my purchases and tell Faith, "You're making at least two people very happy today." I'm guessing more because I'm sure Thomas will share at work.

It's raining when I leave the bakery, which once again makes me glad I've decided to learn to drive. If I already knew how I wouldn't be facing a soggy six-block trek to the hospital and then another five back to my shop. Maybe Thomas can take a break, and we can have a little chat while I wait for the rain to stop. Or if I'm lucky, he might even drive me home.

Kicking into gear, I practically jog the whole way to the hospital. I'm only partially drenched by the time I get there. My raincoat has kept my body dry, but my feet are cold and soaked and so is my hair. I should have stopped at my shop to get an umbrella, but I was so excited to see Thomas I talked myself out of it.

I tell the woman at the information stand who I'm there to see. She clicks away on her computer before saying, "I'm sorry, Dr. Culpepper isn't working. It's his day off."

"It *was* his day off," I assure her. "But a couple of people called in sick. He's covering their shifts."

Her eyebrows furrow in response. "I suppose that's possible, but I'm not showing he's here." Pointing down the hallway, she adds, "Why don't you go and check in at the ER? If he's on duty, they'll know."

I follow the signs to the emergency room and then I wait behind a person practically coughing up a lung. Reaching over to the countertop, I grab a mask and put it on to protect myself. When it's my turn, I tell the man behind the glass, "I'm here to drop something off for Dr. Culpepper."

He barely looks up from his computer. "Dr. Culpepper isn't in today. But if you'd like to leave it, I can make sure he gets it tomorrow."

Hot prickles stab at the top of my head, which is how my nervous system reacts to unexpected news. "Are you sure?" I ask.

"I'm sure," he says curtly.

Why would Thomas cancel our shoot and *our date and lie about having to go into work?* It doesn't make any sense. I thought he was really looking forward to seeing me today. At least that's what he said. A wave of hurt the likes I haven't felt since high school swamps me.

Turning around, I walk away from the check-in area to find a chair to sit down on. If I don't, I might collapse onto what I'm assuming is a floor riddled with a wide variety of antibiotic-resistant germs.

I find a small bench far away from other people and remove my mask. Then I open my hot chocolate and take a sip. I barely taste a thing. Picking up my phone, I text Thomas.

ME

I was thinking about stopping by the hospital to bring you a treat. Are you free?

He texts back immediately.

THOMAS

You are very sweet, but we're totally swamped.

Thomas is lying to my face. Or rather, he's lying through his phone, which is connected to my phone, which is lying to my face. *Why is he lying?*

So, I type …

ME

You could meet me outside and grab it. That way you can enjoy your goodies when you have a break.

THOMAS

I wish I could, but there's so much going on, I'm probably not even going to get lunch today.

My eyes fill with tears as I look around the room. There can't be more than a half-dozen people waiting to be seen. *Is it possible that I've completely misread the signals?* Yet, I can't imagine how that could be. Thomas did kiss me, and it was no peck, either.

ME

Let me know if it lightens up and I'll stop by then.

I briefly consider throwing the box of treats away, but even in my despair that seems like an awful waste. Especially as I suddenly need some comfort for myself.

Not sure of my destination, I find the nearest exit and walk back out into the rain. Instead of returning to work I decide to go home. By the time I get there, I look like a drowned cat.

Once again I torment myself wondering why Thomas would tell me he can't wait to see me today only to make up an excuse not to. As if I wasn't uneasy enough about following my mom's advice. The advice I'm now going to ignore. Another favorite saying of hers is, "When someone tells you who they are, believe them." And Thomas just told me loud and clear that he can't be trusted.

I take off my dripping raincoat and hang it up to dry. Then I take the box from Rosemary's and go into the bathroom. Before I completely lose it, I fill up my tub with my best bubble bath—the one that's reserved for mood stabilization.

After setting up the box of pastries on the floor nearby—I'm going to take at least one bite of each—I take off my clothes and step into the rose-scented foam. I need to devise a plan how best to manage this situation. And the way I see it, I only have two options.

The first is to not confront Thomas. This is probably the option I should go with being that we've only been out on one date. Maybe he had a good reason to lie to me. Perhaps he's having a mole removed and doesn't want me to worry. Or he might be setting up a surprise for me. I suppose it's even possible he's as confused as I am about what to do regarding us and he's taking some "me" time to think things over.

But then righteous indignation floods my brain and leads me to my second option which is confrontation. I'm not usually a person who relishes conflict, and when I'm faced with it, my brain short-circuits. My black and white world does not understand variations of truth. You're either honest or you're not. The end.

Tears fill my eyes as I contemplate Thomas's betrayal. We had so much fun last night. SO much. He must have spent a fortune on dinner and flowers. He hung on my every word like it was gospel. He held my hand and kissed me. He made me feel more special than any man ever has, and now he's taken that all away.

I replay our evening word for word, trying to figure out where I went wrong, but I can't. Even when I expressed concerns about what kind of future we could have, he continued to assure me everything would work out.

That's when it hits me: maybe he's a compulsive liar. I try to convince myself that the problem is with him and not me. But I'm not sure I'm successful.

I do know one thing though. I'm starting to feel like I might need a little revenge of my own. I do not appreciate being played for a fool, and in addition to being very sad right now, I also feel enormously foolish.

CHAPTER THIRTY-SIX

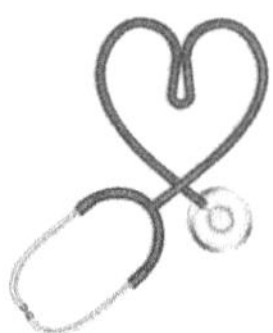

THOMAS

I stand up when I see Kevin walking toward me. "Hey, neighbor," I say. "I stopped by your house this morning for a chat."

"I'm sorry I wasn't there, Tommy." He's wearing a dirty pair of overalls that look like they've seen better days.

That's when I recognize the man he's with. It's Dr. Hall from the hospital. "Edward," I say to him, "It's nice to see you again."

He nods his head. "You too, son." Then he adds, "Pickles and I were just doing a little fishing."

The use of Kevin's nickname catches me off guard. These two must be old friends. "Did you catch anything?" I ask.

Kevin answers for him. "We got a mess of walleye. I was going to bring some by for you later."

"I'm not sure I'd know how to clean a fish," I tell him honestly. "Maybe I can YouTube it."

He waves his hand. "Don't worry, I'll clean it for you."

"That's very nice Kevin, thank you."

"You gotta call me Pickles, boy," he says. "Every time you call me Kevin, I feel like I'm being called into the principal's office."

Dr. Hall jokes with him, "Remember that time we got called in for putting a dead fish behind the radiator?" The two of them laugh like little boys.

"You guys go way back, huh?" I ask.

"We grew up next door to each other," Kevin says. "Eddie here lived in the house you're renting."

"Really? Does your family still own it?" I ask him.

"My sister Judy does," he tells me.

"Does she live in town, as well?" I haven't met her, but I'm not surprised as she listed the house with a realtor.

"She's retired down to Florida. She comes up and spends Christmas with us, but other than that, we don't see much of her."

"Yet." Kevin nudges him in the ribs. "Now that you're going to retire yourself, you'll be seeing her bunches."

"You're retiring?" I ask Edward. He doesn't even look sixty yet.

"My wife wants me to stop working while I'm still young enough for the two of us to have some fun," he says. "I figure she might be on to something."

"Good for you," I tell him. I hope I'm as lucky someday.

Kevin interjects, "Why did you stop by the house?"

I glance between him and Edward and stammer, "I … um … just wanted some advice."

"Why don't we all head over to the tackle shop for some tater tots and we can chat?" He nudges Dr. Hall and adds, "Two heads are better than one, am I right?"

I really don't know if I want to tell Edward about this. Not only don't I know him well, but he's in the same field I'm in. I'd hate for him to spill the tea and alert the hospital board what's going on. Although, nothing is definitive so they can't be mad at me for considering an offer.

Edward senses my hesitancy because he's quick to say, "Or you and Pickles can go yourselves. No skin off my nose."

"You know what?" I decide, "Let's all go. I bet you'd have some good insights for me, Edward." He smiles appreciatively.

I walk next to the two older men in pursuit of a solution to my problem. Because honestly, I've got no one else.

By the time we reach Hook, Line, and Sinker, I'm feeling a little more optimistic about my choice of counselors. I discover both men have been married for over thirty-five years and they both consider themselves happily hitched, as they put it. I knew this was the case for Kevin, but I learn Edward is equally contented.

Kevin opens the door of the rickety-looking bait shop and immediately calls out, "Three buckets of tots, Frankie, hold the worms!" *Gross.*

A hefty older man around Kevin and Edward's age walks out from the back room. He's wearing an apron that is either dirty from cooking or dirty from worms. I can't tell which. "Pickles, Eddie! How you boys doin'?"

Kevin turns to me and explains, "Frankie has been part of our gang since we were in diapers."

I try to imagine how these seemingly very different men have managed to stay close friends. I guess a lot of that has to do with proximity. They all stayed in the town they grew up in so it's easier to assume the disparity of their life choices didn't cause major disruption to their friendship.

Kevin declares, "Our friend Tommy here needs our help, Frankie. So, get those tots and let's see what we can do for him." Great, now I have three old guys weighing in on my life.

Kevin and Edward lead the way to a small table in the corner of the shop. They sit down and motion for me to do the same. Edward asks, "So how's life treating you, Thomas?"

"That's kind of what I wanted to talk about," I tell them.

Before I can explain, Frankie comes out with three small buckets of tots. He arrives quickly which makes me wonder if he made them before we got here. After setting them on the table, he pulls up another chair to join us. Frankie must sense my hesitancy regarding the food, because he declares, "We use different buckets for the worms."

My companions dig in, but I don't. Instead, I tell them, "I've met a very nice woman here."

"Finley?" Kevin asks. When I nod my head, he tells the other men, "That sweet gal from Happy Snaps." They grunt in what appears to be approval.

I continue, "But I'm having a tough time adjusting to life in Elk Lake. It's very different from what I'm used to."

"I bet," Edward says while reaching for a handful of tots.

"Also," I tell them, "I just received an offer from my old hospital and I'm not sure I can turn it down."

"And you want to know what to do about Finley?" Kevin asks.

"Exactly," I tell him.

We bat around the same ideas that Shelly and I did. There are no new insights. That is, until Edward asks, "Have you given any consideration to going into private practice?"

"I haven't," I tell him. "I've been an ER doctor from the start."

"But you weren't happy doing that in New York *or* Elk Lake. Maybe it's time to try another area of medicine."

He's not wrong. "But don't you get bored?" I ask him.

"Not at all. I have a full roster of patients. Like I told you the other day, as their primary care doctor, I get to know them well. I get to know their families, too. It's very rewarding."

"But I don't really know anyone here yet," I say. "I don't know how I'd even get started in private practice."

"Lucky for you, you know a doctor who's about to retire and is going to need to sell his practice."

I feel a jolt of something shoot through me. I'm not sure if it's good or bad yet. "I wouldn't want to take over for you and then decide I don't mesh with being a primary care doctor," I tell him.

Edward nods his head. "You'd want to take some time to come in and shadow me," he says. "I'd give it a couple of weeks to make sure you get a good idea of what I do."

"Except I have a job at the hospital," I tell him. "I'm not sure where I would find the time."

Edward leans back in his chair and stretches his arms

before saying, "Armie Bader is a good friend of mine." *Of course, he is.* This whole town seems to be connected in one way or another.

"And?" I prompt.

Edward continues, "He told me what's going on with Constance." He suddenly leans in before saying, "He'll let you out of your contract if you don't sue them."

"I wasn't going to sue them," I tell him. "I just wanted the harassment to stop."

Kevin interrupts, "Who's harassing you, boy?"

"Constance Brucker," Edward answers for me. All three men grumble like they're hep to that gossip as well.

"Even if it stops," Edward says, "you said you're bored, so corralling Constance will only solve half your troubles." He's right about that.

"So, what are you saying?" My brain is completely jumbled, I need Edward to spell things out more clearly.

"I'm saying you give your notice at the hospital—sign whatever nondisclosures they require—and then you give me a couple of weeks. If you aren't happy with my practice, you go back to New York."

"And give up dating Finley?" The thought hurts more than it should given our brief association.

"What else are you gonna do, Tommy?" Kevin asks. "You gotta work."

"If I do this," I say, "I'm going to need the three of you to stay quiet about it. I don't want Finley to find out what's going on until I've made my decision."

"Don't want to get her hopes up, huh?" Frankie asks.

"I just want to keep getting to know her normally without her calling an end to things too soon."

"Sounds like you want to string her along." Kevin doesn't sound pleased.

I exhale loudly. "That's not it. I just want to have time to get to know her better." I explain, "If I'm still unsure about private practice in a couple of weeks, how I feel about Finley might help to tip my decision."

"Even if we keep quiet," Edward says, "Elk Lake is a small town. Word has a way of getting out."

"While that's possible," I tell him, "I'll talk to Armie and see if we can't keep this on the down low for a couple of weeks."

My fellow plotters don't look convinced. Kevin eventually says, "I think you should just tell Finley what's going on."

And while he's probably right, I've come to know her well enough that I'm afraid if I do that, she'll simply shut me out. "I've already told her I might leave Elk Lake," I tell them. "And she's agreed to take things one date at a time."

Frankie's eyes narrow like he's trying to focus on a dust particle. "It's sounds like you're playing with a live grenade, kid." He explains, "Women say one thing, but they usually mean something else. For example, if you've had an argument and you're pretty sure you've worked it out, you can be certain she doesn't feel the same way."

"Frankie's divorced," Kevin interjects.

Frankie waves his hand in front of himself dismissively. "If you ask your lady if she's okay, and she says she's fine, run."

"Why, exactly?" I ask.

"They're never fine when they use that word. Fine means, 'I'm done talking to an idiot like you and if you say one more thing, I'm going to end you.'"

"It means all that?" I'm guessing Frankie's divorce wasn't amicable.

"Oh, yeah," he says.

Edward jumps into the conversation. "Don't scare the boy, Frankie. Just because Elaine and you didn't work doesn't mean everyone is destined for misery."

Frankie replies, "Women are masters at battle, Eddie. Tommy here needs to know that."

I'm not sure about his advice, but I am sure that Edward might have just offered me a lifeline by suggesting private practice. And even though I've never considered it before, that doesn't mean it isn't the answer to my current troubles.

"I appreciate you all taking the time to talk to me," I tell my cohorts. Then I turn to Edward, and add, "I'd love to come into your office and see what it's all about. I have to talk to Armie first, of course."

He nods his head. "You do that, son. Just give me a call when you're ready and we'll set things up."

I've had more life changes in the last two weeks than in the last two years. Which makes me wonder if I might have been destined to come to Elk Lake. And if that's the case, then surely Finley plays a large part in that.

I still want to think about things for a few days before I see her again. Hopefully my head will be clear enough by then that I'll be on track to make the right decision.

CHAPTER THIRTY-SEVEN

FINLEY

It has been forty days since I've heard from Thomas. Okay, it's only been four, but in my world, that doesn't mean the same thing as it does for other people. I'm starting to think the date we went on was a figment of my imagination. There's no way we had the great time I thought we did only for him to ghost me. I know I don't always perceive things the way other people do, but I'm not a different species for Pete's sake. I do possess basic human comprehension.

Anger has replaced sadness after finding out Thomas lied about having to work. Especially after not hearing from him except for two small texts saying how busy he's been. As such, I made a few minor changes to his calendar. And by minor, I mean I completely revamped it to suit my burgeoning disappointment in him.

"Finley, yoohoo, you in there?" Margaret snaps her fingers in front of my face to get my attention.

I turn to my client in time to see that she's changed into her jungle costume. Bob is standing behind her similarly attired, the boot on his broken foot camouflaged by a large fig leaf. "I'm sorry," I tell her. "I'm a little distracted."

"No kidding." She reaches out and squeezes my arm reassuringly. "You want to take a raincheck and do this another time, honey?"

Bailing on Margaret and Bob would be the pinnacle of unprofessionalism. But then again, so would taking bad pictures of them. "I would hate to disappoint you," I tell her.

"Don't you worry about us," Margaret says. "Bob and I have been binge-watching *Bridgerton* on television. We'd be just as happy to go home and do that."

Bob raises his hand behind his wife, and confirms, "It's getting really good!"

"In that case," I tell them, "I think I'd do a better job for you on another day. I'm just not feeling like myself lately."

"Man troubles?" Margaret asks.

I'm not up to explaining, so I simply nod my head.

"You let me know if you need an ear," Margaret says.

"Thanks," I tell her. "You guys are the best." Allie's mom and dad have become like surrogate parents to me. I appreciate them more than I have words for.

While they get changed back into their street clothes, I check my messages in case today is the day I finally hear from Thomas. I'm not exactly holding my breath so imagine my surprise when I see his message.

THOMAS

I'm sorry I haven't gotten in touch with you sooner. Work has been crazy busy. Can I stop by later today and pick up the calendar?

What work? I've called the ER every day that I haven't spoken to him, and according to them, *Dr. Culpepper has been out sick.* If that were the case, there wouldn't be any reason for him to keep it secret. In fact, one might argue it would be common courtesy to give me a heads up. We did kiss after all, *on the lips.*

For reference, when I called, I wasn't actually going to talk to Thomas. I was going to hang up as soon as I knew he was there. Which leads me to wonder where he's been spending his days and who he's been spending them with. Could he have reconsidered Constance Brucker's interest in him?

I stare at Thomas's text for a long time before responding.

ME

It's supposed to come in later this afternoon.
Why don't I drop it off at your house?

I know his family is supposed to arrive today, and even though he claimed he wanted me to meet them, he hasn't bothered re-stating those intentions. And now, more than ever, I want to see their reaction to Thomas's calendar. I want to witness firsthand how I've spoiled his vengeance. And while there's a tiny little part of me that feels bad for doing what I'm doing, the bigger part of me feels it's a completely warranted reaction.

THOMAS

I guess that would be fine. Are you still up to meeting my family? If not, I could swing by and get the calendar from you later.

It sounds like that's what he'd prefer, but I don't care what he wants right now. His desires no longer hold any importance for me.

ME

I can't wait. Can I bring anything?

THOMAS

That won't be necessary. I'm going to take them to supper afterwards.

I'm going to take them to supper. Not *we're* all going to supper. It looks like I'm not included which once again makes it clear that I don't mean anything to him. *What happened after our date that caused Thomas to change his tune and start treating me like garbage?* I suppose I'm glad I got to know his true character before I gave him the opportunity to break my heart—which while not yet broken, has certainly been smacked around.

I force myself to try to remain nonchalant and unaffected.

ME

Where are you taking them?

THOMAS

I thought we might go to the lodge. You and I had such a such a nice evening there.

I thought so too, but I'm starting to think we were on two different dates.

ME

What time would you like me to stop by?

THOMAS

How about five? I really can't wait to see their reaction to all our hard work.

He adds a trail of laughing emojis that makes me feel deviously proud of myself. Little does he know how hard I worked to sabotage his plan.

ME

Send me your address and I'll be there.

It seems strange that I don't even know where Thomas lives. Last week I felt like I'd known him my whole life, and now he feels like a total stranger to me. My heart once again clenches painfully.

Maybe I'm not meant to date. Maybe there is no happy ending for me. Perhaps my sole purpose in life is to capture other people's joy while never getting to experience it for myself.

If that's true and I'm destined to be alone and lonely, then I really want to make the most out of my revenge against Thomas.

CHAPTER THIRTY-EIGHT

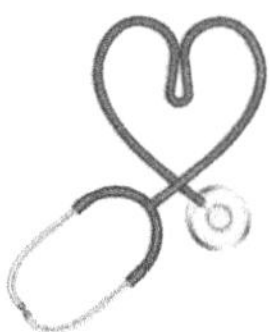

THOMAS

I feel bad I haven't been in touch with Finley more since I canceled our second date. I should have at least called her, but I was afraid I'd say more than I should. Even so, getting to know her better is a big part of my decision about whether I want to stay in Elk Lake. Which makes me doubly excited to see her tonight.

I had originally thought I'd introduce Finley to my parents as a love interest, but now that my future is so uncertain, I think it's best to just say she's my friend, even though Vivie knows the truth about her.

Armie Bader was remarkably receptive to my ending my employment at the hospital. I'm guessing he might have even been relieved because he assured me there were no hard feelings. He also mentioned he would personally choose my replacement. In the meantime, he's hired a traveling doctor to fill in for me.

I'm not going to tell my parents I've left my job. They would take my discontent as a sure sign that I should come home, and I don't need the extra pressure.

I've had a great few days with Edward. Strangely, I don't find what he does boring. It's not like he sees a bunch of patients with exotic illnesses, either. It's primarily been ailments like the flu, eczema, and strep throat, with a few others sent out for additional testing. The same conditions in a hospital setting would have bored me to tears, but it really is different here.

To keep rumors at bay, Edward has introduced me as his associate. I realized it would be a lot easier for gossip to spread if my full name were used, which is why he refers to me as Dr. T. I haven't interacted with the patients a lot. I mostly sit back and watch Edward do his thing. Which is quite impressive.

He doesn't rush his people through, like we do in the hospital. Instead, he chats with them about their lives and their families. He small talks about things going on in town, and he's even offered dining recommendations. Only then does he perform a physical exam.

He told me that by starting out slowly, people are less anxious about why they're at the doctor's office. He shared that those who get nervous, and have higher blood pressure readings because of it, will have more accurate readings after a nice chat. Patients who are inclined to embellish their symptoms suddenly don't.

Edward very wisely told me that people just want to be seen and heard. He said that a lot of them come to a doctor before medical intervention is needed simply to feel like someone cares. He gives them that before tending to their complaints.

One woman told Edward she'd not been feeling well since her husband died eight months earlier. Edward assured her, "We'll do all the necessary tests to find out if there's a problem." Then he added, "But grief hurts. Not just emotionally, it can cause real physical pain."

Helen, his patient, seemed relieved to hear this. She told Edward, "My world stopped spinning when John died, but everyone else just keeps moving forward."

"It doesn't seem right, does it?" he asked.

She simply burst into tears. "I don't expect everyone to feel as badly as I do, but most of our friends have stopped checking in.

Even our kids have kept living like the most devastating thing in the world didn't just happen to me."

"Everyone mourns differently," Edward told her. "Just because they don't show it on the outside doesn't mean they aren't grieving, too."

After he examined Helen, he assured her that her physical health looked great, but he told her that her emotional health needed tending to. Most doctors would have probably told her she was fine and sent her on her merry way. But Edward gave Helen a referral to a counselor, he offered her suggestions about attending a support group, and he even advised she talk to her pastor. Then he excused himself and went to his office.

When he came back, he was carrying a small white bag. In it was a large ginger snap he'd bought at Rosemary's that morning. He gave it to Helen and told her, "They're not magic, but they're pretty great." Then he winked at her and said, "Do nice things for yourself while you grieve, Helen. You're worth it."

She left the building with a smile on her face. Not because she was suddenly happy but because Edward took the time to validate her feelings. He showed her that he cared. He *saw* her and it was a beautiful thing to witness.

I'm only going in for half a day today because I want to get to the store and fill up the house with food for my family. I don't feel secure enough on the highway to pick them up at the airport myself—not that there would be enough room in my car. Instead, I hired Kevin next door to collect them. I can only imagine what my mom is going to think when she gets a load of his old Cadillac.

I leave work later than I had planned because our last patient had a very questionable looking lump in his throat. Edward called a colleague who's an ear, nose, and throat specialist to see him right away.

Once the man left, Edward told me, "I'd bet my left foot it's cancer."

We talked for over an hour about how hard it is when people get a bad diagnosis. Unlike my job in the ER—where we see patients and then either admit them or send them home—Edward continues to track his patients' journeys. Even when they're referred to specialists, he stays on their case. I can see why he finds his job so rewarding.

On my way from Edward's clinic to the grocery store, I see Finley walking down the street. Pulling over, I give the horn a brief tap to get her attention. She doesn't even stop and look. Hurrying to park, I get out and call, "Finley!"

Again, she ignores me. I wonder if she has earbuds in or something. Jogging over to her, I touch her arm and say, "Hey, you. Long time no see."

She stops walking but she doesn't turn in my direction. Instead, with her back to me, she responds, "I've been in the same place I've always been."

Uh-oh, I'm in the doghouse. "I'm sorry I haven't called but I've been super busy at work," I tell her. "I've missed seeing you."

That causes her to spin around so quickly she almost loses her balance. Regaining her footing, she looks at me and demands, "Really?"

"Yes." I have no idea what's going on with her, but whatever it is, it's making me nervous. "I've been burning the candle at both ends."

I'm about to explain the idiom means, when she snaps, "I know what it means."

This is certainly not how I thought it would go when I saw Finley again. She's really mad at me. Other than my not talking to her for a few days, I can't imagine why. And even then, I told her I was going to be busy this week.

I decide a change of subject is in order. "So how does the calendar look? Is it amazing? Can I come into the shop and see it?"

"It's fine," she says with no inflection in her voice to give credence to that statement. "And no, you can't see it now. I have a client coming in."

"You could just hand it to me. I wouldn't have to go through it there."

"No," she replies. "I'll see you at your house at five. I need to go." Then she turns around and practically sprints away from me. I briefly wonder if Frankie might have some insights into what's going on here. Out of the three men I talked to about Finley, he was the one who seemed most battle-savvy.

I figure there's no point in going after her now; she clearly doesn't want to talk to me. Which makes me uneasy about her meeting my family. Maybe I should cancel with her for tonight and set something up for another day. Although, I'm guessing that will only make her madder.

I turn around and get back into my car and go to the grocery store. I buy everything I can think of that will impress my mother and help convince her that I don't live at the very edge of the earth. But being that Elk Lake doesn't carry the same selection she's used to in Manhattan, I probably haven't succeeded.

When I get home, I turn up the thermostat and put fresh logs in the fireplace. Then I make sure the spare rooms are ready to go. At four thirty on the dot, I see Adelaide pull into the driveway. I hurry out to help Kevin get the luggage out of the trunk.

When I reach his side, I ask, "How did it go?"

"We're here, aren't we?" I can't tell if he's acting normally or if he's annoyed at having been trapped with my mother in a car for over an hour.

When the doors open, I hurry around to help my mom. My first thought is she looks totally wrung out. Then she throws her arms around me and declares, "I can't believe we made it."

My dad walks up behind me and claps me on the shoulder. "What a journey!"

Clearly, there's a bigger story than Kevin picking them up in a less than respectable car.

"Where's Vivie?" I ask.

"Lying down in the backseat," my dad says. "She's had quite a day."

"We all have," my mom interjects.

"What happened?" I want to know.

"Let's go inside first," my mother says. "I have to use the restroom."

"What about Vivie?" I peer in the back window and see that she's sleeping.

Kevin walks past us and puts my parents' luggage on the porch. When he passes back in our direction, he says, "Let her rest. I'll walk home from here and get the car later."

I reach into my pocket and pull out forty bucks for his tip, but he waves it away. "Tommy," he says. "I felt bad taking the money for the fare, but you booked it on the app so I had to. I'm not taking a tip, too."

"This is your job, Kevin," I remind him while pushing the money at him.

He still doesn't take it. Instead, he turns to my parents and says, "Morgan, Jason, I hope I get a chance to see you before you go back to New York."

My mother uncharacteristically reaches out and gives my neighbor a hug. "Pickles,"—the use of his nickname is more startling than anything—"thank you for all your help." He hugs her back before shaking my dad's hand.

As he walks away, I lead my parents inside my house. Then I ask, "What in the world happened out there?"

"First point me to the bathroom," my mom says. I do as I'm told and she walks away.

Turning to my father, I demand, "What's going on, Dad?"

"It was a rough flight," he says. He crosses the room and sits on the sofa before saying, "I don't suppose you have any vodka."

My dad drinks socially only, and never before supper, which makes his question truly unnerving. "I bought a bottle today," I tell him. "How do you want it?"

"Straight," he says, once again making me jumpy. "Your mom will have one with whatever juice you have on hand."

This is a true emergency if my mom is drinking hard alcohol. Hurrying to the kitchen, I quickly prepare both cocktails for my parents and then bring them back to the living room. When I get there I find that my mom has returned. She's sitting down next to my dad with her head on his shoulder.

"Reinforcements," I announce while handing over their beverages. My dad makes quick work of his, but my mom takes it slower. Sitting down on one of the chairs across from them, I ask, "What happened?"

"Rough flight," my dad says. "There was a lot of turbulence."

"And that baby!" my mom interjects like Satan's spawn was onboard. "I have never heard a baby scream for over two hours without falling asleep."

I'm starting to understand why my sister is sleeping it off in the car. "That must have been hard on Vivie," I say.

My mom slumps down in her seat, which effectively makes her look like a lost child. "*My* poor baby," she says.

My dad explains, "The infant was right behind us, so the headphones did little to drown out the noise. Your sister did her best to distract herself, but then the turbulence started and it was too much stimulation all at once."

It's been years since Vivie has completely lost it due to external overload, but it *has* happened before. "What did she do?" I ask.

"She pulled out her piece of sandpaper and rubbed it hard enough that her fingers began to bleed. When I tried to take it away from her she screamed at me and just kept rubbing," my mom says.

"I gave her an additional sedative," my dad interjects, "but you know how these things go. Sometimes too much has a reverse reaction."

Many autistic people have heightened reactions to different substances and in some cases, including my sister's, often have paradoxical reactions. For instance, caffeine makes Vivie tired and most sleeping medications actually stimulate her. It took a long time for my parents to find the perfect calming cocktail.

My heart sinks at hearing this. "Poor Vivie," I say. I feel responsible for this happening. Had I not moved here, she wouldn't have been on a plane to come see me. She would have remained comfortably at home in the bubble she knows.

My mom takes a sip of her drink before saying, "Your sister is such a fighter and she does so well most of the time. This is going to feel like a real setback to her."

"I was going to take you all to supper tonight," I tell them, "But maybe we should order in, instead."

"That's a good idea, Thomas," my mom says. "I think Vivienne might need a couple of days to recuperate."

Trying to play the good host, I ask, "While we wait for suppertime, can I get you guys something to snack on?"

My mom is the first to respond. "Do you have any cheese?"

If I didn't already know what a tough day they'd just had, her response would be enough to alert me that all was not well.

"I have cheddar," I tell her.

My mom snuggles into dad and replies, "Perfect."

CHAPTER THIRTY-NINE

FINLEY

At a quarter 'til five, I grab Thomas's calendar and then lock up shop before heading over to his house. I cannot wait to see the look on his face when he realizes what I've done. I feel strongly that you can't lie to me and make me cry my eyes out and get away with it. If I've learned one thing on my autism journey it's that I will not let people treat me like a subpar species.

Every step I take toward my destination seems to rile me more. By the time I'm a block away, I probably look like a soldier marching into battle.

There's a giant black Cadillac in Thomas's driveway, which alerts me he must have other company. I can't imagine who though. As I pass the car, one of the back doors swings open, nearly knocking me over. I jump back to avoid getting hit.

A confused looking woman about my age steps out. She sways on her feet a little before sitting back down. "You must be Thomas's sister," I say to her.

She looks up at me and nods her head. "Is this Tommy's house?"

"It is," I tell her. My first impression of Vivienne is that she's nowhere near as functional as Thomas said she was. In fact, she seems almost simple in her confusion.

I scoot inside next to her before shutting the door again. According to Thomas, Vivienne also enjoys the cocoon effect of small spaces. "I'm Finley," I tell her. "I'm a friend of your brother's." I feel bad calling myself his friend given my current state of anger, but I don't want to upset Vivienne by laying the truth on her.

She takes my hand in hers and simply holds it for a minute. "I'm Vivie," she says before adding, "Thomas really likes you." I'm not quite sure how to respond to that.

"How was your flight?" I ask.

She seems to be trying to remember when her eyes pop open like they're going to make a run for it. "Not great."

"Turbulence?" I guess. That's my least favorite part of flying.

She nods her head and adds, "And there was a baby screaming behind us the whole flight."

A wave of panic hits me. I'm not sure I could have managed the combination. "Are you okay?" I ask her.

She shakes her head. "I'm not great. My dad drugged me."

Ah, maybe that's why she seems a little off. "Good thing he was there," I tell her.

"Yeah." She doesn't say anything else for what seems like several minutes.

I finally announce, "I'm on the spectrum, too." As much as I don't like to share what I consider my weaknesses, I feel like it's okay to do with another of my kind.

Vivie nods her head. "Thomas told me." Then she seems to catch herself. "But I wasn't supposed to tell anyone."

I laugh. "You can tell me. I already know."

She appreciates my attempt at humor. Then she turns serious. "I haven't had trouble like today since I was a kid. I'm pretty disappointed in myself."

"You should be more upset with that baby and the pilot who couldn't maneuver around the bumps."

Vivienne asks, "Do you travel a lot?"

"Almost never," I tell her.

"Do you feel like you're missing out?"

"All the time. But that's our burden, isn't it? We've been taught to believe everyone else is normal and we're not. So, if we can't do the things they do with ease, we're made to feel like we're on the outside."

"I do really well at home," Vivienne says. "I've got my routine and all my coping mechanisms in place. If I get overstimulated, I know where to go and what to do. But being thirty thousand feet in the air somehow hinders my ability to self-soothe."

"I probably would have locked myself in the bathroom," I tell her.

"That's not allowed," Vivienne says. "I researched it and if you do that they arrest you when you get off the plane."

I think about that for a minute before deciding, "It might be worth it."

Vivienne turns to me and studies my face. "I like you, Finley. I think we should be friends."

My heart rate picks up speed. That's not something I hear every day. "I'd like to be your friend, Vivie." Although, I'm not sure how that's going to work with my being at war with her brother. "Should we go inside?" I ask.

"I suppose so." Looking at her watch, she adds, "I've been sleeping for a while."

I get out of the car first and then I reach out to help Vivienne. The last time she stood up she was kind of woozy. Then I tuck Thomas's calendar securely under my arm before leading the way up to the porch. Stopping at the front door, I give it a quiet knock.

"They'll never hear that," Vivienne says. She proceeds to bang on it like she's trying to break it down.

A very classy-looking woman in a knit pantsuit opens the door. This must be Thomas's mother. Under different circumstances I might be a little afraid of her. But when she sees us, she immediately wraps her daughter in her arms and asks, "How are you, honey? Feeling any better?"

"I am," Vivienne tells her before pulling out of her embrace. Not all autistic people like to be touched and I'm wondering if she's one of them.

A good-looking older man, who looks an awful lot like Thomas, walks over and repeats his wife's inquiry and embrace of his daughter. She lets him hug her but seems relieved when he releases her.

The couple quickly turns to me, and Thomas's mom asks, "Who are you?"

I suddenly feel like I'm intruding and I don't quite know how to answer. Luckily, Vivie does it for me. "She's a friend of Thomas's."

His mom cocks her head to the side and narrows her gaze like she's inspecting me for fleas, before saying, "I'm Morgan." Then she gestures toward her husband. "This is Jason."

"I'm Finley," I tell them. "I think maybe now isn't the best time for me to be here."

It looks like Morgan is about to agree but then Vivienne takes my arm and declares, "It's the perfect time." She looks at her parents and adds, "Finley and I have had a nice chat in the car. We're friends now, too."

Apparently an endorsement from their daughter is all it takes to be welcomed into the fold. Morgan announces, "We're drinking vodka and eating cheese. Can I get you something?"

"No to the vodka and yes to the cheese," I tell her, while following her into the living room.

Thomas walks in moments later and calls out, "Vivie!" He runs to her side and hugs her. He holds on longer than his parents, which his sister seems to appreciate this time.

"Did Mom and Dad tell you?" she asks.

He nods his head. "It sounds like an awful flight. I'm sorry."

"It's not your fault. You weren't the one crying," she says.

That's when Thomas notices me. "Finley, you're here, too." He sounds nervous. I guess I can see why given our exchange this afternoon.

It's amazing how fine a line there is between heartbreak and anger. And while I've crossed that line into rage territory in the last few days, my heart still aches.

Thomas looks at the package under my arm and says, "Can I take that from you?"

So much for my plan to unveil it to them all at the same time. But I realize how inappropriate that would be given the current circumstances. Handing Thomas the calendar, I say, "I think maybe I'll go now."

Morgan interrupts. "Nonsense! You can't go until you've had some cheese."

Thomas looks at his mother with confusion. Then, instead of showing me the door, he gestures for me to sit on one of the giant overstuffed chairs. As I pass by him, he leans down and whispers, "I'm happy you're here. I've missed you."

Liar. But even though I'm mad at him, shivers run from the base of my neck to the tips of my toes. I'm practically vibrating in response to his nearness. I feel like I'm betraying my own best interests.

Instead of sharing his sentiment, I tell Thomas, "I'm happy to meet your family. They seem lovely." *You, on the other hand …*

Vivienne pushes her brother aside and comes to sit on the chair next to me. She tells Thomas, "Finley and I are already friends." He looks between us with a smile on his face but it's clear something is off. In fact, the energy in the room is downright weird, and I'm pretty sure this time it's not just my perception.

"Are you feeling okay now?" Morgan asks Vivienne.

Her daughter shrugs. "I might have to take the train home."

Jason interjects, "You just let me know and I'll book the tickets for us." This is clearly a family used to making concessions for a person they love.

Thomas picks up a tray full of cheese off the coffee table and brings it over to me. I only want one piece but I grab three. I take a bite before saying, "Wisconsin has the best cheese."

"It's surprisingly good," Thomas's mom replies.

Thomas stares at her like she just professed a love for mud wrestling.

"Are you planning on joining us for supper, Finley?" Jason asks.

Before I have a chance to answer, Vivienne says, "Please, do. It will be such fun."

The current vibe of the room indicates no such impending enjoyment. So, I tell them, "I think Thomas has planned to take you all out for supper."

"We're going to stay in," Morgan says. "It's already been a big day."

Vivie shifts in her chair and puts her feet up on the coffee table. "I don't want to ruin everyone's plans. I can stay here and go to bed early if you want to go out."

Thomas makes eye contact with me and holds it, while telling his sister, "We can go another night, Vivie." Then he adds, "And we'd love for you to join us, Finley."

Part of me feels like I should run and never look back, but I don't. Instead, I find myself drowning in the depths of Thomas's hazel eyes while saying, "That would be nice, thank you."

What am I doing? I'm mad at Thomas for lying to me. I'm mad that he didn't call in four days.

I warn myself not to fall for his smooth ways. The problem is, I'm not sure I'm listening.

CHAPTER FORTY

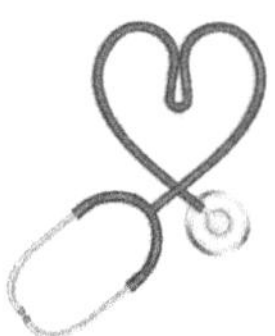

THOMAS

I'm happy to finally be spending time with Finley, especially after her reaction to seeing me earlier today. Although, I don't think she shares my sentiment. She seems annoyed every time I say something to her.

Pulling an array of carry-out menus out of my kitchen drawer, I bring them into the living room in time to hear my mom ask Finley, "What do you think we should get, dear? I'm guessing you've lived here longer than Thomas."

"I've lived here for three years," Finley tells her before adding, "Elk Lake has surprisingly good Chinese food. I like the kung pao shrimp."

My family immediately jumps on board with the idea and I place the order. "Use my name," Finley says. "They'll give us more fortune cookies that way."

"You're a regular, huh?" my dad asks with a smile on his face.

"Sunday night is kung pao night," Finley responds.

We continue to nibble on our snacks while we wait for our food delivery. My mom has eaten more cheese in one sitting than she's probably had in the last ten years combined. While I know she's going to regret it in the morning, she's currently enjoying herself. She asks Finley, "How do you and Thomas know each other?"

Finley side-eyes me, seemingly unsure of how to respond. So, I say, "The hospital hired Finley to take my picture for their wall of fame."

"You're a photographer?" my dad asks excitedly. "Do you enjoy it?"

"I love it," she tells him. A telltale blush comes to her face. I'm guessing she's remembering our sessions together.

"What's your favorite part?" my mom wants to know.

Finley starts to run her fingers back and forth across the arm of her chair. That's when I notice she's also petting the hem of her sweater with her other hand. *Oh, yeah, she's nervous.* "I love the babies," she says. "They're perfect in every way."

"She also has a booming business taking boudoir photos for couples," I tell them.

My mother's eyes narrow critically. "Surely that can't be lucrative."

"It really is," Finley tells her. "So much so I've recently expanded the size of my studio."

My mom seems skeptical. "What kind of pictures constitute boudoir shots?"

Finley opens her phone and types something in before handing it to my mom. "These are from my website," she tells her.

My mom scrolls through the phone slowly. "These are actually quite tasteful."

Finley nods her head at the compliment before explaining, "It's a very intimate kind of session. People want to express their love for each other in a visual way so they can look at it from the outside."

Vivie announces, "You've just given me a great idea for a painting."

"What's that?" Finley asks.

My sister replies, "I was thinking it would be fun to paint an ordinary couple looking into a mirror and have their reflection be their fantasy." She pauses for a moment before saying, "In fact, you know what? I'd like to paint an elderly couple and have the mirror image be of when they were young and first in love."

"Oh, Vivie," Morgan says. "I love that idea! You could do a whole series like that."

"I could," my sister says. At this point she sort of glazes over and remains quiet, which means she's deep in thought. I love when this happens because I know Vivie is in her happy place, mentally traveling to other worlds.

Finley stares at her, too. Then she announces, "A lot of autistic people are very creative."

My parents both turn and look at her. I'm not sure what they're thinking, so I say, "That's very true." The room goes unnaturally silent after that.

My mom finally asks, "Are you on the spectrum too, Finley?"

Finley surprises me by saying, "I am." Then she adds, "It's been a journey for sure."

My dad nods his head in agreement. "Have you known your whole life?" he asks her.

"I found out in high school," Finley tells them.

Vivienne finally joins the conversation again and says, "It's nice to have a friend who knows what my life is like."

Finley continues to tug at her sweater. "Do you have a lot of friends, Vivienne?"

My sister shakes her head. "Not really. I have a hard time understanding other people's motivations. You know, like do they really like me or are they making fun of me. I've found it's just simpler to stay away."

"That's how it is for me, too," Finley says. "Although, I've recently become friends with a very nice teacher in town. Her parents are my best clients."

"I'm your friend, too," I hurry to interject. Finley shoots me a withering glance, making it clear the jury is still out on that one.

"And we're friends," Vivie tells her. At least Finley looks happy when she hears that.

"I hope we'll see a lot more of you while we're here," my mom tells Finley, which is kind of surprising. She's not a person who welcomes others into private family time.

"I work," Finley says. But then she notices Vivie's disappointed expression, and adds, "But I'm sure I can make time."

"We'd love to come into your place and see what you do," my dad says.

"Maybe I can take a nice family picture of you all," Finley says with a smile. "My treat."

"That's a lovely offer," my mom tells her. "We would like that very much."

It's too bad I still haven't quite made up my mind about Elk Lake yet, because my family sure seems like they'd be on board with Finley as my girlfriend.

When the doorbell rings, Finley stands up to get it. I already paid over the phone, but I follow behind to help carry the bags. After opening the door, Finley greets, "Hey, Flip. You didn't by any chance check the fortune cookies did you?"

The high-school-aged boy says, "Nope. I didn't know the order was for you."

I interject, "I asked for extra fortune cookies like you told me to."

She turns to me. "How many did you ask for?"

"Just extra. I didn't specify the number."

Finley looks into the bag and counts them. "There are thirteen," she says. Then she holds the open sack up to the delivery boy and tells him, "Take one out, please." He follows orders without hesitation, which makes me wonder if this is a ritual between them.

I hand Flip a ten. After he walks away, I tell Finley again, "I'm really glad you're here."

Her only reply is, "I like your family."

I can't go on the rest of the night like this, so I ask, "What's wrong? Are you mad that I didn't call? I know I should have but I was really harried at work. I texted a couple of times and told you that."

Finley's gaze narrows until she looks like she wants to punch me. "Remember the day I texted about dropping off goodies at the hospital?"

I nod my head nervously. "I do."

"I was texting you *from* the ER. They said you weren't there and you weren't on the schedule at all for that day."

Uh-oh. I know I shouldn't have lied to Finley, but I did it to protect her. Oh heck, who am I kidding? I did it to protect myself. I didn't want her to give up on the possibility of us before I had a chance to decide if I was going to stay in town. I was being a selfish jerk and I've been found out.

"I can explain," I tell her. But before I do, my father calls out, "What's keeping you two? I'm starving in here!"

Finley doesn't stay to hear me out. Instead, she walks right past me and into the living room. I trail after her.

My mom has cleared off the coffee table and put down some silverware and napkins. She says, "Let's eat comfortably tonight." Yet again, my mother is acting nothing like herself. If this were any other time, we would all be sitting properly in the dining room.

I start to open the bags and arrange the containers so everyone can grab their orders. Finley takes hers, along with a fork, and goes back to sit on her stuffed chair. My family does the same.

Once we're all settled, Vivie suggests, "Maybe tomorrow we can go for a walk on the beach. Doesn't that sound like fun, Finley?"

"No," Finley tells her plainly. Then she explains, "I don't like sand."

For some reason, I feel the need to add, "She doesn't like foil either." Finley glares at me like this wasn't my information to share.

Vivie doesn't seem to notice. Instead, she asks Finley, "What textures do you like?"

"Soft ones," she says.

Vivie tells her, "I like rough ones." Then she looks down at her hands. My parents must have washed and bandaged them for her. "Except for today. I tried to calm myself down with some sandpaper."

"Thomas mentioned you liked rough textures." Finley releases a full body shiver.

My parents have been sitting and watching this exchange like they're witnessing a miracle. My mom finally tells Finley, "I'm glad you and Thomas found each other. You are a lovely addition to our family, Finley."

I nearly choke on my cashew chicken. Not because my mom is being nice, but more because it seems like she already assumes Finley and I are an item. And with the way Finley is treating me, that couldn't be farther from the truth.

Finley must interpret her words this way as well, because she's quick to say, "Thomas and I are only friends."

Opening his supper, my dad says, "Whatever you are, we're very happy you're here."

Finley looks like she wants to cry, and she's not the only one.

CHAPTER FORTY-ONE

FINLEY

I like Thomas's family a lot. Too bad he's a big, fat, thick-haired liar. I know he said he could explain why he wasn't at the hospital like he claimed he was, but I don't see the point in hearing him out. In my world you're either a liar or you aren't. There is no in between.

After we eat, Thomas's parents excuse themselves to go upstairs to change. I'm relieved Vivie doesn't do the same. But then Thomas asks his sister, "Are you ready to witness my April Fool's prank on Mom and Dad?"

Vivie claps her hands together excitedly. "Yes! That would be the perfect ending to this stupid day. Although, if it's too mean, maybe it will be more than Mom and Dad can handle."

"I think you should wait," I tell him. "Your parents are tired. You should let them recover first." As mad as I am at Thomas, I really do like his parents and I don't relish the idea of causing them more distress. Also, I'm no longer sure I want to bear witness to Thomas's shame.

"I think they're recovered enough," he tells me. "Plus, this way, they'll have a whole week to get over it before they go home."

"They are pretty resilient," Vivienne says. "Go ahead and do it." She looks positively thrilled.

Thomas stands up and walks to the staircase. Then he calls up, "Mom, Dad, come on down! I have a surprise."

"Coming," his dad shouts back.

When his parents join us again, they're both in their pajamas. Morgan says, "I don't usually entertain like this, but it's been an exhausting day."

"If I'd brought my jammies with me," I tell her, "I'd put them on, too. You look very comfortable."

Sitting down on the couch next to his wife, Jason says, "Now, what's this surprise you have for us?"

Thomas walks over to the side table and picks up the bag containing the calendar. Then he comes back into the room. "What Finley and I didn't tell you is that we've been working on a special project together."

His parents look at us expectantly. A pang of doubt stabs at me, but I brush it away. *Thomas deserves this.* He tells them, "In fact, it's gone so well, I've been offered a new opportunity."

Both of his parents look confused. Handing the bag to his mother, Thomas says, "Open it up and see."

Morgan moves toward the edge of the couch and gingerly takes bag. Then she pulls out the calendar and simply stares.

"What do you think?" Thomas asks excitedly.

Her expression shifts rapidly. Oh yeah, she's mortified. Which is exactly what I wanted her to be.

Thomas tells her, "Finley has shown that around to a few contacts and I've been offered a modeling job. I'm going to take a hiatus from work and do it."

Thomas's dad, who's also looking, asks, "Are they hiring you to play the village idiot?"

"What? No." He explains, "They were impressed with my

skills and they've offered me a modeling contract. Isn't that exciting?"

Morgan looks like she's about to lose it. But then she asks, "Are they blind?" She stands up and hands Thomas the calendar. I can't make eye contact with him.

Thomas takes the calendar and is quiet for long enough, I'm tempted to make a run for it. I know I've just ruined his revenge, but he deserves it after what he did to me. Except Thomas holds his ground and unexpectedly announces, "They said I'm the best male model they've ever seen." It looks like he's going to brazen this out, which goes against common sense. Even so, I'm actually impressed by his chutzpah.

With copycat cringes on their faces, Morgan says, "You cannot give up being a doctor to do this. Thomas, dear, you're not that good. In fact, these photos are horrible!" She looks at me like she wants me to agree with her.

At this moment, I'm not quite sure what to do, so I tell her, "My contact said that Thomas's look is exactly what they're looking for."

"Son." Jason stands up and walks to his son's side. "I think they're making fun of you."

I suddenly feel bad for ruining this for Thomas. He did take me out on the best date I've ever been on. That's why I decide to announce, "April Fool's!"

Everyone in the room turns to me with a look of shock on their faces. So, I continue, "Thomas is pulling an April Fool's joke on you." Pulling out my phone, I take it over to his parents and show it to them. "Here are the real pictures my client saw."

Morgan and Jason take the camera and start scrolling while Vivie runs over to stand behind them. There are comments like, "Oh, dear," and "These are actually quite good," when Jason declares, "You can't leave the medical profession to be a male model. That's lunacy!"

I feel Thomas staring at me while he tells his parents, "I told

Finley how we used to play pranks on each other and she thought this would be a funny way to get even with you."

Morgan looks up at me anxiously. "So, it was all a joke?"

"Just this calendar," Thomas tells her. "The real one is no joke."

Morgan opens and closes her mouth several times before she finally says, "It's been a long day. I think I need to go lie down."

Jason stands up and helps his wife to her feet. "I could use some rest as well." Their disappointment is palpable.

This prank clearly isn't having the bang Thomas hoped it would, and I know that's all my fault. But I still don't feel too bad for him. I am sympathetic toward his parents though.

Thomas motions for his mom and dad to sit back down, which they do tentatively. "Remember when you took us to Ohio instead of Hawaii?" he asks them. They both nod their heads slowly.

Thomas tells them, "That was pretty traumatic and I've wanted to get even with you ever since."

"So, you're going to leave medicine and become a male model?" It's clear Morgan thinks her son has gone off the deep end. "That's seems extreme, Thomas."

"Stupid, more like," Jason adds.

"Brilliant!" Vivie claps her hands together excitedly before saying, "Look how gorgeous he is! He could be the next Fabio!"

"I don't know who that is," Jason responds.

Vivie uses my phone and looks up pictures of the vintage romance novel cover model and shows it to her parents.

"I might throw up," Morgan groans before saying, "It's one thing to get even with us and another to lose your mind."

"*Cleveland*," Vivie announces. "You took us to Cleveland when we thought we were going to Hawaii."

"We took you to Hawaii two weeks later," Jason says, sounding confused.

"But you didn't tell us that until after we came home from Cleveland." Vivie is holding her ground.

Morgan is still struggling to put this all together. "So, because your dad and I played the prank of all pranks on you when you were kids, you're going to pay us back by becoming a male model?"

Thomas simply smiles. "Mom, I could make a fortune!"

"You're a doctor. You already make a fortune!" Jason says.

Thomas and Vivie share a look, and Thomas says to her, "What do you think we should do?"

Vivie shrugs. "I think you really should become a male model. Your pictures are gorgeous."

"Thank you, Vivie," Thomas tells her. "But what should we do with Mom and Dad?"

She turns to her parents and declares, "We'd like an apology and a promise there will be no more April Fool's pranks ever again."

Morgan stands up again and heartily declares, "I'm truly sorry."

Jason joins her. "Me, too." Then he looks at his son and pleads, "But son, you can't leave medicine."

Thomas's expression shifts to one of victory. "Because I believe you're sincerely repentant, I accept your apology." He adds, "There's only one thing left to say. April Fool's!"

Morgan nearly collapses in her relief. "It was *all* a joke, then?"

"All of it," Thomas tells her. "I'm sorry I pulled it tonight. I thought it might go over a little better than it did."

"I love it!" Vivie says running over to Thomas to hug him. "It was brilliant and it made my whole day better!"

A lone tear slides down Morgan's face when she says, "If it made you happy, honey, then I'm happy, too."

Thomas's parents may have played a horrible prank on their kids once upon a time, but the truth is, they are amazing parents. They love their children and they champion them—which was clear with how they took care of Vivie during her crisis.

Jason suddenly starts to laugh. He keeps going until he's nearly bent in half. He catches his breath several moments later and says, "That really was something, Thomas. I bow to the master."

"I need another cocktail," Morgan says. "And maybe some more cheese."

Thomas's parents and sister sit back down on the couch and start going through the cross-eyed pirate calendar again. Their enjoyment is contagious. But even so, Thomas isn't laughing.

Instead, he walks over to me and says, "Finley, I'd like a word."

CHAPTER FORTY-TWO

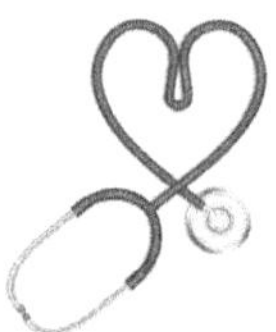

THOMAS

There's no longer any doubt in my mind that Finley is furious with me. And it's time to find out exactly why. "Will you join me on the porch?" I ask her.

She hems and haws before saying, "I think maybe I should get going."

"Not yet." I take her by the hand and physically pull her from the room. I grab a couple of throws as we go. We don't stop until we reach the porch swing.

Once we're both seated, she stares at her feet and asks, "What do you want to talk about?"

She can't be serious. "Why did you do it?" I demand.

"It all worked out, Thomas," she says like this makes her actions okay.

"It did, but not quite the way I thought it would. Would you like to tell me what's going on in that head of yours?"

Finley suddenly turns toward me and jabs a pointer finger right into my chest. Then she yells, "You haven't been at the hospital all week!"

Uh, oh, I've been caught. "You know about that, huh?" I

should never have lied to her. I hurry to explain, "I wanted to tell you where I was, but I didn't want you to get your hopes up."

"Get my hopes up? For what?"

I inhale deeply before telling her, "My old hospital called last week and essentially offered me my dream job."

"So you quit working at the hospital?" Her eyes start to water. "You're moving back to New York?"

I reach out to take her hand, but she pulls it away. I wind up holding onto her sweater. "I thought I might try something else first."

Looking at me with panic, she demands, "Not modeling?"

"Not modeling," I assure her. Then I tell her all about Edward Hall's offer for me to buy his practice. "I've been over at his clinic this week trying to figure out if I'm interested."

Her anger seems to leak out of her like a hole in a balloon. "So, you didn't agree to accept the job offer back in New York?"

I shake my head. "I'm not sure I'm ready to leave Elk Lake."

"Because of me?" Finley's eyes flood with new tears.

"Because of you," I assure her. "I just didn't want to tell you about Edward's offer yet, because I wasn't sure I'd be suited to private practice."

Finley takes a moment to drape one of the throws across her shoulders. Once that task is complete, she stares down at her hands and asks, "Did you like it?"

I'm painfully aware of how much I hurt her by not being completely truthful. But I also realize she wouldn't be this mad at me if she didn't really care for me. That knowledge fills me with a welcome warmth. "I liked it a lot," I tell her.

"It must be very different from what you've always done." She sounds worried that I won't like it enough to be happy here. But suddenly I know I want to stay in Elk Lake more than I've wanted anything in my life. I want to see what grows between me and this kooky photographer. Heck, my family already loves her, too. Not that I'm ready to declare *that* emotion quite yet.

"It's different, for sure," I tell her. "But I left New York because

I was burning out working in a big city ER. I had the opposite problem here. I was bored in Elk Lake's ER."

"Not to mention you were being pursued by Constance," she adds.

"That didn't help," I tell her. Then I explain, "The thing with private practice is that it's much more personal than working in the hospital. Edward really gets to know his patients and he cares about them. I feel like maybe this is something I've been yearning for without even realizing it."

Finley reaches out and touches my arm lightly. Then she asks, "Does that mean you're going to buy his practice?"

"That's what it means," I assure her. I didn't know until tonight that was going to be my choice, but spending time with Finley again has completely sealed the deal. I like her so much and she's such a great fit in my life.

"Does that mean we're going to go on a second date?" She suddenly sounds so hopeful I want to scoop her up in my arms and kiss her.

"As soon as my family goes back to New York," I tell her.

Finley moves her hand down my arm until she's holding my hand. Grasping onto it she says, "I want to plan our second date." Then she asks, "Would it be weird if I wanted your family to join us?"

"Very weird," I assure her. "But they all seem to love you. I'm sure they'd be happy for the invite." I'm touched Finley wants to take charge of our next outing. And I'm oddly delighted that my parents and sister will be with us. Finley fits our family dynamic to the point that she already feels like one of us.

"I'm sorry," Finley says quietly. "I should have never messed up the prank against your parents. That wasn't very professional of me."

"It wasn't," I agree. "But it was understandable. I lied to you and I'm very sorry about that. My intentions were pure, but I went about things the wrong way. I will never lie to you again."

Finley leans into me until she's resting her head on my shoulder. "I forgive you," she says. "But in the future, it's probably best to just talk to me and tell me what's going on."

"That's exactly what I will do," I tell her. "I promise I've learned my lesson." I could sit out on this porch with her for the rest of my life. Even the fact that she's on the spectrum is perfect for me. I know so much about it from growing up with Vivie that it seems totally normal to me.

"When are you planning this second date of ours?" I ask her. I know I have to entertain my family this week, but I am really looking forward to seeing her again as soon as I can.

"How about tomorrow night?" she asks. "I'll need the day to pull it all together." Clutching my arm, she quietly says, "I can't believe you're staying just to spend time with me."

"You'd better believe it," I tell her. "Finley Harper, you are an amazing woman and I can't wait to get to know you better."

She glances up at me nervously. "You might run away when you do."

Leaning down, I gently kiss her forehead before telling her, "Give it your best shot. But you should know I don't scare easily."

I think about what Vivie went through today. I would never be embarrassed if Finley shared a similar intolerance to sound, even if she screamed in public. Instead, I would want to double down and protect her from anything that caused her distress.

Right now, there are no words to describe the overpowering sensation of optimism I feel for my future. And only a small part of that is due to moving into a new avenue of medicine.

I was brought to Elk Lake for a reason, and that reason is currently sitting next to me.

CHAPTER FORTY-THREE

FINLEY

Ever since my diagnosis, I've fought feelings of insecurity that I wasn't like everyone else. But spending last night with Thomas and his family changed all that. The Culpeppers have embraced me in such a way that makes me feel normal—or whatever it is I perceive that to be.

I fell asleep replaying the conversation Thomas and I had on his porch. I don't like that he lied to me, but I understand he thought he was protecting us both by doing it. The fact that he's staying here for me, even after I sabotaged his revenge, is totally crazy. He is an exceptional man, and I'm going to do everything in my power to let him know how much I appreciate his belief in us.

I roll out of bed and put on a brand-new pair of pink socks. Then I wrap myself in my furry robe and check the weather to make sure there's no rain coming our way. Once I know it's going to be a beautiful day, I get busy making some calls.

When I'm all done, I text Thomas and tell him to meet me at my shop at five.

The Culpepper clan walks into Happy Snaps at four fifty-two. Morgan comes straight toward me and immediately takes my hands in hers. "How nice of you to plan an adventure for us all, Finley."

As soon as I make eye contact with Thomas, a jolt of joy floods my nervous system. "Do you mind if I tell them what tonight is?"

With a giant smile on his face, he says, "Go right ahead."

I turn toward his family and announce, "Tonight is Thomas's and my second date."

"We figured you were more than friends," Vivie says with a wink.

"We just thought you wanted to keep it on the down low for a while," Jason adds.

"I think it's better for us to tell the truth," I say. "I like the truth." I give Thomas another meaningful look and he shoots me a double thumbs up. "Is there anything *you* wanted to tell your parents, Thomas?" It's okay if he wants to wait to tell them about taking over for Dr. Hall, but if it was me, I'd want to get it over with.

Thomas clears his throat and announces, "I've left my job at the hospital. I'm done working in the ER."

"You can't mean you're coming home?" Morgan strangely sounds like she wouldn't support this, which is confusing since according to Thomas she wants him back in New York more than anything.

"I'm not leaving Elk Lake," Thomas tells her.

"Good," she says, before adding, "You can't leave Finley." Her opinion means a lot to me, especially as she barely knows me.

"Why exactly are you leaving the hospital?" Jason wants to know. "And please tell me it's not so you can become a model."

Thomas explains, "I've met a general practitioner who's planning on retiring soon. I've decided to buy his practice."

"That's a big change, son," Jason says. "Have you spent time with him?"

"I have," Thomas assures him. "Not only do I love the pace

and predictable hours, but also think I'll enjoy getting to know my patients better."

Jason nods his head. "As long as you've thought it through." Then he asks, "When do you start?"

Thomas puts his hands into his pockets and shifts his weight from one leg to the other. Even though things appear to be going well, I can tell he's still nervous. "I've already started," he says. "Edward has been introducing me to patients and next week he's going to shift some of their care over to me. If things continue to go as expected, I'll buy him out in two months' time."

Vivienne walks up to her brother and gives him a hug. "I'm excited for you, Tommy. I think this is going to be a great opportunity."

"Thanks, Vivie," he tells her. "But this means I won't be moving back to New York."

"That's okay," she replies. "I've been here now, so I know I can come visit again. I might even stay with you for a month or two over the summer just to see what life in a small town is like."

I know what a big deal that would be for Vivie, so I tell her, "I can make space for you in my studio to paint, if you want." She nods her head enthusiastically.

"Well, if Vivie is planning to visit for an extended time, surely Morgan and I can do the same. We could rent a house so we don't cramp your style, son," Jason says with a wink.

Morgan adds, "My home is where my family is. And if that means spending part of the year in Wisconsin, I'll do it."

I give Thomas's family a quick tour around my shop and reiterate the offer that I want to take their picture. We decide to do that over the weekend. When we're all done, I tell them, "I've ordered a car service to drive part of our group. I don't think we'll all fit in Thomas's car.

"You drive with Tommy," Jason says. "Morgan, Vivie, and I will take the other car."

"I just need to get ready," I tell them. "I'll be back in a few minutes."

I hurry into the back room and put on my knee-length rain boots; I pair them with a matching long yellow raincoat and hat. Then I put on a pair of yellow dishwashing gloves. Yes, I look odd, but I'm going to need it for what's to come.

When I join the Culpeppers up front, Thomas takes one look at me and starts to laugh. "You look like that girl on the salt box." Then he asks, "Should we have dressed differently?"

"You're fine," I tell him. It's clear he's wondering what's going on, but he doesn't ask.

We all walk outside as soon as the car arrives. It's the same big black Cadillac that Vivie was sitting in yesterday when I went to Thomas's house.

It pulls up to the curb and Mr. Picknell gets out. I know him because his son hires me to take pictures of his grandchildren. I greet him, "Mr. Picknell, I didn't know you worked for a car service."

He waves at me, "Call me Pickles, Finley. And I just do this part time. I also work as a drivers' ed teacher."

"Seriously?" I ask. "I'm going to sign up for driving lessons as soon as I get my permit. Maybe you can be my teacher." And if he is, surely I shouldn't call him Pickles. That seems disrespectful.

"I'd love to teach you to drive!" he assures me. Then he turns to Thomas's family and greets them.

"Pickles!" Morgan announces. "How nice to see you again." The use of Mr. Picknell's nickname sounds funny coming from a lady like Morgan. But it just goes to show you that you can't judge a book by its cover. Thomas's mom might look like a society woman, but she's really very down to earth.

As Mr. Picknell opens the back door and the front passenger door for the Culpeppers, I tell him, "You know where you're going, right?" He nods his head. So, I say, "We'll be right behind you."

Getting into the Mustang, Thomas asks, "Where *are* we going?"

"To the parking lot by the lake where you and I went the night you took me for a drive."

"We're having our second date in a parking lot?" he wants to know.

"No," I tell him. "That's where we're parking. Now no more questions until we get there."

Thomas does a pretty good job of driving us. He still slows down about a block before he gets to a stop sign, but hey, at least he has his license.

The rest of our party is already waiting for us when we get there.

After we join them, Mr. Picknell asks, "What time should I be back?"

"How about seven?" I suggest.

"See you then." He waves as he pulls out.

Morgan says, "I don't mean to be a complainer, dear, but it's very cold out here."

"We'll have you warm in no time," I tell them. Then I start walking toward the beach.

Thomas catches up with me. "You don't like the sand."

"I don't, which is why I'm dressed like this." I raise my rubber-gloved covered hands into the air.

"I don't understand?"

I stop walking and turn to face him. Then I explain, "You said that you love the beach, and I wanted to do something you would enjoy. Now, do you want to stand here or do you want to see what I have planned?"

CHAPTER FORTY-FOUR

THOMAS

I can't believe Finley went to such lengths for our date tonight. Seriously, she hates the sand and yet she's planned a whole evening on the beach because she knows how much I like it. She's even wearing the craziest outfit I've ever seen just so she can get through it.

Finley leads the way to a large fire pit with five Adirondack chairs surrounding it. Then she walks up to it, pulls a lighter out of her pocket and lights it. It immediately bursts into giant flames. "Everyone sit down and warm up," she orders.

We all find a space by the fire and take a seat. Meanwhile, Finley walks toward a large red cooler that she must have placed there earlier. She opens it up and pulls out five thermoses. As she hands them around, she announces, "Hot chocolate to warm your insides." Then she pulls out a pack of marshmallows for anyone who wants them.

"This is lovely!" My mom sounds as excited as a little kid. "It's just like how we do it in the Hamptons. Except, you know, it's summer and not forty-five degrees."

"Thomas told me how much he loves the beach," Finley says. "I wanted to show him that I was paying attention."

"Very nice, Finley." This comment comes from my dad.

"We're just getting started," Finley tells us. Then she sits down in the open chair next to mine. She pulls out her phone and sends a text before telling us, "I realize that it's important to stretch my boundaries and I haven't been doing that as much as I should."

"It's hard to do," my sister says.

"There's nothing wrong with staying within your own comfort level," my mom tells her.

Finley opens her hot chocolate and takes a sip before responding, "Yes, but we live in a world that doesn't exactly honor our differences. It's really on us to try to meet people more than halfway." She raises her thermos to Vivie as if giving her an air toast.

"Just so long as you don't go too far out of your comfort zone," I tell Finley while reaching over to take her yellow-rubber-gloved hand in mine.

We continue to enjoy the fire and conversation when a delivery truck pulls into the parking lot. Moments later, two men walk toward us carrying various bags. Finley directs them to put them down next to her chair.

As they walk away, she tells us, "Dinner has arrived!"

Unpacking the first bag she pulls out long, foil-covered, oblong shaped objects. With a cringe on her face—I'm assuming because of the foil—she hands them out. "Hot dogs!" she announces. Then she distributes plastic ramekins full of ketchup, mustard, and relish.

"Are these especially good hot dogs?" my mom asks while holding her supper like it's a live grenade.

Finley shrugs. "I don't know. I hope they're good."

"Is there some significance to hot dogs?" my dad wants to know.

"They're part of Thomas's favorite meal," she tells him confidently. Then she opens another bag and pulls out several plastic bags containing pink cotton candy. She distributes these next.

"Cotton candy and hot dogs?" Vivie declares excitedly before asking, "I don't suppose you have any strawberry lemonade, too?"

"Funny you should ask," Finley says before opening the final bag. She hands out bottles of strawberry lemonade.

My parents both look completely baffled, so I remind them, "This is what we ate at Coney Island when you took us there when we were little. I told Finley it was my favorite meal."

"You threw it all up on Dino's Wonder Wheel," my mom reminds me.

"I did," I confirm. "And while the food was nowhere near as delicious coming up as it was going down, I truly did love that meal." I turn to Finley and say, "Thank you for remembering and thank you for going to all this trouble to show you care."

She's beaming like she just won the lottery. "I like when people pay attention to things that are important to me. I try to do the same." *If only the rest of the world was that attuned.*

We all enjoy our meal and ensuing conversation and when we're all done, Finley walks around with an empty bag for us to throw our garbage into.

Moments later, Kevin shows up. He toots his horn twice to get our attention. As my parents and Vivie stand, my mom says, "This was a truly enjoyable evening, Finley. Thank you very much."

My dad adds, "I think a trip back to Coney Island might be in order. Maybe this time Finley could join us."

Finley shakes her head sharply. "No, thank you. I don't like amusement parks."

"Don't hurry home," Vivie says as she walks by us. She stops and gives Finley a hug. "Thank you for being you," she says. As far as votes of confidence go, this appears to be the perfect thing for her to say.

Finley responds, "Thank you for being you, Vivie. Knowing you makes me feel almost normal."

I love that my sister—and, dare I say, girlfriend?—have

formed such a fast bond. This is one of the many things that makes me think the Universe knew what it was doing by sending me to Elk Lake.

Once my family leaves, Finley and I sit back down in front of the fire. I ask her, "Do you want to get going to?"

She shakes her head. "Not yet."

"But you hate the beach," I remind her.

"Not as much as I used to." She offers me a secret smile as if I'm responsible for her softening.

But then a gust of wind hits and sand blows over us. Finley abruptly stands up and declares, "Now it's time to go."

"Should we clean up here first?" I ask.

Putting the garbage bags into the cooler, she says, "The men are going to come back and pick everything up." Pointing at the fire, she says, "But you could put some sand on that to put out the flames."

I hurry to follow orders and then I take Finley's dishwasher-gloved hand and escort her off the beach. As soon as we get to the car, she brushes herself off and removes her outerwear. Then she gets into the car.

Once we're inside, I blast the heat before telling her, "This was the best date I've ever been on. Thank you."

"I don't know if I believe that," she says shyly, "but it was pretty good."

"I can assure you it's the only date I've been on that included my family." I reach over and take her bare hand in mine. Giving it a squeeze, I tell her, "You aren't like all the other girls, are you?"

"It's not for lack of trying," she grumbles.

I stare deeply into the sea green depths of her eyes. "Quit trying," I tell her. "You're lightyears beyond everyone else and I never want to see you try to snuff out your light. You're too special for that."

Then I lean over to Finley and kiss her. The sensation is positively electric and I don't ever want to let her go. I don't know if minutes, hours, or days pass. I just know that we're totally connected, our spirits intertwined and dancing around us.

When we finally pull away, Finley says, "You know what we have to do now, don't you?"

"Run off to Vegas and get married?" I'm only partially teasing. As of this moment, I cannot imagine a time when Finley won't be a prominent fixture in my life. Just the thought of living without her makes my heart hurt.

"Not until our twentieth fake date," she jokes. Then she says, "We have to learn how to drive a car."

"It sounds like Kevin is on board," I tell her. "But being that we can't do that tonight, how do you think we should spend the next couple of hours?" I pump my eyebrows at her suggestively.

Finley smiles coyly. "Oh, I think you know." Then she leans over and we kiss again.

If you told me last year what I would be doing now, I wouldn't have believed it. But life has a way of taking you places you don't see coming. I figure as long as you try to keep your boundaries open and don't run when obstacles arise, there are rewards waiting for you. And without a doubt, Finley Harper is one of my greatest rewards.

EPILOGUE

FINLEY

Thomas and I are going out tonight to celebrate our first official year as a couple. We're going back to the lodge to pay homage to our first date.

The last twelve months have taught me an amazing amount about life. For instance, it does not always go according to plan, and that's a good thing.

My path has not been typical, but that's not only because I'm on the spectrum. I'm different because we're all unique creatures. No two people are alike and that's something we should celebrate, not feel diminished by.

I look into the mirror and check myself out. I'm wearing a copy of Thomas's blue cashmere sweater, but this one is in my size. He bought it for me for our one-month anniversary, and it's now the softest thing in my wardrobe. I hurry to grab my gift for him and go down to the curb. As much as he's practiced, he still isn't a great parallel parker.

As I leave my building I see Thomas has already arrived, and true to form, he's parked at an almost ninety-degree angle. He jumps out of the car and comes around to the passenger side. "Don't judge me," he says. "I'm going to keep practicing."

I reach up and give him a kiss—an activity I will never tire of. "We don't judge each other, remember?" Then I tell him, "I will love you even if you never learn how to park."

He opens the car door for me and once we're both inside, he asks, "Can we exchange gifts now?"

"Pretty please!" I say excitedly. Then I hand him my box.

Thomas takes it and opens it up. Inside are two calendars. The first is the initial one we shot for his parents that I never had printed. The second is a project Thomas and I have been working on over the last few months. We've taken inspiration from Margaret and Bob's photo shoots and have been reenacting romance novel covers of our own. The final product is pretty amazing.

Thomas opens that calendar and exclaims, "I don't care what anyone says, we could do this for a living."

"We do look pretty great," I tell him. "I can see why Margaret and Bob never seem to tire of it."

"I will model for you anytime you want me to," he says. And I believe him. Thomas has been nothing but supportive and excited about what I do. He puts the calendars away before handing me a small box of his own.

I take it greedily but before I can get the lid off, he says, "This isn't the only gift."

"You spoil me," I tell him with a smile on my face. Then I untie the bow and open the lid. Inside is a car key.

As I hold it up, Thomas tells me, "It's the key to this car. Now that you've become such a great driver, I think it's time for you to own it."

"You're giving me my dream car?!" I have no words.

Thomas points to the glove box. "The rest of your gift is in there."

I excitedly open the glove compartment, and sure enough it's full of all my favorite snacks. There are granola bars, mini boxes of raisins, and my favorite strawberry wafer cookies. "You remembered!" I say before throwing my arms around him. "You are the best boyfriend in the whole world!"

He holds me tightly before whispering in my ear, "You missed something,"

Turning back toward the glove compartment, I start to take out my snacks, and that's when I see it. A small robin's egg blue velvet box. My whole world feels like it's stopped moving, and the gravitational fluctuation that results makes me a little dizzy.

"Open it," Thomas says.

So, I do. Inside is the most beautiful diamond solitaire ring I could ever imagine. It's huge, too. "Thomas ..." I start to say but the rest of the sentence gets caught in my throat.

He takes my hand in his. "Finley Harper, you have been the most unexpected, delightful, and all-around surprising gift of my life. I love you and I never want to spend a day without you. Would you do me the great honor of becoming my wife?"

My body erupts in a sensation of pure joy. "I would be honored to be married to such a fabulous and sexy model," I tell him. "My answer is yes, Thomas."

He takes the ring out of the box and puts it on the appropriate finger before saying, "I will always be your model, but I think I'd better keep my day job, too." Thomas loves being a general practitioner. He's become friends with a surprising number of people doing what he does.

In the end, Elk Lake has given us both the gift of a lifetime. It has brought us together and we are going to create our own family here as a tribute.

Pity Ploy is coming in September!

Pre-order today.

ABOUT THE AUTHOR

USA Today Bestseller Whitney Dineen is a rock star in her own head. While delusional about her singing abilities, there's been a plethora of validation that she's a fairly decent author (AMAZING!!!).

After winning many writing awards and selling nearly a kabillion books (math may not be her forte, either), she's decided to let the voices in her head say whatever they want (sorry, Mom). She also won a fourth-place ribbon in a fifth-grade swim meet in backstroke. So, there's that.

Whitney loves to play with her kids (a.k.a. dazzle them with her amazing flossing abilities), bake stuff, eat stuff, and write books for people who "get" her. She thinks french fries are the perfect food and Mrs. Roper is her spirit animal.

Join her newsletter for news of her latest releases, sales, and recommendations. If you consider yourself a superfan, join her private reader group, where you will be offered the chance to read her books before they're released.

www.ingramcontent.com/pod-product-compliance
Lightning Source LLC
LaVergne TN
LVHW020705110826
845149LV00012B/2113

* 9 7 9 8 9 9 1 2 3 2 8 8 3 *